Kenneth Foust

Uncontrolled Substance
The Solution

Kenneth Foust

authorHOUSE®

AuthorHouse™
1663 Liberty Drive, Suite 200
Bloomington, IN 47403
www.authorhouse.com
Phone: 1-800-839-8640

First published by AuthorHouse 11/14/2008

ISBN: 978-1-4343-4952-1 (e)
ISBN: 978-1-4343-4950-7 (sc)
ISBN: 978-1-4343-4951-4 (hc)

Library of Congress Control Number: 2008930703

Printed in the United States of America
Bloomington, Indiana

This book is printed on acid-free paper.

A SPECIAL THANKS

TO

W. L. FOUST

FOR THE INSPIRATION

Preface

In my abbreviated description of this one of a kind novel (Uncontrolled Substance) you will realize it's more, much more then just an out of control drug problem. It's set in a not so distant ulterior world that demands results, not unlike present day. Results that cannot be accomplished without assistance. It begins with a young partisan man who was raised by his father and trained by the government, for what would be a new and challenging beginning for all, but as most trainees he knew nothing of this new beginning.

However, before this change would take place, in desperation of stagnating and after losing the love of his life, he takes leave from the space program and heads straight to the one place the government doesn't want him to see, the planet below, and his new temporary assignment with the Drug Enforcement Administration. There he learns everything concerning the good, bad, and very bad of what the government has allowed to take place on the planet. The truth about the mother planet slowly creeps in throughout the story. How people are genetically designed to fit the needs of the drug trade. How generations of drug usage has left many needing more, even the tainted blood of others.

On his first mission captain Harrison stumbles upon one of the genetically contrived humans, known as half breeds. Shortly after bringing him back from the jungle hideout he is killed, but not before leaving Harrison a clue as to why the drug lords are always one step ahead of the DEA. The clue takes him to A-T, the corporation that produces the DEA vehicles, and discovers how the government has hindered the agency. However the government's extreme solution is not uncovered until virtually the end, now captain Harrison must race against a swiftly moving clock, in his attempt to halt the well thought out government program.

In his attempt to unravel the plot captain Harrison finds not one but two new loves, Megan, a beautiful blue eyed co-worker, and second the freedom that he never realized existed, neither of which he can now let go. He also finds the plot is much too advanced for him to reverse, he can now only retaliate by stopping those who are responsible, in the hope that this will end the termination.

An ageing society depends heavily on highly developed drugs. With enhanced drugs you don't just keep up, you excel. Imagine being anything you want, who wouldn't desire that? Who could control it? However, as with most things there's a price to be paid. The enhanced drugs are very expensive and the improvements are short lived, thus it must be taken continuously. The side effects or should we say aftermath is not the drug lords' problem, that belongs to the government. To be more precise the DEA. For this, the DEA has formulated (clean-up crews) their name pretty much describes their job. These men are well trained, and extremely well armed. Everyone fears the clean-up crews, and with good reason. Concerning drugs the DEA has full authority and the clean-up crews are the force behind it. Clean-up has become very cold and callus in doing their job, which is to eliminate druggies and their addictive crop effectively. However, this is not permitted without evidence. First the agents must locate and record the drug manufacturing in progress or discover a drug lord present, before the crews are called in. Everyone knows, all to well, that DEA doesn't take prisoners, the crews eradicate everything.

Having this much power, chief Boyd of the DEA is an open target for everyone in government, especially the Head Counselor who knows chief Boyd would never consort with the government plot. The Head Counselor aligns himself with the drug lords in order to eliminate Chief Boyd and the DEA, and at a later time the drug lords themselves. It's a double-cross on a global scale.

Meanwhile, Chief Boyd uses Captain Harrison, considering his knowledge of the space program, as his trump card when the Head Counselor takes control of the space program and turns it against the DEA. However no one realized that the government raised and trained Captain Harrison, they know exactly what he knows and what he is capable of. Captain Harrison completes the task that he unknowingly has been trained for. The Head Counselor has all bases covered, except one. Harrison has fallen in love and doesn't want to leave Megan, or the planet which represents his freedom. However, the Head Counselor has sealed everyone's fate, and staying is not an option. Harrison's definitive act before having to leave the planet is to try and stop the Head Counselor.

Uncontrolled Substance gives the only written account of what the future will bring from continued abuse, concerning enhanced drugs, genetics, and government cover ups. Read on, if you dare.

Thank you for your time.

KennethFoust.com

Chapter One

Reflections from a distant moon glisten off the barren peaks that pierce the evanescent atmosphere. No one witnesses the small black object that escapes the dark tranquility, its pitted outer hull invisible against the night sky as it invades the shadows without a trace. Traveling several times the speed of sound, the arrow-shaped craft proficiently maneuvers the Nevado del Huila.

The vehicle has been specifically designed for penetration and termination, and is one of many weapons employed by the Drug Enforcement Administration (DEA) in its efforts to curtail the centuries-old dilemma of chemical abuse. The pandemic has reached a disaster level on the planet. Among the mounting issues attributed to illegal narcotics are widespread official corruption, staggering mortality rates, and countless human deformities. The dependency has also rendered large sectors of the planet's population nonproductive. To counter this, the government has issued a martial directive: liquidation of all violators.

Soon the vehicle will reach its destination, on this pilot's maiden mission with the agency. Inside the thickly shielded craft, the pilot feels anxious, although he does not anticipate any real difficulty. It has been several months since a major encounter with the drug traffickers, who it seems have become very proficient at avoiding the DEA.

The 180-degree wraparound viewer is on standby, so as not to distract the pilot. Guided only by instruments, he is totally reliant upon them.

The pilot's trained eyes routinely glance at the command panel, analyzing it in an instant. His attention focuses on the radar scan. Throughout the years, these pristine peaks over which he is traveling have taken the lives of many pilots. A small blue halo suddenly appears in the center of the dimmed viewer. As the halo heightens, it begins to pulsate, alerting the pilot that he has now reached his first preset nav point.

¤ ¤ ¤

The DEA headquarters in Houston is well-fortified, and a comfortable distance from the main buildings of the city. The heart is located on the top floor, beneath the heavily guarded landing port, five stories aboveground. Most of the building is underground, with a naturally maintained temperature perfect for the storage of weapons, food, water, vehicles, and surplus parts. However, the largest sector of the building is used for repairing vehicles, and has a second service entrance several hundred meters away in the security office building. The balance of the structure is officers' sleeping quarters, with an infirmary on the ground level. The dimly lit offices on the top floor show little spirit. There's not much activity at 4:45 a.m., except in one large central room that is the control center of DEA headquarters.

It's filled with computer-monitoring stations and charts and screens used for the satellite tracking of agents and suspects. At the core is a massive concentrically circular desk, where twenty-four-hour rotating shifts continuously receive information and provide directives to the agents.

Only two people are working the control center now, but the daily activity will pick up rapidly with the rising of the sun, at which time all desks will be occupied. On a normal day, a minimum of twenty-five analysts are keeping track of the 180 active agents, processing and coordinating their actions.

¤ ¤ ¤

Megan and Winston are pulling their normal graveyard shifts in the control room. Megan's sitting attentively at the concentric desk, monitoring the agents, while on the other side Winston has immersed himself in one of the abundantly padded seats at a remote desk. He's monitor another screen, however his head is nodding back and forth. They're both wearing their DEA uniforms, but Winston's pants are quite wrinkled, and he keeps the cuffs rolled above the top of his boots. His black pullover shirt matches his wrinkled pants.

Megan glances up and smirks. "Hey, Winston," she says, "did you forget to check the mirror before you left home?"

Winston doesn't open his eyes. "Look, I'll tell you just like I tell everyone else. A single man doesn't have the time to worry about his wardrobe."

"With that wardrobe, you'll stay single."

One eye opens. "Maybe. But maybe meeting someone isn't high on my list of priorities. No one sees you in here, so why does it matter?"

Megan smiles. Her ploy has worked.

With both eyes open, Winston plants his feet firmly on the floor. His abundantly padded chair is no longer comfortable.

"You women are all alike. Don't want a man to have a moment's peace."

Even the chief talks to Winston about his unprofessional appearance, but he doesn't push the issue. Good officers are hard to come by, harder still to train, and Winston is one of the best. Besides, the agency is always understaffed.

Megan isn't looking to meet anyone romantically, especially at 4:45 a.m. However, she looks perfectly professional in her cleaned and pressed uniform, even at this hour. She's beautiful too with her naturally curly, long black hair and polished fingernails. Her radiant eyes, bluer than the sky, reflect an inner beauty few people possess.

A loud metallic bang echoes through the quiet floor. Megan doesn't flinch, doesn't even glance at the chronometer. She knows immediately who has entered. He always arrives at the same time each morning, allowing the heavy metal door to slam shut, wanting to make sure everyone on duty acknowledges his presence. Like the others, Megan knows the chief's history. Many years ago, authorities decided the only way to end the vast amount of corruption infesting the government was to have one person solely responsible for combating the drug problem. Therefore, the DEA became the only branch of authority headed by one man. The Commander-in-Chief of the Drug Enforcement Administration, he answers to no one with respect to his job. In this way, Chief Boyd is the most powerful man in government.

¤ ¤ ¤

Boyd is prompt to scrutinize everything as he enters the control room, his morning coffee in one hand, a computer data pad in the other. The cup overflows; some of the coffee sloshes over and runs down his hand. His face scowls. The thin-haired, wide-shouldered chief is slightly overweight, but his tall stature covers for it and he is otherwise still in good shape.

Megan gives him a customary smile.

"Good morning, Chief Boyd."

He looks her way but makes no reply. Instead, he places the data pad on her desk and wipes the spilled coffee from his hand as he marches over to the wall map that reveals the location of all agents, along with their names and vehicle numbers. He uses the glass covering of the map as a mirror to fix his collar and adjust his tie, a routine Megan has witnessed religiously since her first day in the control room. Today is different, though. Boyd flinches, and then shakes his head. It isn't the location of any one agent that's troubling him. She knows Boyd. He undoubtedly knew where every agent was even before he looked at the chart. No, it's something else, she thinks.

A red, pulsating light catches his eye. Pointing at it, he turns to Megan.

"Who is piloting this JT.24?"

"That's Captain Rod Harrison. He's new, just added yesterday."

"On whose authority?" His tone tells her the explanation better be good.

"I, well, mine, sir. I knew you were covered up, with everything going on, so I authorized it."

His look tempers to a keen edge. "Never again. Notify me first, always." She types a command into her keyboard. A split-second later, Harrison's service record appears on the viewer to the right of the planetary map.

Boyd reads over Harrison's impressive record and then looks at the accompanying picture. He chuckles.

"He doesn't look nuts to me, does he to you?"

He reads on without waiting for the answer. Moments later, he walks over to Megan's desk and motions for her to clear the screen.

"I can't figure it out. Why would a fighter pilot from a prestigious starship like the Wingate ever volunteer for this hellhole job?" Megan merely glares his way. "Well, go ahead, let's hear it. I know you've already unearthed everything about this guy."

"What makes you think that, sir?" She hides her grin, but not well enough.

"Listen, I've been an agent longer then you've been alive, and I haven't lost it yet. I saw the way you looked at his picture. I also noticed you didn't have to look up his ID number. You just punched it in. Then, when I asked you if he was nuts ... Well, if looks could kill, I'd be stone cold by now. So come on, talk."

"Okay, okay, you still got it," she admits, laughing. "All I know is that they're reviewing his record for a promotion. Meanwhile, he's on a ninety-day liberty that ends the same time as his enlistment. If he gets the promotion, he'll re-enlist. If not ... Well, maybe he's using the ninety days to check out other branches of government. And he's not married."

Boyd ignores her last comment. "After ninety days of this place, the Wingate will look like a paradise to him. He'll go back ... at any rank."

"You may be right, Chief. But maybe he'll find a reason to stay."

"I see." Boyd notes the inescapable look in her eyes. He suspects Harrison's thick black hair and dark eyes give the Captain an air of mystery Megan can't resist. "Well, what level of DEA training did he make it through?"

She glances at her screen. "Just the two-week rundown on the DEA procedures. We didn't expect him to get too involved in ninety days."

Boyd nods. "Why waste resources if he's not going to hang around? If he signs on permanently, we'll put him through the academy." Another glance, this time at the map. "That vehicle he's got ... the JT.24. Where did it come from? Thought we took those out of service some time back."

Megan looks over. "It's been grounded a long time. Walter had his maintenance crew download the new programs and put it back online. So I assigned it to Captain Harrison."

Seconds later, the chief mutters, "Yeah, I guess. I didn't even know we had any of those left. The youngest recruit always gets the oldest vehicle, but I'm not sure that was a good idea in this case. That one's severely outdated."

Like everyone else on staff, Megan is no stranger to being second-guessed by the chief. She takes it in stride.

"I thought about that, sir. But in the development exam, Captain Harrison showed top scores. And according to his documents, he's flown numerous vehicles. Besides, it's built like a battleship. The hull is over fifteen centimeters thick. He should be all right."

"Hey, Chief, no problem," comes a voice from the dark. "Captain Harrison got the crash course, and now he's got the perfect vehicle to do it with!"

Boyd whirls around. "Winston," he shouts, "What department are you in?"

Winston rises immediately to his feet. "Search and Rescue, sir."

"Isn't there something in Search and Rescue that you should be doing? Now?" Winston knows he crossed a line. "Ah, yes, sir, I think there is." He wastes no time leaving.

Megan sighs and looks up, hoping her blue eyes will have their usual effect. "Sir, are you going to be in one of those moods all day now?"

"Megan, it's not a mood. Nothing makes me more furious than someone badmouthing the DEA, especially one of our own people. Morale is low enough."

One of the many display lights on Megan's desk begins to blink. "Looks like our newest pilot's about to turn off his tracking signal."

Boyd nods. His face is somber. "I disapprove of them doing that, but what choice is there? We have to stop monitoring them while they're making their descent. The drug prefects' technology has gotten so sophisticated in the past few months, changing our satellite link and scanner codes proved a waste of time. Last thing an agent wants is to be announced by a tracking signal."

They watch the screen together, trusting Harrison will make it. During the last four months, the DEA has lost as many agents performing routine surveillance. The fact that Captain Harrison is temporary, and therefore expendable, isn't the issue. Chief Boyd can't afford to lose anymore people.

¤ ¤ ¤

Harrison shuts down the tracking signal, his hands move fluid across the cluster of instruments. Some are operated by touch screens; others are voice-activated. Every instruction he initiates is recorded, every command posted on the viewer to his left. It doesn't matter that he's had only two weeks to familiarize himself with this particular panel. Literally thousands of hours in the cockpit have programmed his body to respond to a ship's controls by instinct.

As he prepares the small craft for its next duty, he covers the checklist in his mind. "All right, we made it out, let's cut power," he whispers, then eases off on the death grip he didn't realize he'd had on the control wheel.

With two blinks of the display light, the screen indicates power-off.

"Okay, ground temperature 30 Celsius, hull temperature 290," Harrison mutters. The hull's temperature must drop to 30 degrees Celsius or he'll be detected by a heat scanner.

The air-speed indicator announces that his descent is precarious.

"Reconfigure structure, trim for glide."

The green display blinks twice, indicating the successful deployment of wings. He immediately sets the air speed at 250 knots. The gravity drive will keep the vehicle at this speed until changed.

Now that he's slowed enough to actually visualize things, he turns on the viewer and smiles. The JT.24 might be old, but he likes this feature; it's like opening a curtain that starts at the back of his right shoulder and travels all the way around to his left. It's similar to sitting in a cockpit with a glass bubble instead of the heavy steel lid that is actually there. The view is magnificent: The Mountains are barely visibly behind him, and the sun is peeking over the horizon. The curvature of the planet cast a giant shadow across the seemingly endless forest below. It will be at least forty-five minutes before the early morning light reaches the dense forest floor. As the JT.24 periodically pierces the sparse white clouds that the early morning sun hasn't yet evaporated, he experiences the sensation of speed for the first time that night.

Prior to descent, the final item on the checklist is activating the heat scanner. A red tint is imposed over the screen, and immediately four deep red circles appear. Harrison's eyes widen; he hadn't expected anything to be identified so quickly. The scanner has located four heat sources: three small sites, and a rather sizeable one at least the length of several city blocks. Harrison quickly feeds the coordinates into the computer and locks the JT.24 on course, then forces the control wheel forward, causing the small craft to begin a long plunge.

After several minutes of stealthy descent, he levels off just above the treetops at 100 meters. It'll be only a few minutes before he reaches the first hot spot.

He utilizes the time to put on his helmet and hook up the air lines. Harrison is the only agent with a pressurized suit. The thick, bulky black flight suit from the Wingate is designed for space travel, but saved the cost of making a new suit for the ninety-day assignment.

He checks his shoulder weapon, located under the wide, gold-colored epaulet on his left shoulder. The Stinger appears to be working properly, but he takes care not to load it. The weapon emits a small beam of light that releases a pencil-size load of caustic matter, equivalent to acid.

His final check reassures him — the charge light on his handheld laser is transmitting, indicating that it's operational. The fighter pilot's laser weapon is larger and more powerful than the DEA-issued laser. It's designed for long range, unlike the DEA weapon.

Once again, the red beacon warns he's arrived at the first hot spot. He leans over to switch on the high-speed camera, and a twenty-centimeter monitor comes alive. With his finger on the "Load" button, he waits. The red display turns green, and he pushes the button to activate the camera. It immediately begins taking pictures.

"Okay, okay," he mutters. "It's time to go to work. Wonder what they're making down there."

In a split second he passes over the hot spot, he gets little more than a glimpse of the jungle clearing. But the camera develops the pictures and displays them on the viewing screen instantaneous. They confirm that the camera got more than a glimpse — twenty-six pictures in all.

"Hey, an entire village," he whispers. "No one around. But, it's still early."

Displayed to the left of the pictures is the chemical breakdown from the microscopic particles picked up by the chemical sensors, listed alphabetically with their percentage rate indicated alongside each. He peers at the readout. "Carbon, pollen, salt — conventional soot — and sulfur. The usual. But no drugs. Good."

While the autopilot sets the vehicle on course to the second hot spot, Harrison clears the screen and resets the high-speed camera. It'll be a few minutes before he reaches the next target, and he leans back to breathe. That's when the doubts begin intruding into his thoughts.

Did I do the right thing by coming down here, or should I just stick with the space program? Man, I don't know anything about the DEA. I haven't been on the ground for more than a few days at any one time. And now, I'm supposed to go one-on-one with drug dealers. I dunno ...

Like his grandfather, and the father he never really knew, Harrison has spent most of his adult life in the space program. His mother died in childbirth, and Harrison's father placed him in a private school until he entered the academy.

"I don't know what I was thinking," he whispers. I know nothing about drugs. There's no drug problem aboard the Wingate. He thinks; I know exactly what Dad would be saying if he thought I'd signed on with the D.E.A.

For some unknown reason, his father's opinion has recently weighed heavy on his heart — heavy as the love he'd once had, and then lost, he now feels the need for some accord in his life. Maybe his uncertainty is from losing Laura, the pretty blonde with big green eyes who pilots one of the many supply ships. They met while on a routine re-supply mission for the Wingate. Things had gotten too serious for her. She wasn't ready for a permanent relationship, or so she said. He allows himself to open the memories of Laura Renee, knowing it isn't a healthy practice. He removes a thin black oblong box from his chest pocket. The hologram of Laura begins to speak. He yearns to see that perfect smile, hear her voice, and feel the passion once again. Harrison isn't ready to let go. She's the reason he's here now, and perhaps Admiral Kachel and all the run-ins with him in the past six months.

Harrison's boss is the last person he wants to think about now, especially in relation to Laura. But Kachel is Laura's boss, too. Even worse, Kachel seems to have a vendetta against everyone. Most of the crew could steer clear of him, but Harrison never got the hang of keeping his mouth shut when he thought something was wrong. Everyone says it's a throwback to his grandfather.

Back then, Harrison thought, you could get away with it.

He believes there is no way Admiral Kachel will grant him the promotion to shift commander presently, so the threat of leaving the Wingate after his enlistment couldn't hurt.

The blinking red display brings him back to reality, and he prepares to push the camera-load button again. The microscopic particles are the most important evidence. They tell the real story, and he doesn't want to miss a thing. Besides, obsessing over small details helps keep his mind off what's really bothering him.

The green light appears, he touches the camera activation button, and in a repeat of the first site, it's over almost as soon as it begins. The readings parallel the first village like a carbon copy. Even the air quality and chemical breakdown are identical. He resets the camera, hoping in the back of his mind that the next two locations are this quiet. If they're the same, all he has to do is turn on the satellite tracking and head for home. Not too bad for his first solo mission.

For a third time, the crimson light begins to blink. His hand pauses over the button, waiting for the green display before pushing it. Instantly, a warning light flashes: "Narcotics Detected!"

He sighs. Well, so much for hope ...

Chapter Two

In the air-quality column, the chemical analysis shows concentrated amounts of cocaine dust and high-grade production methamphetamine in heavy percentages, along with enhanced alkaloid.

"All right, we have a drug lab and manufacturings in progress," Harrison says, straightening up in his chair.

Cutting off the autopilot, he commences to slow the vehicle's airspeed, resetting the heading by 180 degrees to re-enter the hot spot. He quickly examines the pictures with two objectives in mind: to find the best way in without being detected, and to determine the optimum location for recording evidence. The wrong choices could cost him his life.

The estate is quite large, with one main dwelling harboring a satellite-tracking disc on its broad, flat roof. He sees a few secondary buildings and an array of other objects he can't discern. A black light screens the area, which even his high-speed camera can't fully penetrate. He can only assume these are the occupied secondary buildings within the perimeter.

Unlike the previous two quiet villages, the heat scanner unveils sporadic activity in the fields. The pictures reveal a heavy guarded rooftop, and a poppy field hidden behind the thick tree line. The poppies are not natural vegetation.

Harrison now realizes how different this is from fighting pirates and escorting supply ships; he wonders if his impetuous decision to temporarily volunteer for DEA duty will backfire. At least in space, he had a good idea of what to expect. Focusing on more immediate concerns, he brings the small craft to a near stop in order to prepare for a vertical landing on a small clearing just behind the tree line that faces the rear of the main residence and is out of view. Or so he hopes.

It is time to start recording — and watching his back every second.

Bringing the camera up and around, he sweeps across the poppy field. The workers are just standing in the field, likely waiting for daylight. Beneath the black-light screen, he can see the individual buildings now. The nearest, adjacent to the main house, has a huge open retractable door. Inside, he sees what looks to be pods being treated for opium, prepared by a special laser used to enhance the drug by eliminating impurities while stimulating the morphine. Containers of chemicals used to cut the drugs for mass distribution are everywhere. These also become part of the evidence. The heat scanner verifies every object's position with a number, just as it had done earlier with each village, and the high-speed camera records everything that's on the grounds, even in the obscure light.

¤ ¤ ¤

Inside the estate's mansion, beads of sweat begin to form on the security officer with well-developed muscles as he stands in the empty hall. He doesn't want to wake his boss with bad news, but reluctantly punches in the number that releases the door. It opens to a master bedroom suite. The officer warily approaches the oversize brass bed inside.

"Sir? Mr. Radcliff ... Sir?"

A sheet-swathed figure stirs.

"I'm sorry to wake you, sir, but the radar detected something, but now we can't verify its location."

A tall, thin man with a dark tan rises from the bed. He growls with his thick European accent, "What! What's its location?"

"Ah, we don't know, sir. It passed overhead, and then disappeared off the screen."

Radcliff's head jerks up; his eyes bore into the shorter man's. "What? You're telling me you can't find it? Activate those new VLT modules. God knows we paid enough to get them."

The man sighs. "I've already done that, they aren't picking up anything either."

"What about the satellite tracking?" Radcliff quickly makes his way to his adjacent office with a full-size picture window on one wall, a black marble desk with a mahogany chair, and several exquisite paintings on the opposite side of the room.

"There's nothing showing from satellite tracking either, sir," the officer replies as he tries to keep up. "And the heat scanner isn't picking up anything," he adds, anticipating his boss's next question.

Peering out the third-story picture window at the workers below, Radcliff barks, "Well, maybe he kept going, or maybe there was never anything there. In either case, you woke me for nothing. Victor, you're an idiot!"

"No, Mr. Radcliff, there was something on radar."

Radcliff scowls. "Then alert the guards, and give me those damned binoculars. Now!"

¤ ¤ ¤

Harrison turns on the satellite tracking and opens communications. The recorded information instantly transmits to Houston.

¤ ¤ ¤

"Chief, you better come here."

"What is it, Megan?"

"Got a live one, sir," Megan says, as Boyd rushes out of his office to stand beside her. She glances up at him, then back to the screen, fingers moving madly over her keyboard.

"Who is it?"

"It's Captain Harrison." Megan's voice is short. "He just turned on the signal, communications are open."

"Put it on the big screen."

Three keystrokes later, they can see everything Harrison can. After two more clicks, Boyd calls into Megan's wireless microphone, "Not bad, not bad at all, Captain. Talk about beginner's luck! This makes you an honorary DEA agent. We're dispatching a clean-up crew to your location. Now, you get out of there as quickly as you —"

Harrison isn't listening; his attention is focused on the high-speed camera, which is taking shots of the figure standing in the full-length window.

In a split second, Boyd has followed Harrison's gaze. He's talking fast now. "Captain, hold that view and get a file comparison on him."

Harrison punches in the information and almost instantly, the computer creates a close-up reproduction of the man standing in the window and compares it with the DEA's files. Just as quickly, the computer displays the man's name and record on Harrison's viewer. Next to the man's name — Radcliff — are the words "Wanted by DEA," followed by: "CODE ONE FOR IMMEDIATE TERMINATION."

"Can't you read, Harrison?" Boyd shouts. "Terminate him NOW!"

Harrison is taken by surprise, but he's never disobeyed a direct order. He stabs the ready-weapon button. Two long, thin slits open on each side of the vehicle's curved hood and equally long, shiny black barrels rise out of each compartment. As the barrels slide into position, they move toward each other, locking into place a half-meter apart. Two cross hairs appear on Harrison's viewer.

He watches the load meters build power while the computer works on the formula to lathe the light; the old gas lasers have to be pumped. He curses in frustration. The newer solid-state weapons (like the ones he's used to) do all of this instantly. Termination is one area that his brief rundown on DEA procedures didn't cover, and the reality of what's expected of him is becoming clear.

The green weapon-ready icon illuminates the large firing button in the center of the control wheel. Harrison is too close to aim both lasers at the man. Trusting it will work, he rotates the knob to place the left laser-sight dead on the figure in the window, leaving the right laser to hit the wall to the right.

Radcliff turns as he sees the reflection of Harrison's blistered barrels through his binoculars. As Harrison presses the fire button, Radcliff drops from sight.

The first blast thunders through the full-length picture window, spraying glass into the room as an immense, white-hot ball of fire follows. The fireball crosses the room and slams into the far wall near the top, quickly turning into black smoke that is sucked out of the hole just made. The second fireball strikes to the right of the window, creating a two-meter hole in the outer wall.

Only now do the security spotlights come alive. They begin sweeping the area, illuminating workers running frantically throughout the compound. Most are screaming.

¤ ¤ ¤

Harrison prepares to lift off, but keeps an eye on the viewer. A small heat source leaves the room Harrison just nailed, crossing in front of several windows.

It's Radcliff, Harrison frantically thinks, but no one should have gotten out of that room alive.

The heat signature, moving rapidly, disappears roughly midway through the large structure. Harrison re-aims and hits the fire button again. The lasers blast a prominent hole in the brick wall, exposing a layer of burnished steel underneath.

Harrison curses. "No wonder Radcliff disappeared. He's in a damnable reinforced steel room!"

Hissing, a laser eruption cuts through the tree line and a blinding white flash darkens Harrison's viewer. The blast was close. Too close.

He leans forward to see where the shot came from. As he scans up, he sees what he hadn't noticed before: laser cannon mounted on the rooftop. The remainder of the brick wall above the hole he made begins to peel off and fall to the ground. In a whirlwind of dust, the entire steel armor of the building is exposed.

"It's a shaft leading to the roof, Chief," Harrison yells into his microphone. "I think I see where the guy is going. Man, they planned for everything, didn't they?"

A second shot is fired from the rooftop cannon. It perforates the tree to his right and cuts a deep slice in the vehicle's right wing.

"Oh, yeah," Harrison roars, "I didn't expect there'd be this much action in the good old DEA."

He hears Megan shouting in the background, "Get out of there, Captain, let the clean-up crew handle it!"

He pays no attention. Aiming his lasers directly at the cannon, he unleashes another attack. This time, there's a massive explosion from the rooftop. Harrison watches the main portion of a barrel plunge from the roof and hit the ground. Several smaller pieces fly up and away from the house. Immediately after, the entire roof is engulfed in smoke and flames.

As he engages the control wheel, the small craft lifts off as double doors on the building to the right of the house opens. A large barrel tip begins emerging into view. It has to be either a laser emitter or a particle projector beam.

Either way, he has to get out of range, and is determined not to abort without first terminating Radcliff.

Once he reaches the treetops, Harrison aims the lasers at the roof. Another explosion shakes the rooftop, but this time, it isn't a laser; someone has just launched an escape ship.

"Captain, I know what you're thinking," Boyd yells. "Stop it right now and get the hell out of there!"

"It's Radcliff, sir, it's got to be," Harrison mutters through clenched teeth. As he pushes the throttle to full power, the small vehicle rises slowly, but promptly picks up speed as both ships shoot straight up toward each other. Harrison braces for the impact, but the other ship veers onto a course toward the mountains.

With Boyd shouting commands at him through his earpiece, Harrison glances down. The display indicates full power, but full speed will take a few more seconds. He locks the scanners onto Radcliff's ship. They indicate that it's a much newer and, undoubtedly, more sophisticated model. If Harrison doesn't dispose of him quickly, Radcliff will escape.

"Sir, if I don't stop him now, I won't get another chance," Harrison yells as he turns on the radar and sets the lasers on automatic targeting.

"Captain, if you don't get out of there now, I'll —!"

The green ready-light glows. Harrison pushes the fire button. The lasers let loose with a white blast that whistles through the early morning air.

Just before the blast reaches Radcliff's vehicle, a plume of fire spurts from the exhaust as the afterburner is triggered. The vehicle begins to pull away, and then suddenly makes a full-throttle dive. The lasers from Harrison's ship continue on out of sight. They leave only a faint afterimage on the view screen.

Harrison shoves the control wheel downward, forcing his ship into a nosedive. He hopes to keep Radcliff in sight; however his vehicle is much older. When Radcliff levels off, Harrison's scanner locks on again, but before he can fire, a laser barrage is hurled straight at him from the rear cannon mounted high on Radcliff's ship. He wrenches the control wheel hard left, but the fierce energy of the blast strikes the tail section, knocking him back to his original course.

Quickly regaining control, he aims for the ship again. A warning klaxon blares from the monitor panel, showing that the power-plant temperature is dangerously high. He ignores it. Because the after-cooler is damaged, the recycled air has a heavy oily taste. He lines Radcliff up for one last shot before losing him to the mountains, and fires.

Radcliff's ship drops again and the rear cannon returns fire. This time, Harrison isn't so lucky. Both lasers are incinerated in a direct hit to the bow. The viewer goes dark; all lights on the instrument panel fade out, leaving the small cabin pitch black inside. But the emergency lighting activates immediately, and the red warning lights on both sides above his head begin flashing. He hears the sound of the vehicle's power plant winding down. To the left of the viewing screen, the words "Gravity Drive Activated" appear. The computer has initiated the gravity-drive system.

To his lower right side, a single screen revives: the only monitor to reboot is the one mounted underneath the vehicle. The high-speed camera, self-contained and insulated from the rest of the ship, hasn't been damaged. At least I can still see the ground, he thinks.

The communication system is out. This means he can't contact Houston for assistance. He grins wryly. On the upside, they can't contact me, either, he thinks. At the moment, he really doesn't want to hear Chief Boyd's reaction to what has just happened. His pilot training has taught him to act first, and apologize later. It's better than waiting for permission. The ship is damaged, but still maneuverable, and he is unhurt. With the gravity drive working, he can try to intercept the clean-up crew. The gyrocompass won't show him the way back, but will keep him from going around in circles.

He turns the JT.24 around and sets the course back.

As he flies over, he notices breaks in the jungle below; there are a few large, rocky hills, and ... something else — Radcliff's ship, directly to his lower right, skimming just above the ground.

"He sure didn't get far," Harrison grumbles. "But his vehicle doesn't look damaged ... what in the world is he doing?"

Harrison notices a huge opening in the gradual slope of one of the smaller hills. Radcliff's vehicle is heading straight for it.

"No wonder they can't catch this guy," Harrison whispers. "The scanners can't penetrate that much rock." With that split-second realization, he knows he's been given a second chance.

He turns the control wheel to the right and pushes it forward, initiating a downward spiral just above Radcliff. Harrison hopes to strike Radcliff's vehicle with a glancing blow from the top while it's in such a vulnerable position. The maneuver might just knock it off course and into the hillside. But with no altimeter or spin indicator, and the high-speed camera mounted on the bottom of the vehicle, Harrison knows it won't be easy.

He misjudges by a few meters, but the JT.24 still makes a solid, glancing strike. He's surprised when Radcliff's vehicle explodes.

Harrison's ship catches the explosion's shockwave and is slung through the treetops. The JT.24 is history; the only remaining function is the red warning light that reads, "EVACUATE IMMEDIATELY." But Harrison doesn't see it, as he's been knocked unconscious.

Most of the debris from Radcliff's ship is scattered across the hillside. The propulsion system remained intact, and dropped straight down into the entrance in the hillside.

Harrison's lifeless ship quickly loses momentum, and begins an unscheduled visitation into the forest below. After splintering several treetops, it starts to tumble, eventually collapsing into a dry, rocky riverbed. The aft section bounces off a large boulder, which cracks open the power plant. With the cockpit lid knocked ajar several centimeters, poisonous gases from the power plant flood in. Harrison's suit, designed for space emergencies, detects the gas and automatically seals and pressurizes. Moments later, the oxygen streaming in his face brings him back to reality. The only thing he sees is the "EVACUATE IMMEDIATELY" warning light in the otherwise pitch-black cockpit.

He retrieves his laser from its half-crushed compartment and turns on his helmet's emergency lights. He wants to stand and force the cockpit lid open, but his left leg is pinned to the seat by the control wheel. When he moves, the pain makes him cry out. He quickly adjusts his seat back all the way, and puts his right foot up on the control wheel. With gritted teeth, he pushes against his knee with both hands. The wheel eases forward just enough to free his leg. His helmet muffles the curse he can't hold back.

The vehicle's damaged lid moves easily, but the outer hull is scalding hot. Doesn't matter, he thinks. He has no idea if anyone saw him crash, or how many gun-wielding individuals might be on their way to him. He moves from the cockpit, then rolls off the hood to the punishing hard ground. No damage to his suit, except a bit of melting on his left shoulder. He wishes he could say the same for his knee.

He limps toward the thick jungle. After stumbling a few hundred meters, hears a faint whistling noise; it's vague at first, but rapidly turns ear-piercing. He wheels around just in time to see the JT.24's titanium hull fly apart amidst an enormous explosion. He dives behind the nearest shelter — a fallen tree. After several seconds of silence, fragments of his ship begin streaking through the trees like a metal hailstorm, cutting the leaves and slicing into the tree trunk in front of his chest. The surrounding foliage promptly absorbs the echo from the blast, leaving no audible evidence to mark his position. He sighs, relieved.

Harrison is surrounded by an oppressive silence. All he can do is wait and hope that the clean-up crew will get close enough to be contacted through his helmet communicator before anyone else arrives. He removes his helmet, and the humid air hits him like a murky wall. He was prepared for the heat (over 30 Celsius by the readout in the vehicle), but not the humidity. He knows within a few minutes, the inside of his flight suit will be dripping with sweat.

The jungle is just beginning to wake. His first shift as a DEA agent has been excruciatingly long, and it isn't over yet. He is still too close to the crash site. If a scanner could locate the wreckage, it could locate him. He decides to follow the dry riverbed in the direction of the compound. Exhausted, he drops onto a fallen tree, intending to only rest for a moment. He allows his eyes to close. The sounds of the jungle increase with the light of day. Birds and other animals are moving about and the wind is rustling the thick vegetation around him. The air is even hotter than before. He can feel the perspiration running down his lower back as he thinks about how different and beautiful this place is, especially when compared to the planets he is familiar with. Everything here is alive. You could smell it: green scent, cloying, but still clean. He takes a deep breath to analyze the fragrance in a way his suit's sensors never could.

A small red streak of light burst over the log close enough to burn the back of his hand. He hurdles the log he was leaning against, then begins searching the immediate area for any movement. He notices that his helmet, his only possible connection with the clean-up crew, is on the other side of the log. In his panic, he'd forgotten to grab it. He is well hidden behind the massive log, but the helmet gives him away.

He cautiously reaches out and retrieves it just as a second burst strikes the falling tree in front of him.

This time, Harrison is able to see that it comes from behind a small tree about a hundred meters away. He draws his laser pistol, switches off the safety, and turns on the targeting optics in the scope.

He moves further into the jungle so the darkness there might conceal him better. He pauses for a moment to look around, and using the gun's scope, he spies two men in army fatigues following him. It's a miracle that Harrison can perceive them in the deep greens of the foliage.

One man is still; the other man is looking around and talking. "Do you think it's the DEA?"

"I don't know," answers the other, who is also looking.

"Do you think he's the one that got Radcliff?"

"I don't know."

"Do you think we hit him?"

Irritated by his companion's endless questions, the first man motions for him to move out. Harrison knows they haven't located his exact position. Good. Maybe they think I'm wounded because I haven't fired back, he thinks, holding his breath.

The second man peers around with squinted eyes, and then mistakenly moves out into Harrison's line of sight. Harrison squeezes the trigger. The blast impacts the man in the chest, hurling his body several meters.

The first man, stunned, crouches low and crawls back to take a better look at the situation, but quickly realizes there is nothing he can do for his companion. From the waist up to the neck, the corpse is charred. Where the man's stomach and chest once were, now only a large black cavity remains. The bewildered look on his face showed evidence of a quick death. For the moment, Harrison thinks he has a chance to get out alive.

But Harrison finds out there were three men, as a sudden small burst pierces the tree just above his head. This time, it comes from the side of the tree that he is standing on. He's outflanked, and trapped. If he moves out of range from either one, he'll be moving into the other's line of fire.

Looking for a safe place to retreat, he sees a cluster of rocks behind him. There's a long clearing between him and the rocks, and running in a thick flight suit is like running in wet concrete. The man in front will have a clear shot at him, with plenty of time to take aim.

Harrison loads the shoulder weapon, sets it on automatic, and then shoves his laser into its holster. "You've got one shot, don't let me down," he murmurs to the stinger. It will now lock onto the first heat source that moves. He begins his slow sprint for the rocks. The man stumbles out from behind the tree he's using as cover. Raising his laser, he takes careful aim at Harrison's back, confident that he has ample time.

Harrison's shoulder weapon, sensing the man's body heat, is activated. As the man adjusts his arms to take aim, the stinger releases. Traveling at half light speed, it strikes the man just below the chest with a brilliant flash, followed by a shower of sparks.

At first, the man tries desperately to wipe it away, but the stinger has already begun its agonizing absorption into the man's body, consuming its way through his chest. He cries out in disbelief at the stench of his own flesh burning.

Harrison lunges for the mound of rocks just as the man falls backward to the ground, still clutching his weapon. The third man, out of Harrison's view, has watched the episode and silently fades back into the jungle.

Harrison examines the rock pile and decides it will serve as a good stronghold. He needs to get out of the area, but dares not venture any further away from the crash site; if he does, the clean-up crew might not find him. And, as he doesn't know the exact location of the third man anymore, he feels it best to stay here.

Looking straight up, he sees that the sunlight passing over the treetops is making a miserable attempt to reach the ground below. Except for the clearing in front of him, from where he stands, everything is dark, including his future.

After about an hour, he realizes that the shooting, combined with his presence, has unbalanced the daily routine of the forest inhabitants. Not unlike the situation he himself is in right now, everything being so different and unlike the life that he is accustomed to. The life, which had appeared to be laid out from day one, is now as distant as night from day. He thinks it's so disconnected down here. Why didn't anyone ever tell me how different? No one said a word, not even my father. He had to know how beautiful this place is. An unbidden thought comes to him: Maybe that's how they get cadets into the space program. Or possibly that's how they keep them, by never letting them know.

An unfamiliar sound breaks into his thoughts. The animals seem to vanish, and the jungle grows quiet, except for an unbroken reverberation that is steadily increasing in volume.

Harrison waits uneasily as the sound draws nearer, trying to decide whether to run, but the noise suddenly stops. A risky glance over the rocks reveals a large laser, mounted on some type of land crawler, now positioned approximately three hundred meters from the clearing. It's aimed directly at him.

Knowing that running would mean sure death, Harrison elects to stay and measure his enemy. Accompanying the weapon is an army of men. They're swarming through the jungle on the opposite side of the clearing, but seem hesitant to cross it. Perhaps they know Harrison is watching them, or they are afraid for some as yet unknown reason of crossing.

The enormous laser cannon fires at the rocks, as do the twenty-five or so men. Their attack is relentless. Harrison is pinned down and unable to return fire. Harrison thinks: The clean-up crew will surely be here soon. Can I afford to wait? That's when the rock face above him begins to splinter. Soon, more rocks begin to chip away. He positions his hand on the boulder in front of him but it begins to crack. His stronghold won't last much longer. He desperately looks for an opening, but realizes that it would be impossible to get over the barrier and into the forest without being hit. His fortress has become his prison, and likely his final resting place.

Chapter Three

"Megan, your shift has been over for almost an hour, go home." Megan's replacement takes her station behind the main control desk and secures the wireless earpiece to her head.

Megan gives the large wall map a long, disapproving look. "I know, Angie. I was hoping that Winston would report on that missing agent."

Angie glances at the map and nods. "I see. Sector Four ... that's a bad spot."

One look at Megan's face tells Angie her comment showed poor judgment. "Oh, don't look so somber. You know Winston ... he's one of the best. If that agent's out there, he'll locate him."

"Yes, but last night was his first solo mission, and I...I assigned him that old JT.24."

Angie reaches out to shove Megan's shoulder. "Go on home, I'll keep you informed."

"Thanks, Angie." Megan rises from her chair and trudges to the door.

¤ ¤ ¤

Harrison's hopes fade as the men start across the clearing. Suddenly there's a large, diffused flash of light followed by a loud crack like lightning striking. Most of the lasers, including the cannon, fall silent. When a second burst is followed by a loud echoing bang ripping through the trees, the remaining laser fire ceases.

As Harrison rises from his crouch, a third flash lights up the jungle, he drops behind the now battered rock fortress. Moments later, a mammoth tree struck by a fourth eruption falls to the ground. This time, Harrison sees the origin of the flash. The shiny prow of a large ship slowly moves overhead and into plain view in the sky above him.

Soon, the immense ship blocks the sunlight, and the clearing darkens. Three enormous black letters show on the ship's underside. Harrison can only see one at a time through the crowded tree line. First, a "D." By the time the third letter — "A" — appears, Harrison grabs up his helmet and turns up the communicator just in time to hear a voice calling.

"Captain Harrison, is that you? Are you all right?"

"Yes, I'm all right. And very glad to see you!"

"After locating your vehicle, we dismissed you for dead."

"Another minute and I would've been."

"Houston said they detected only one explosion, but the clean-up crew said they thought there were two. We identified the first as Radcliff's ship — or what was left of it — I've been searching the area for some activity."

"I'm lucky you found me in all this —" Harrison looks around "— stuff. What about Radcliff, did you find him?"

"Yes, we got a positive ID on the remains. But the computer overview didn't recognize his ship. The entire back portion must have dissolved." The voice turns admiring. "What did you hit him with, anyway?"

Harrison pauses. "Wait a minute. If you're not the clean-up crew, then who are you?"

"Oh, sorry. The name's Winston, from Search and Rescue."

Harrison glances at the sky. "Where are you going to put down in something that big?"

"I'm not. Not here anyway. Got another agent to retrieve."

As the enormous ship begins to move, Harrison yells into his helmet. "Hey, what about me? There might be more out there —"

"We've checked the area. You'll be all right, just stay put. I've already notified Houston of your location. They're sending you a replacement vehicle."

Uneasy about being left behind, Harrison can only watch, his eyes fixed on Winston's heavy ship until it vanishes from sight. He decides to take a look around, just to make sure there aren't any unwanted guests still about. He approaches the huge laser, and whistles: It's burnt to the ground, nothing left but the tracks on the crawler. He turns to see the crumbled rock face, his only protection during the siege, and suddenly drops to his knees in amazement; in spots, their fire had virtually breached the pile of boulders. He continues his investigation, but with less enthusiasm than before.

The fire from the still-smoldering trees is crackling and smoking; he can smell the damp wood burning. That's the perfect weapon for this thick jungle area, he thinks. Much like a lightning bolt, it creates an ionized path before shooting a charge along the channel. When it hits the damp forest floor, it propagates in all directions, frying everything it contacts. Finding no one in the area alive, he decides the only thing to do now is sit back and wait for his vehicle.

Several hours later, he's convinced himself that he is actually getting used to the heat, but worries the ringing in his ears might be a sign of heat stroke. It isn't. A moment later, another ship moves into sight. It's DEA all right, but this one has a smaller vehicle in tow — one that makes his heart pound the instant he recognizes it.

As his transport sets down in the clearing, Harrison's eyes follow the flowing lines to its end. The smooth edges begin at the nose and shoot straight back to form the five-meter-high wings ending at the tail of the aerodynamically designed craft. On top of the fuselage, the cockpit lid slopes upward to a height of about one meter, then stops abruptly halfway. With the twin tail fins angling outward in a V-shape, the vehicle has a unique look compared to most other crafts.

A tall, thin man with sunken cheeks and an artificial arm appears at the rear door. Harrison moves toward him.

As soon as Harrison is within hearing range, the man introduces himself as Walter. Harrison notices that the right side of Walter's face is deeply scarred, probably from the same explosion that had severed his right arm.

Walter's short on small talk. He points with his good arm to the smaller craft. "Well, Captain, this is your new vehicle. Actually, it's our newest model. Most all the agents have them by now, there's very few of the old vehicles left. I'll be happy to show you around the instrument panel."

"No thanks, that's not necessary. I've flown the SJ.26 before."

Walter's eyebrows arch. "But how can that be?"

"I'm a pilot commissioned to the Wingate."

Walter tries to hide his admiration. "Well then," he mumbles, "I guess there's not much I can tell you about the SJ.26."

"No, but I thank you for delivering her."

Harrison passes Walter quickly and begins climbing the ladder to the cockpit.

"Oh, before you go, Captain Harrison, just one more thing."

Harrison turns his head, with one hand on the cockpit opening.

"Can you point me to your old vehicle? I'd like to salvage it out, especially that new camera."

Harrison doesn't know what to say. Apparently, no one has informed Walter about the JT.24. "Well, ah ... I think the clean-up crew took it with them."

Walter looks skeptical, but says, "Fine." He starts for the tow vehicle.

Harrison wastes no time lifting off; he wants to relocate Radcliff's hideout. On the way, he checks in with Houston. Angie takes Harrison's report, then advises him, "Megan is ... concerned. She'd really like to hear from you when you get in."

Harrison pauses. Angie's expectancy is apparent, but he doesn't know what to say. He only met Megan when he first signed on with the DEA, and when he received his first assignment. But he definitely remembers her. "Well, ah," he finally says, "I'm going to be a while."

"Why's that?" Angie snaps. "You're supposed to return to Houston."

"I'm going back to the location where Radcliff's vehicle went down. Winston didn't find all of his ship, and I think I know why. I want to look around."

It is silent for a moment before Angie speaks again. "Look, you're new," she says, "but what you're doing is highly unusual. The clean-up crew takes care of all that."

"The clean-up crew doesn't know where to look."

Angie waits, but Harrison doesn't explain. "Well," she finally says, "you don't have long. Keep your communicator on at all times. I'll notify you when the clean-up crew begins their final pass, you'll have to be out by then. You're safe as long as they're in the area, but when the crew's done, you'll have to be on your way back."

"That's not a problem."

"I hope not. If anything goes wrong, the chief will have my head. Do you understand?"

"I do, Angie. And thanks. Out."

There is another pause, then a reluctant "Out."

¤ ¤ ¤

He begins in-depth thought about Megan. He's only met her a couple of times, but remembers she is very pretty. It surprises him that she's interested. He'll definitely call her — after he gets the answer to his most pressing question.

Before he can even envision what might happen after that call, he's arrived at the site where Radcliff went down. Pieces of the drug lord's ship are still scattered across the hillside. No one else is around; apparently, the clean-up crew is still working the original site.

Harrison doesn't expect to find anyone alive, but has many questions about the drug operation. What he saw before he was knocked unconscious was the back section of Radcliff's ship drop cleanly into the hill; he suspects this is where the answers lie. He sets the vehicle down in front of the hill, adjacent to the once-open sanctuary. It's now caved in from the explosion of Radcliff's power plant.

After a bit of thought on how best to breech the hill, Harrison mutters, "Well, a good offense seems to be the only alternative." Then he readies the lasers and aims them at the rocks. The weapons onboard the SJ.26 is much more responsive, with several times the JT.24's intensity. Three blasts trigger a violent explosion inside the cavern, and a modest hole appears in the wall of rocks just aboveground.

The explosion is far louder and more destructive than he had expected, blacken boulders litter the hillside. Harrison departs the vehicle and starts uphill on foot, while watching his back. As soon as he enters the small opening, he realizes the reason for the massive explosion. The underground caves are filled with natural gas, which is now exiting through the hole. His suit detects the strong readings, more so the closer he gets. He notes the blackened walls as he climbs down. He debates his safety, but decides the suit will alert him if the gas reaches dangerous levels.

The opening he enters is an empty cavernous room. Probably where Radcliff stores his ship. It seems to be the center of a large complex, with tunnels leading away in three separate directions. The tunnel to his left has caved in. A hasty inspection tells him the one to the right is either incomplete, or the blown-open doorway at its end leads to a very small room. He walks the short distance to the open door. Inside, the room resembles the interior of a furnace. Everything inside — tables, cabinets, even what look to be bodies — is embedded into the far wall, having been propelled by the intensity of the blast.

Harrison accepts the third tunnel straight ahead as his only hope of getting some answers. Its length is immeasurable: Only a small amount of light trickles from the vertical shafts spaced every few meters in the ceiling. Undoubtedly, they're designed to let light in and allow gas to escape. Now, most of the shafts are obstructed by debris. A small mound of dirt and rock has fallen into the hallway just below each shaft.

There's less damage further in. Harrison quickly examines most of the rooms and hallways, not finding much until he reaches what looks to be some from of operation center. Several broken computers and file cabinets line the walls. Then he notices the bodies. Wishing he hadn't followed his instincts to investigate, he forces himself to move in for a closer look.

What he finds confuses him even more. "They look as if they've been dead for days, not a few hours," he whispers. "And they're so old ... What are they doing here, anyway?"

But as he realizes he's the one responsible for their deaths, a sudden wave of guilt washes over him. He looks straight into one of the men's distorted face. The tongue is swollen from the lack of oxygen. It reminds Harrison of the time he'd been dispatched to a mining asteroid, due to concerns for the colony that was working it. The colonists had been out of contact for several weeks. By the time he arrived, it was too late. Some of the miners had died in their sleep from the poison gas. Those who didn't were gathered in one corner of the room, just like these — dead and lying huddled together, as if trying to find protection within each other.

Harrison is young, but as a fighter pilot, he's seen more than his share of death. And it's still hard to take, especially when he encounters something like this: Even when they know death is coming, they choose to stay together. "It must be a natural reaction for people to cling to each other when they know there's no way out," he whispers. "But there's not always strength in numbers. Sometimes you have to depend on yourself." He forces himself to turn away and rise from a kneeling position.

The room has two other doors. One is closed. Skirting the bodies, Harrison moves into the room whose door is standing open. It's also an office, covered in dust, but nothing like the other ones. This one has very nice decor, possibly Radcliff's own office. This is what Harrison is looking for. He checks his readings. There doesn't seem to be as much gas in this office, but he keeps his helmet on anyway.

There's a large metal cabinet recessed into the far corner behind a heavy wooden desk. It's locked, which is a good sign, no one locks an empty cabinet. This makes Harrison want to open it even more, but he doesn't dare use his laser to sever the lock as the unstable complex could collapse. He returns to the main room, finds a metal bar that has fallen from the ceiling, and carries it back to the office to use as a pry bar.

After a short fight with the safe-like cabinet, he's finally able to open it.

"Man, the clean-up crew obviously hasn't gotten here," he roars, and whistles at what he's holding: several documents with names and dates, an electronic logbook that looks like quantities of drugs ordered, a small amount of cash, and what looks to be a computer disc sealed in a small blue box. Harrison debates waiting for the clean-up crew, but decides to go ahead and take the items. Besides, his DEA training not only includes evidence collection, but also authorizes him to do it any time he suspects a crime — and this definitely qualifies.

He stuffs the stash into several of his many zippered pockets and heads out. But as he walks past the closed door, he hesitates. "Better take a look in here, too," he says.

The thick metal door resists, but a final healthy shove opens it just a crack. A sudden gush of air knocks him back.

He's glad for the cushioned suit. "The room must have been pressurized," he says. Curious, he leans forward to look through the crack. With the pressure equal in both rooms, resistance is gone and the door swings open easily now. Moving cautiously, he enters. It was likely that the door had been sealed from the inside, to keep out the gas.

As Harrison inspects what appears to be a storeroom, he notes an air shaft in the distant wall. A pile of dirt and other rubble has fallen down the shaft and flooded out into the room. The dust, now being sucked up the shaft, catches his eye.

When Harrison walks closer to the inlet, he notices a body the size of a small child lying face down, partially buried in debris. He knows that confronting this will be difficult. The child must have first sealed the door, and then tried to exit through the air shaft. But when the dirt shaft caved in, that ended his escape. For the second time, Harrison regrets firing the lasers into the mountain hideout.

Harrison quickly rushes over to see if the child is still breathing. He is, and Harrison's heart lightens. As he lifts the body, he realizes it isn't covered with dirt from the waist down, as he'd first thought. But from the waist down, there is ... nothing. By the looks of the clothing — slacks rolled and pinned where the thighs should have been — the child never had any legs.

Harrison lays the child down and turns him over, then suddenly gasp. Although the torso is the size of a small child, the face is that of a grown man, possibly in his early twenties.

The young man reluctantly opens one eye and forces out a barking cough. Harrison unhooks the air line from his helmet, allowing the fresh air to blow on the young man's face. Another moment and a short cough later, the man looks up at Harrison, cries out weakly, and pushes himself away; using both hands, he keeps moving back until he hits the wall.

"Hey, hey, slow down there," Harrison says, holding his hands out in an open gesture. "I know I look a little scary ... this helmet and suit would be enough to shock anyone. But believe me, I'm not here to hurt you."

The young man doesn't respond. He just keeps staring at Harrison, obviously terrified. For the first time, Harrison takes note of the man's appearance — black hair with a dark tan. The hair holds his gaze. Even with his otherwise disheveled appearance, the man's short hair is neat. It's almost as though he'd just combed it, which isn't likely. Harrison also recognizes signs of malnutrition. The man is very thin, with eyes sunken into two large, dark circles. Even against his dirt-covered skin, his eyes look wasted. He's injured from the cave-in, or possibly from something else. His notably large head has several sizeable abrasions on it, and a crucial amount of blood has run down his face and dried there. This worries Harrison.

"Can you talk?" Harrison asks, rising to a standing position.

The man stares at Harrison for a moment before answering. "Yes," he finally says

"Are you all right?"

The man reaches up and wipes a smudgy hand over his face, wincing as he passes over the cuts. "Yes. Yes, I think so."

"I'm going to take you out of here."

"Why?" comes the quick reply. "Aren't you DEA?" The man's voice grates over each letter.

Harrison nods, wondering why the man's eyes have turned to slits. "Yeah, I'm with the DEA."

"Since when does the DEA rescue anyone, especially half-breeds?"

"I ... I don't know what you mean."

"I know why you're taking me in. I'll save you the trouble and tell you right now — I don't know anything. Nothing!"

Harrison takes a long breath, trying to figure out what to do. Finally he says, "I don't know what you know or don't know, and I don't care right now. But there's some kind of gas leak in here. We have to get out of here, now."

Harrison reaches down to pick the young man up, but his hand is slapped away. "Don't bother, I can manage on my own," the man barks.

And it seems that he can; he pushes himself upright and begins a sort of stumbling walk, using the palms of his hands for feet.

But the sound of falling rocks erupts from the tunnel. Fearful that the weakened passageway will collapse, Harrison reaches down and snatches up the man with one arm while making his way to the door. The man squirms, almost causing Harrison to drop him.

"Look," Harrison yells, already breathing hard from running. "I respect you want to do it yourself, but this whole place is going to cave in on us. We got to hurry."

"Then let's go out the other way."

Harrison stops and looks down befuddled.

The man jerks his head back in the direction from where they'd come. "The air shaft. That's what I was trying when the rocks fell on me. But it might be closed now. There were a lot of rocks."

A huge boulder-sized rock falls out of the ceiling fifty meters ahead, virtually blocking the tunnel. Harrison has no choice but to trust what the man says. Hoping he might still be able to squeeze both of them through the air shaft, he turns back.

With the man still in his arms, Harrison hurries back to the storeroom. He sets him down and begins to dig out the shaft.

He clears away the dirt. "These walls are steep. Looks almost straight up. I'll push you ahead of me," he says.

"I don't know. If you're DEA, maybe I should just stay here and let the mountain collapse on top of me."

Harrison takes a deep breath. "Look, I don't know what your problem is, or what you might have been told about the DEA. But you don't have anything to worry about. You have my word on that."

The man nods slowly. "I guess I don't have a whole lot of choices, do I?"

Harrison places the man in the shaft first, and then pushes himself up until the man is sitting on Harrison's shoulders. The man places his hands against the walls for leverage, and they continue up together.

Near the top, the shaft widens enough for them to continue in a rough side-to-side movement. At the top, Harrison removes a thin metal grating, and both crawl out onto a grass-covered hilltop. The fresh air and sunshine feel fantastic, and Harrison breathes deeply. But when he looks over, his fellow escapee is cowering, covering his eyes with both hands.

"What's the matter?"

"It's ... been a long time since I've been out."

Harrison hesitates for a moment, and then says, "Well, stay here, and I'll get the vehicle."

"Where could I go?" The man pulls his hands away and grins at Harrison. "No legs, remember?"

Sitting in the tall grass shading his eyes, he watches as Harrison makes his way down the hill and over to the SJ.26. Minutes later, Harrison lifts off and quickly sets down on the hilltop. The man has crawled several meters from the shaft, perhaps thinking to elude, but Harrison acts as if he hadn't noticed when he climbs out and says, "Well, you ready to go?"

"Go where?"

"Back to DEA headquarters in Houston."

"Why? I can't tell you anything."

Harrison studies the dense jungle below them. Other than the animal noises, there is no sign of life. "You can't stay here."

The man moves his hand away from his eyes and with a defeated look peers at Harrison. "If I go back with you, I'll ... die."

"Huh? No, you'll be all right."

The man looks away, debating, then turns back. "You mean ... you're not going to give me to the clean-up people when you're done with me?"

"What are you talking about?"

Now it's the man's turn to be confused. "Me? What are you talking about? What kind of agent are you?"

"Well ... I'm not an agent yet, I'm a pilot. Captain Rod Harrison." He picks up the small man and heads for the vehicle.

"You sure have a lot to learn, Captain Rod Harrison."

Harrison decides to ignore that for now, but the insinuation troubles him. It has to be a misunderstanding. He leans behind the pilot's seat and sets the man down. The man tenses, so Harrison explains, "I'm not sure if the body harness in the copilot's seat will hold you since you don't have ... Well, I just think this place will work better."

The man nods.

Harrison begins readying the vehicle for takeoff. "So, now you know my name. What's yours?"

"We're not allowed names. I'm called Sixteen."

Harrison turns from the instrument panel. "Why are you called Sixteen?"

"Because I'm the sixteenth operative."

This is getting stranger and stranger, Harrison thinks. "I don't understand."

Sixteen sighs. "Didn't they teach you anything?"

"Apparently not. So why don't you fill me in."

"My mother was a drug user, like her parents, and their parents before them."

"I see. Your parents both used drugs, and that's why you're ... malformed?"

"No, you don't see. My father isn't a drug user. If he were, I would have turned out like those people working the fields, the drudges. They're just vegetables. They'll slave all day. Do anything for their daily ration of drugs. No, my father is Radcliff, and he doesn't use drugs, just people. That's why I have a good mind, that's all Radcliff wants."

They're in the air by now. Harrison signals Houston and informs them he is on his way in. Then he turns back to Sixteen. "So, you're the sixteenth child?"

A nod.

"You mean Radcliff fathers children knowing they'll be defor — knowing they will be genetically altered, just to use their minds?"

"It's not just Radcliff. All the traffickers have genetically altered beings. We get enough enhanced DNA to be half a person. The half they need. We're a lot less trouble to them being incomplete." He points to his missing legs. "That's why they call us their half-breeds. Deformed from the waist down."

"Where's your mother?"

Sixteen doesn't say anything at first.

"I don't know. I never met her. They took her after I was born. Least, that's what they did with the other ones."

"And you were the sixteenth one?"

"Yes, from Radcliff. But we all have different mothers."

"Why didn't Radcliff simply clone himself?" Sixteen doesn't try to conceal his cynical grin. "He knows we're more intelligent than he'll ever be." Harrison gives up checking his instruments and turns completely around. "So, do half-breeds need a daily amount of drugs, like the drudges in the fields?"

Sixteen nods. "Most do."

"Most. How about you?'

"No. I've learned to live without it. I began cutting back years ago. Without Radcliff knowing." He smiles.

"Hold on." Harrison turns forward and prepares to set down on the DEA rooftop.

Sixteen peers over his shoulder at the computer screen. "We're here already?"

"Yes." Harrison can see Sixteen is scared; he's starting to shake violently. "Look, I don't know what you've heard about the DEA, but you're with me now. Just stay quiet. I won't let anything happen to you."

He doesn't reply; Harrison simply lifts him out of the vehicle and starts toward the only building near the center of the huge landing deck.

The guard is a stout-looking man with a nametag sewn onto his shirt identifying him as Richard. With a "Hello, Captain Harrison," he holds the door open. "Looks like you brought company."

Sixteen doesn't say a word. Harrison only smiles. "Yeah, I guess I did."

As soon as they enter the modest structure, Harrison looks down at Sixteen. "See, it's not going to be that bad."

Behind them, Richard closes the door, but slower than usual. The expression on his face is quite blank.

Inside, they head straight to the elevator. Harrison pushes one of the many panels, and then enters the first door that slides open. Sixteen, watching, says, "Where are we going, Captain?"

"We're going to get those cuts taken care of first. You can call me Rod."

"We don't have to do that. I'll be all right, we could just leave."

"Don't worry, it's not going to hurt."

"That's not what I'm worried about, and you know it."

¤ ¤ ¤

When the elevator doors open at the infirmary, all eyes are on Harrison and Sixteen. One of the nurse mumbles under her breath; another places her hand over her mouth and whispers, "What's a pilot from the Wingate doing bringing that thing in here?"

But their professional training quickly takes over, and a nurse approaches the ragged duet. "Sorry about the way we acted, Captain. We've heard about mutants, but most of us have never actually seen one."

Harrison glares at the nurse, whose eyes are still riveted on Sixteen. "Why is that?"

The nurse shrugs. "Oh, we've had some brought in, but they usually go straight upstairs."

Harrison wonders what that means, but places Sixteen on the chair and allows them to finish examining him. He's surprised and a little annoyed at their reluctance to attend to Sixteen's facial cuts, but decides not to make a stink about it.

A doctor enters the hall were Harrison is waiting, as well as a nurse rolling a stretcher. "Captain Harrison, we were told you'd be coming in," the doctor says, giving Sixteen a sideways glance. "Just put him down here, we'll take care of him."

"No!" Sixteen jumps up onto his hands and tries to leap off the chair he's sitting on.

Harrison turns to Sixteen. He isn't happy about them being separated at this time, but apparently, this is procedure. "Look, just go with them. I have to talk with Chief Boyd, then I'll be back to check on you, all right?"

It takes several more minutes of convincing, but eventually, Sixteen allows himself to be placed on the stretcher.

As they roll him away, Harrison's unease grows, even though the room has a two-way mirror and he's able to watch everything.

"Captain Harrison?" He turns around. A woman, wearing a DEA uniform, has marched up behind him.

"Yes."

"Hi, I'm Angie."

"Hey, it's good to finally meet —"

"The chief wants to see you right away."

Harrison stops. "All right. I'll be up as soon as they're finished here." He points to the scene in the mirror.

Angie shakes her head. "No. He'll be taken care of. You must report to the chief right away."

Harrison looks back into the room to see that they're finally bandaging Sixteen's head. Fighting his instincts, which advise him to tell Angie to wait, he says, "I guess he'll be all right. I'm on my way."

Angie steps into the elevator with him, she is silent throughout the accelerated ride to the top floor. As soon as Harrison knocks on Chief Boyd's door, it's clear that his boss is hot about something. He yells, "Get in here, Harrison!" It's an attitude Harrison is familiar with.

Harrison opens the door and quickly enters what seems to him a very modest-looking office for such an important man: an oak computer desk and monitors take up most of the space. "Yes, sir. You wanted to see me?"

"Well, first off, I'd like to congratulate you on getting Radcliff, and second, what the hell do you think you're doing bringing that mutant in here?"

That didn't take long, Harrison thought. "Well…sir…I couldn't leave him out there to die."

"Yes you could. And if it bothered you so much, the clean-up crew was heading there right after they finished up the compound."

"I…thought he might know something that could help us. He's one of Radcliff's people."

The chief leans back in his chair, but doesn't invite Harrison to sit. Not that Harrison was expecting it.

"Well, Captain, is there anything else you'd like to drag in? Maybe a dog or a cat?"

"Are…Are you serious sir?" It makes Harrison realize just how little he knows about the DEA. He remembers the documents and money and quickly regains his composure. Trying to reclaim some decent piece of professionalism, he begins pulling them out of his various pockets as he walks toward the cluttered desk. The articles are placed in front of the scowling man. "I found these at Radcliff's."

Boyd leans forward, but doesn't touch the items. "What's all this?"

"Documents and drug money. Names and amounts ordered. Evidence. Leads."

The chief sighs. "Harrison, there's nothing we don't know about Radcliff's operation. With Radcliff dead, this is of no use to us…just like your friend."

Harrison stands quiet; he has run out of reasons. "What will you do with him, sir?"

"The DEA doesn't take prisoners. Remember that, Harrison. We don't have the space, and certainly don't have the drugs they need to detox. Or maybe you expect the DEA to go out on the streets and purchase them so we can keep our prisoners from destroying the place?"

"This one doesn't need any drugs, sir."

"Harrison, wake up. They all need some kind of drug, or they'll die. But not before they go nuts and tear the place down. You have no idea what they're capable of." He points to the small pile. "Now, take all of this and get out of here. There's a liquid paper recycle in the control room."

Harrison gathers up the papers and turns toward the door. He's shocked by the chief's statement about prisoners.

"Wait, this is yours, too." Boyd shoves the money over to Harrison. "Any money the agents find is theirs to keep. It's our way of retaining them. Without it, no one would have this job." He pauses, and then slowly stands. He chooses his words diligent. "One more thing, Harrison… Sorry about being so inflexible. But we only bring in prisoners for one purpose…questioning. And I decide which ones, understood?"

Numb, Harrison can only say, "Yes, sir."

When Harrison enters the elevator, his stupor makes him nauseous. Now, he realizes what he has done. And that Sixteen was right. They'll put him to sleep like an animal, he thinks.

But this situation is so far out of his league, he has no idea what to do about it.

Chapter Four

Harrison, in deep thought doesn't hear the elevator door open; he looks up and sees the infirmary. He heads immediately to the window.

The doctor steams up from behind and ask, "Are we ready?"

Harrison turns toward him. "Ready for what?"

"For this." He holds up a hypodermic needle. "You brought him here for questioning, didn't you? Well, he's ready."

"Ah…yes," Harrison replies. "Of course. Let's get on with it."

The doctor points Harrison into the stainless steel room where Sixteen lays. The half-breed has been strapped to a metal table; not excepting his fate he is now biting his lower lip in angry.

The doctor, tapping the needle, asks: "Are you familiar with how this drug works?"

Harrison whips his head from Sixteen to the doctor. "Pardon me?"

The doctor smiles. "I heard you're new. Figured you'd want a rundown of what to expect. Now, as soon as I administer the drug, he'll begin telling everything, starting with the most recent and going back to the beginning. But you'll have to record it. He'll have a vast amount of information, and he'll go very fast. You only get one chance."

"What do you mean … I only get one chance?"

"Well, after he tells of an experience, he'll lose it for good. It's kind of like emptying his head."

Harrison glances over to give Sixteen a comforting look before turning back to the doctor. "What happens when he gets to the end?"

The doctor smiles again. "Oh, don't worry. You'll have your information long before that. After you've obtained your data you can leave…we'll handle it from there. You see, as he regresses, his body functions will deteriorate. It can be very messy."

"You mean he forgets that too?"

"Everything," the doctor replies with a nod. "When he reaches the primal stage, his brain functions will shut down. And he might fight toward the end. That's why he's strapped down."

Harrison gives Sixteen another collusive look. "Well, ah … I'll have to be alone with him. You can't hear anything he's going to say. It's … classified. Sorry, you'll have to leave."

The doctor shrugs; obviously disappointed he'd have to miss out on something good. "I'll just be a second administering the drug and I'll be out."

"No, that won't do," Harrison states, fighting to keep a level tone. "I'll have to inject him myself. I've done this before."

"I don't know. If it's not done properly, it'll be very painful for him."

Harrison just stares, and then holds out his hand.

With a resigned sigh, the doctor passes Harrison the needle and points at Sixteen's neck.

"All right, this is where it goes. No need to hit a vein, but injecting here gives it a direct route to the brain. Call me when you're done, I'll be right outside."

As soon as the doctor leaves, Harrison points the needle at the floor and releases the serum, then tosses the empty syringe on a nearby table. He then turns to Sixteen.

Sixteen's tempered frown lessens, for the first time. "Boy, for a while there, I thought I was dead."

Harrison shushes, and then gives him a tense smile. "We'd better be quiet. I don't know if they can hear us. I told you I'd take care of you, and I keep my promises."

Sixteen looks around, his eyes resting on the door behind Harrison. "So, what are we going to do now, Rod?"

Harrison doesn't answer right away; he's busy undoing the straps that secures Sixteen to the gurney, and wondering if he's doing the right thing. The chief's words are blaring through his head. What if they're true? What if Sixteen does need some kind of drug to keep him from going crazy? After searching his conscience, he realizes that, by helping him escape, he'll be disobeying a direct order. But the chief's order goes against everything he holds true and worthy. Destroying a pirate's ship in a dogfight is one thing. Taking part in killing an innocent half-breed is abhorrent to Harrison. If there are going to be consequences, he'll just have to pay them.

Finally, he turns to Sixteen. "What are we going to do! We're getting out of here, that's what. But first, you're going to play dead."

He glances at the sheet covering Sixteen's torso, then takes it and wraps Sixteen in it, covering him completely.

"I don't think I know how to play dead," Sixteen whispers.

Harrison whispers back, "You don't do anything. Nothing at all. Don't even breathe." He then turns and heads for the door, Sixteen securely under his arm. "Remember, not a sound."

Now in the hall, he makes certain no one is nearby, and then quietly departs for the elevator. Midway down the hall, he breaks into a half-run.

Just about the time he thinks he's librated Sixteen, he hears, "Captain Harrison."

He twists just as the doctor reaches for the sheet-wrapped bundle under his arm.

"What are you doing, Captain? We'll dispose of the body," the doctor demands as he attempts to pull Sixteen out of Harrison's hands.

"I…I need the body," Harrison stammers.

The doctor slows but continues to tug gently. "Well, if it's an autopsy you need, we'll do that right here."

"No, it's not that. We…We're testing a new weapon, and we need bodies."

The doctor stops pulling altogether. "All right, but at least let us package it up and send it down to Weapons for you."

Harrison shakes his head. "No, uh, it's non-standard testing. And there's no time to waste. The bodies have to be fresh … I mean recent … and I was told to personally see to it."

The doctor takes one step back, his face more formal than before. "Well, why didn't you say so before now?"

"No one is supposed to know. Keep this to yourself." He continues for the elevator. Immediately after the elevator door open topside, he hears, "Hello, Captain Harrison, what do we have here?"

Richard doesn't look quite as understanding as the doctor was, and he reaches toward the bundle. Harrison has always thought the guard was a little strange; the way he talks is bad enough, but that blank stare that never changes … Harrison wonders if standing in the hot sun all day has poisoned his brain. But for now, Harrison ponders how many shots from his shoulder weapon it would take to see that blank stare go away for good.

"No," Harrison says, backing away. "It's personal."

"Sorry, I'll have to see," Richard replies. "It's the rules, you know. Everything in and out, I have to check." He lifts the sheet and identifies the top of Sixteen's head.

Harrison starts to feed him the line about an experimental weapon and fresh bodies, but catches himself just as the guard drops the sheet back down and says, "Oh, you're going to dispose of him. All right, you can go."

Harrison's shocked, but also grateful — he tries to hide both emotions as he thanks Richard and heads for the outer door.

When he reaches his vehicle, he sets Sixteen behind the pilot's seat and climbs in. "Sorry about this, but you'll have to stay in the sheet a while longer. We're getting out of here before anything else can go wrong."

"It's all right," Sixteen replies, his voice muffled. "But where are we going? Back to the compound?"

Harrison stops a moment. "No. There is no compound. My place."

"Where's that?"

"Not far from here."

"What kind of place is it?"

"It's a nice place, a community complex." That's all Harrison can think to say about it.

"What's that?"

"It's a place where a lot of people live in one building."

"How many people?"

Again, Harrison is reminded that Sixteen is little more than a child, frightened about his uncertain future. Or perhaps, like a child, he never imagines that he has one. "I don't know," Harrison says his voice thick with emotions he didn't realize he possessed. "I guess about four hundred people live there. You ask too many questions."

Sixteen doesn't say another word, and the next few minutes pass in silence. In fact, he doesn't budge from under the sheet until Harrison states, "We're just about there."

In the reflecting glass, Harrison watches as Sixteen whips off the sheet. A second later, he feels the young man climb up to look over his right shoulder.

"Wow, Rod, your house looks like a giant pot with legs."

Harrison smiles. "I never thought of it that way. Is this the first time you've seen the desert?"

"Yes," he replies. "Or a city, or anything except for the jungle. I mean, I know what this stuff is — I've seen pictures — but they all looked alike. Big and round, with large support columns underneath to hold them up. Each one has got to stand at least twenty meters off the ground."

Harrison nods, impressed. Apparently, the young man's light sensitivity isn't a permanent problem. Without knowing why, he is deeply glad it isn't.

"Are we going to land on the roof?"

"Yep," Harrison says, and begins maneuvering toward the landing pad on top of his building. "We'll be doing a vertical descent." To Sixteen's quizzical look, he adds, "Straight down, just like we did on the DEA landing pad."

The young man nods and continues to watch; he's in awe of the things he's heard about, but never seen. And when he can, Harrison watches Sixteen's reactions, finding pleasure in them.

"Man, I can see it now," he shouts so close to Harrison's ear that it hurts. "All the buildings are connected by large tubes."

"Yes, they're called transit tubes. And next time you're going to blow a hole in my eardrum, care to warn me?"

Amazed, Sixteen asks, "Is that all houses inside? Like, where people live?"

Harrison shakes his head. "Well, I've only lived here for a short while. Been on training missions most of the time. But yes, this is where most people live. There are also places for eating, drinking, and buying food, and lots of stores. Some buildings are for making things and growing food. Everything you need. I live about halfway down in this building."

"Wow! What's the tube for?"

Harrison smiles. "To transport people from one giant pot with legs to another." Sixteen laughs. It's the first time Harrison has seen him look anything but scared or angry. That indefinable feeling happens again, and Harrison finally realizes what it is: a combination of pride and fondness. In his life as a fighter pilot, Harrison has been familiar with the first, but the second has always eluded him. Until now.

As they near Harrison's rooftop, he says, "Hold on, we're starting down."

After a simple landing, Harrison exits the vehicle and turns around to see his passenger emerging. "No, wait," he says, and Sixteen pauses, afraid.

"No, everything's all right. It's just time to play dead again." To Sixteen's dismayed face, he adds, "Look, it's safer for now. And just until we get to my place, all right?"

Sixteen's reply is a sullen nod as he slowly pulls the sheet around himself. Harrison can't fail to notice how much stiffer Sixteen's body is as he grabs up the bundle and heads for the elevator.

What Sixteen doesn't understand is that Harrison can't even go home without facing a checkpoint. In his history lessons growing up, Harrison read about a time when this wasn't needed. But as this isn't the case now; he must keep Sixteen concealed until they reach his private quarters.

Harrison approaches the elevator hoping to obtain easy access from the door guard, who is seated behind a small but thick glass window with a dullard's look permanently fixed on his face. It's abundantly obvious that he has performed menial tasks all his life, and would undoubtedly be very happy to sit there until the day he retires. But, for now, Harrison needs him to open the second security door leading to the elevator. So he has no choice but to work with him.

As they enter the hall, the guard stirring, says, "Name?"

"Rod Harrison."

"What's in the bag, Mr. Harrison?"

"Laundry."

"Looks kind of heavy for laundry. Let's have a look."

Harrison moves the sheet to slightly expose his laser pistol. Then, in the most pleasant voice he can muster, says, "You calling me a liar?"

"No, I didn't mean it that way."

"Then please open the door."

The door splits in the middle and both halves disappear into the wall on either side. Harrison steps onto the elevator, sweating in spite of the controlled temperature of 22 Celsius. "Level 30," he says.

The elevator quickly arrives at the thirtieth floor; from there, it's only a short walk to his apartment. After searching most of his zippered pockets, he finally locates the key card in the top left one that opens the door.

As soon as they're inside, he sets Sixteen on the couch. "All right, you can get out now," he says.

In Sixteen's haste to unwind himself from the sheet, he falls off the couch and onto the hardwood floor. The sound echoes off the polar-bear-white walls. But Sixteen doesn't yell out; his awe and wonder at what is around him keeps him quiet.

Harrison grins. "Well, how do you like your new home, at least for a while?"

"Hey, it's great! But ... how long can I stay? I mean, that guard sounded mad. What if he tells somebody how you acted?"

"Don't worry, we'll find you a permanent home. And let me handle the guard, all right?"

The young man gives him a quizzical look. "A permanent home? Won't I be going back to the jungle sometime?"

Harrison thought for a moment. "I don't think that would be beneficial for you at this time."

"I know people there, you know," Sixteen said, defiantly. "That's where I was headed when you stopped me."

"Stopped you? You mean rescued you."

Sixteen grins. "All right, rescued."

"But would these people keep you?"

"Of course, as long as I know where the drugs are."

Harrison sighs. "That's what I thought. Well, you're my prisoner now, and you have to work for me. But no drugs."

Sixteen looks around. "What will I do here?"

Harrison has always lived and worked alone. He thinks for a moment. "Yeah, what will I do with you? What did you do for Radcliff?"

"I kept track of his inventory and its location," Sixteen replies proudly.

"What can you do without the computers?"

"Huh? No, I didn't use a computer to do it. We weren't allowed to record anything. Evidence, you know."

Harrison is incredulous. "Are you telling me it's all in your head?"

"Of course. What did you think they used us for?"

"You kept track of the entire operation? In your head?"

Sixteen nods. "Every gram in and out and where it's located."

Harrison now realizes what the good doctor meant by a vast amount of information. "That's ... amazing," he says.

Sixteen just grins.

"Ingenious, too," Harrison adds. "If the DEA locates the hideout, they still have no proof. That's quite ingenious. Did you keep track of his money, too?"

Sixteen laughs. "Yeah, I bet you'd like to know that."

Even though, as a DEA agent, Harrison should definitely want to know that, he doesn't care at the moment. "Look, don't worry, we'll find something for you to do."

Harrison notices the blinking light on his viewer; he walks over and touches the screen to turn it on. Megan's face appears on the screen. "Ah, hello, Captain Harrison," her recorded message says. "I just called to congratulate you again. I was watching your daring escapade. If you'd like to talk, I'd love to hear from you."

He pushes the numbers displayed. Just as Megan's real-time face appears, he grabs the screen and turns it away so she can't see Sixteen.

When she sees who it is, her blue eyes light up. "Oh, hi there, Captain," she said. "I was hoping you'd call."

"Hello, I just got in and found your message."

"I'm glad you're all right ... and I'm very glad you returned my call."

"Of course I returned your call," Harrison says. "What can I do for you?"

"Well...I thought since we both have the rest of the day off, and if you feel up to it, we could go out. Kind of a celebration. That evidence conviction you made is the biggest trafficker this year, you know."

"You heard the chief, beginner's luck." Out of the corner of his eye, Harrison watches Sixteen moving toward him in a flurry of white sheets. He holds up his hand, and Sixteen plops onto the floor. The sullen look is back, but he is being still. Harrison turns back to the screen.

"Well, ah, I'm a little tied up right now."

He can see her disappointment, but her reply is cheery. "If you don't feel up to it or if you don't want to, I'll understand."

"No, no, it's not that at all." He glances over at the bundle of sheets piled on the floor and convinces himself that it'll be all right. He turns his attention back to Megan. "Sure, that sounds great."

Her smile is brilliant. "You mean you want to?"

Harrison struggles to keep a normal tone. "Of course, what time?"

"About seven o'clock? I know a discreet place we can go. Since you haven't lived here long, you're probably not familiar with it. Do you want me to come by and get you?"

Harrison glances at Sixteen. "Ah, no. Don't go to any trouble. Why don't I meet you there?"

"All right, if you want. Just take the Number 9 transport from your dwelling and it'll drop you right in front of the place. See you at seven."

"All right, seven o'clock it is. I'll see you there."

The screen goes blank and Harrison looks down. "Look, you should be fine for a couple of hours. Before I leave, I'll make sure you know where everything is."

Sixteen sighs. "Oh, all right. She sure is pretty."

Harrison grins. "Yes, she sure is. Now, are you hungry?"

"Yeah. I could eat a little. But fresh fruit's the only thing I can eat. Radcliff designed me that way."

¤ ¤ ¤

While Harrison watches his new friend clean out what little fruit he has — and it is far from fresh — a yawn overtakes him. "Well, buddy,

I've been up most of the night and all day. I'm badly in need of some rest. How about you?"

"That sounds good to me," He reply's, looking around, "but where will I sleep?"

"In the living room for now. The sofa's pretty comfortable. We'll get you a bed at some point."

¤ ¤ ¤

Four hours later, the alarm blares. Groaning, Harrison reaches over and turns it off, then rolls to the other side of the bed.

The first thing he has to do is figure out when he needs to be at the Number 9 transport station. Bleary-eyed, he glances over the notes he jotted down when he spoke to the man in the transport office. "Good, that transport picks up on the hour and half-hour," glancing back at the clock. That means he'll have to catch the 6:30 transport to get there on time. An hour to get ready. He looks out of his bedroom door and sees that Sixteen's still sleeping.

Harrison doesn't exactly feel rested himself, but by the time he's cleaned up and into his dress clothes, he feels ready to tackle the task of finding the transport station. He checks the front room again. This time, his new roommate is up and wandering about.

Harrison reaches into the pocket of his flight suit, fumbling around, trying to locate his key card. His hand runs across the forgotten papers, then the money, but no key. He smiles to himself.

"Hey, it's not much, but it'll buy dinner," and stuffs the money in his jacket pocket, throwing the papers on the table. He dives into the last pocket, his final hope at a door key. His hand brushes against a small, hard, rectangular object that too he'd forgotten about. He steps into the living room and yells, "Hey, Sixteen!"

He looks up just as Harrison throws the small blue box over to him. "What is this?"

"It's a module," Sixteen replies.

"For what?"

"Well, different colors are for different tasks." He turns it over and peers at the back. "But I don't know what this one's for. I've never seen blue before."

"What does a module do?" Harrison asks, as he steps through the doorway into the room.

"Depends on how it's programmed. They're usually used in flight control."

Harrison's eyebrows furrow. "Funny, I've never heard of them." His face grave, he urges Sixteen to continue.

"When it's activated, it sends out a separate signal that tells the speed and its heading. They're totally self-contained and separate from the other electronics." Sixteen glances at him again. This time, he notices Harrison's clothing. "You look different, why are you dressed like that?"

"I'm going to be gone for a little while. That's it, nothing else?"

"Oh yeah, also. They're used for tracking, too. Like if you have an unmanned crawler on a planet and you lose it off the satellite, all you'd have to do is turn on the module. It would relay its last known location, speed, and direction, and with that, you could calculate where it is."

"Is there any way of figuring out what this one fits?"

He thinks for a moment. "Yes, but I need a computer."

"I have one in the other room." Harrison points at the doorway.

"I'll need a plug for this end."

Pulling the end open he exposes the many-pronged plug-in, but Harrison isn't looking. He's stepped back into his bedroom to do a final check in the mirror.

"What kind of fruit do you like to eat?" Harrison calls out. "I can pick it up on the way back."

"Ah, any kind's good. Some mangos if you can get 'em. And I need a ten-prong plug-in."

Harrison pokes around the corner. "What are you talking about?"

"This." He holds up the module. "I'll need a plug-in for this, or I could use this one." Grabbing a hold of Harrison's viewer cord.

"No, not that. I need that one. But I have a viewer in the bedroom that you can cannibalize. How long is all this going to take?"

"There's no way of telling. See the ten prongs? They only use six of them. The other four are dummies. But there's no way of knowing which six, and in what order they belong. So it could take me a long time, or I might get lucky and hit it right off."

Harrison smiles and the feeling that everything is going to turn out fine returns. "And you thought you wouldn't have anything to do. When you get done with that, I'll have something else by then. But right now, I have to get going, or I'll be late. I'll see you when I get back."

As the front door closes behind him, Sixteen yells, "Don't forget the fruit!"

¤ ¤ ¤

On the way to the transport, Harrison wracks his brain trying to think of a more permanent place for his friend. When he first steps off the transport, his mind is still distracted, until he sees Megan and the place she's standing in front of. Suddenly, his dress-up clothes feel shabby in comparison.

He recognizes her face, but that's about all. The rest of her looks... different. A long satin strapless with a slit up the right side clings to her every curve like a second skin. The dress is almost transparent. It boasts a daringly low front, but he is unable to see much due to the thick, bristly collar that only incites his imagination further. Her shiny black hair is done up, and she's wearing what smells like a very expensive perfume.

She smiles the moment she sees him. "Glad you could make it."

"Me, too. I almost didn't recognize you without your uniform."

She looks down, then back up. "Yes, I guess I do look a little different. Shall we go in, Captain Harrison?"

"All right, but call me Rod."

Another smile. "Rod it is, then."

Once inside, Harrison notices the admiring glances from tables around them. Megan ignores them. Soft music plays in the background as they talk. Harrison reveals to her the good side of life as a fighter pilot, while trying not to bore her with the small details. Megan tells about her life on the planet, as well as her DEA duties. Although he agrees her life hasn't been nearly as exciting as his, it doesn't seem that important. She is so beautiful, she could be talking in a foreign language and he'd still hang on every word.

After dinner, they dance a little, but she seems more interested in talking. After the third dance, Harrison escorts her back to their table and then excuses himself to visit the men's room.

A sizable knot of people in the hallway leading to the restroom blocks his way. They don't seem to be waiting in line, so Harrison gently pushes his way through. When he finally reaches the front of the crowd, he tenses up. At the door stands a man dressed in a white suit with an oversized matching hat.

Harrison knows immediately what's going on. The gaudy white suit is apparently well recognized; everyone around seems to know who and what he is. So does Harrison.

The first woman in line, well dressed and very pretty, passes him a roll of money, and then whispers something in his ear. The man pulls out a gun, rotates the barrel and pulls back the cylinder. He then places the barrel to her neck and squeezes the trigger. She inhales deeply, turns and walks away. He's now looking at Harrison, "Are you next?"

"Hey, you're blocking the door," Harrison states. "Step away!"

The man allows Harrison to brush by, but then follows him in. The small room is made up primarily of glass and marble tile, which reeks of a bleach and iodine mixture.

"What's your pleasure, big fellow?" The man holds up the white gun and cracks a grin.

Harrison doesn't answer.

"Come on, everybody needs something, what do you need?"

"I need you to go away."

The man's grin only fades for a second. "You don't know what you're missing. You've never been enhanced, have you? I'm offering you an opportunity to experience life as it's really meant to be—perfect."

"No thanks." Although the man owns an expensive suit, his lack of education is obvious to Harrison. It's apparent he has become rich late in life, and has no idea of the consequences his actions as a drug pusher will cause.

The guy is bull-headed, as well. His face lights up. "I know, how about a psychic? Or, you want to be a great lover tonight? You can, you can be anything you want, and it's free. Just for you."

"Now why would you do that?" Harrison knows why; his DEA orientation had told him. But he wanted to egg the pusher.

"Why would I give you drugs for free? I treat my customers' right, that's why!"

"Just for your customers?" Harrison replies. "I'm not your customer."

"But you will be."

Harrison almost smiles, wondering if the man's spiel would be as confident if he knew that Harrison was DEA. But he chooses not to mention it. That would only alarm the crowd, and there's no telling what they might do. Plus, he has Megan's safety to consider.

All that changes quickly. "I got just the thing for you," the man says. As he's talking, he's rotating the barrel around. He pulls the cylinder back, and then quickly sticks the gun to Harrison's left shoulder.

Harrison knocks the gun away, and then comes around with a driving right cross that connects with the man's lower jaw. With the solid hit, the man sails back into the toilet stall as his gun drops hard to the floor.

Everyone suddenly gathers at the bathroom door trying to grab a glimpse of the action. When Harrison looks up, nobody is making a sound; all eyes are securely fixed on the gun filled with drugs.

Harrison snatches up the gun and shoots it into the wall, smashing the barrel on the marble sink. The crowd watches with ravenous eyes as drugs of all strains flow into the sink and down the drain.

¤ ¤ ¤

When Harrison returns to Megan, he tries to act nonchalant, but everyone is pointing and staring at him. Megan can't help but notice.

"What happened, Rod? I heard someone say, 'Trouble in the bathroom.'"

"Oh, nothing. Just an over-aggressive drug pusher."

Megan nods and sighs. "That's pretty common around here. Around everywhere, actually. Those drugs have become so sophisticated, there's almost nothing they can't do. And everyone wants something, even if it is temporary. It's an epidemic that has no boundaries." She stops suddenly and smiles at him. "So, you handled it?"

He nods. "Didn't see any sense in arresting him here. But I've got a good description, I'll report him."

"Yes, that's probably the best way. Even in here, a public arrest could cause a stampede."

He reaches out and lifts his water glass, then holds it out to her for a toast. "Yes, and that's the last thing I want to happen tonight."

"So, I heard what happened today," Megan states. "With the half-breed, I mean."

His eyes are quick to meet hers. "Things sure get around fast."

"My friend who's on the day shift...Angie...she told me about it. I think you talked to her?"

He nods.

"If you don't mind me asking, what did they do with him? I...I hear things don't go well for them when they're caught. I've never seen one myself... "

He looks away. "Well...he came out all right."

"All right? What do you mean by that?" Megan knows they wouldn't allow a half-breed to just stay there. The only way he could have gotten out all right was...And then it hits her. "What did you do? You didn't, did you?"

Harrison tries to cover, but his puzzled look doesn't work. So he says, "Didn't what?"

"You know the half-breed. You've hidden him somewhere, haven't you? Or taken him home?"

Harrison's stunned. He just stares at Megan.

"Is he at your place?"

"I...I, uh —"

Megan jumps up, almost knocking over her water glass. "Let's go!"

"Go where?"

"Your place. Come on!" She turns and begins making her way toward the door.

"Megan, wait. I'm not sure that's such a good id —"

Harrison throws some bills on the table and quickly follows.

For the second time, Harrison is terrified for Sixteen, and his terror keeps him from thinking straight. She's talking about him like he's some sort of druggie I just picked up off the street. Maybe when she meets him she'll like him, and she'll see that he doesn't need any drugs. Maybe she won't report him...or me... Maybe ...

It's a fifteen-minute ride back to Harrison's place. Megan whispers excitedly the whole time. Harrison, numbed by the fact that someone has discovered his secret so easily, can only nod and mutter a few answers. When they arrive, Harrison opens the door and goes in first, with Megan close behind.

"Where's the light?"

"They should be on," Harrison replies, his voice guarded. "When I left, every light in the apartment was on."

Harrison shuts the door and pulls Megan down into a crouch beside him, then draws his laser. He uses the small transparent sight screen to search the room.

"He's ... He's gone."

"The half-breed?" Megan whispers. "How could he have gotten out of here?"

Harrison rises without answering; Megan follows as he sets the living room lamp back upright and plugs it in.

"Oh my god!" Megan gasps. "Looks like a tornado's been through here!"

Everything in the apartment is destroyed, even the couch; stuffing is everywhere. Broken glass covers the floor.

"I'll be right back," Harrison starts for his bedroom.

"Hey, wait —"

He holds up his hand and disappears inside the room. A moment later, he emerges and heads for the small kitchen. When he returns, his face is ashen. "Every room is the same. Totaled. And Sixteen is gone."

"Who?" Megan asks, puzzled.

"The half-breed. That's his name. His number. I don't —"

He heads for the one place he hasn't checked yet, the bathroom. Megan strains to listen, but Harrison is strangely silent for a couple of minutes, until he says, "Megan. In here."

"Did you find something?" She rushes to the open door.

"Yes."

She walks into the bathroom and sees what Harrison is looking at. Sixteen is hung with a viewer cord. It's secured to a hook in the bathroom wall. Underneath him is the linen cabinet. Apparently, he'd been perched on the cabinet until it was knocked over. He's still swaying. Harrison reaches out and stops his movement. The cord has cut deep into Sixteen's neck, but there is no blood, not on his neck, nor his clothes. Harrison notices he's cold, and as white as the sheet he was wrapped in only hours earlier.

Harrison is so shocked he doesn't flinch when Megan grabs his arm. "Come on, Rod, let's get out of here. You can stay at my place tonight."

"No. No, I … can't leave him like this. I have to —"

"No, you don't. I'll call my friend at the office. No sense in tormenting yourself. We have people who can take care of this, no one will ever know."

"I…I think I should stay."

"Why? There's nothing you can do for him now. It's not your fault. You didn't know."

He turns her way. "Didn't know what?"

"Half-breeds need drugs or they'll die. But not before they — will do this." Megan had realized early on that Harrison was different than most men she'd known. And she'd guessed it was partly because he was innocent of the way things really were on the planet. Seeing his reaction made her hope even more that their friendship will blossom into something special, and that this incident won't have an ill effect on it.

She squeezes his arm. "Come on, Rod. It'll be alright. Really."

Without answering, he allows her to lead him from the apartment.

¤ ¤ ¤

Neither has anything to say on the transport ride to Megan's place, but after they arrive and she places him on the sofa with a drink, he asks, "Megan, are all half-breeds like that?"

Megan, standing with her back to him turns on a small stereo; she rejoins him just as the soft music begins drifting out. "Like what, Rod? Dependent on drugs?"

Harrison shakes his head. "Yes. It…doesn't seem fair. Why do the traffickers do that?"

Megan thinks a moment. "I … don't know. Possibly to keep them under control, you know dependent on them. "

Harrison manages a swallow of his drink, then says, "Yeah, maybe so."

The horrible death of his new friend has drained the passion from him. There isn't much point in trying to talk. When Harrison finally admits he's tired, Megan points him to the guest room, then shows him where the bathroom is.

He closes the door, turns out the light, and then lies quietly across the bed. He doesn't expect to be able to sleep. It's far from what he had imagined the first night alone with Megan would be like. The day's outcome continues to go through his mind. He can't understand why he'd been so trusting as to leave Sixteen alone, in a strange place, in hiding like that, without even really knowing him.

"I only knew what he told me, and I accepted every word," he whispers to the dark ceiling above him.

Could Sixteen — could any human have done that much damage? He desperately wants to believe that the friendly and intelligent Sixteen wouldn't be capable of trashing an apartment and then taking his own life. But from Megan to the doctor…yes, even Chief Boyd had implied half-breeds were loose cannons. And if not Sixteen, who could have done something like that? His thoughts swirl in his head: No one had access to my apartment. The door was still locked. Was the chief right?

The chief's words run through his head: They all need drugs or they'll die, but not before they go nuts and tear the place down.

An hour later, Harrison gets up and discreetly opens the sliding glass doors. When he sees they lead to the balcony, he eases out onto it. Even in his shock and grief, Harrison can't help but be impressed: Every balcony extends beyond the one below it, and the balcony's acrylic floor gives an unobstructed, if narrow, view of the ground below.

And that's where his focus rest for the next few minutes, while he remembers vague thoughts and feelings that he'd forgotten about. His mind stumbles, one by one, into the holes he's buried his feelings in. Feelings that were not permitted to show in an all-male academy, or to his peers aboard the Wingate.

When he finally looks up, he notices a few sparse white clouds caused by the warm air rising off the vast desert floor, which lays claim to an even larger percentage of fertile grassland as each year passes.

"It's about a hundred meters down."

Startled by the voice coming from the other side of the balcony, he quickly looks over to see Megan standing there.

"I didn't mean to disturb you. My bedroom's at the other end." She points, and for the first time, he notices the other set of double doors. "I come out here every night before I go to bed. With the shift that I work, I can watch the sun come up."

She has changed from her evening gown to an even sexier nightgown. The warm breeze encourages her dark curls to gently brush her shoulders.

However, most important to Harrison at this moment, is her being kind to him. Not pushing him, just being there if he needs her.

"I thought coming out here might help me to relax," Harrison says, walking over to stand beside her.

"I…I called the office. My friends will be going over to your place soon. Do you want to talk about it?"

"Not much to say. I just screwed up, that's all."

"No, you didn't. You just learned a hard lesson. I mean, you're a fighter pilot. Unless you worked with them, you wouldn't have known anything about half-breeds."

Harrison shakes his head, and no matter how she tries, refuses to meet her eyes. "No, it's more than that. I believed in him, and that scares me. I didn't think that someone could deceive me that easily. I though he would be all right."

"Things are different down here, and so are the people. But you couldn't have known."

Harrison nods. "I realize that. It's nothing like the academy or the space program. But I always believed I was a good judge of character. I've never been so wrong about a person in my life."

"You never encountered people like these before," Megan persists. "I mean, it's not like being in space. The half-breeds don't have bars on their collars, or nametags. It's a lot harder to judge people without the stripes on their sleeves or seeing the medals they've earned."

"I should have listened to the chief." He turns to her. "I must seem like a fool to all of you. But Sixteen made it clear that he no longer needed drugs."

"Maybe… Maybe he honestly believed that he could do without the drugs. If you believe in something that strongly it's easy to convince others, even if it's not true."

"You're right about that." Harrison looks back out over the desert lights.

Megan turns around and heads for her sliding-glass doors. "You might as well get used to it."

He calls after her. "You mean there's more?"

She pops her head out of the open doors. "I mean, Sixteen just confused you. The people who work in the drug world are trained to manipulate you. It's what they have to do."

That night, both Megan and Harrison have a troubled sleep.

¤ ¤ ¤

The next morning, there's a knock on an office door somewhere in Capitol City. The voice inside says, "Come!" A well-dressed man with a pencil mustache and finely trimmed beard steps into the office.

"Come in, Mr. Jackson, I'm glad you stopped by."

"We have to talk, Mr. Pressnell."

The man behind the desk frowns when he sees Jackson's expression. "Not here. Let's take a walk."

Once outside, Mr. Pressnell says, "Now, what's your problem?"

"You mean our problem," Jackson replies, his moustache twitching. "The DEA got Radcliff."

"So?"

"So? What do you mean so? Do you know who did it?"

"Yes. I'll see that it doesn't happen again."

The pencil moustache squirms in shock. "That's it! That's your answer? You'll see to it that it doesn't happen again? How are you going to do that? Besides, without Radcliff, we have nothing."

The second-in-command of the most powerful agency in Capitol City sighs. "Roger, please listen. Not too long ago, Radcliff was nothing ... a small-time producer, a minor player. I made him. There's a million Radcliff's out there. We'll just create a new one."

"But how? We need one now."

"I'll take care of the particulars. I had Harrison recalled. His paperwork's being processed now. Can't move too quickly, it would look suspicious. You just take care of your end."

Jackson hesitates. He's worked hard for his position, but at times like this, he wishes he'd never gotten it. "You know I'll take care of my part, but there's something else. Harrison has a tracking module."

"That's not your business. I'm handling it now. Did you pick up your orders?"

"Yes." He tries to mask his feelings of failure. It bothers him that he's sold out.

"You don't look so sure. Do you want out?"

Jackson shakes his head.

"That's what I thought." He smiles. "No one ever does. I'll see you next trip, Mr. Jackson."

¤ ¤ ¤

For the most part, Harrison keeps busy for the next two days. Earlier, he'd hoped for more time alone with Megan and getting to know Houston, a city he knows little of. He also suspects she feels the same way about him, and he wants to follow that trail as far as it will go. But Sixteen's death bothers him. Most of his time is spent at work, trying to keep his mind off what has happened. Harrison hasn't seen Megan since he left her home the next morning, and has managed to avoid Chief Boyd — until now. But on his way in from another non-productive night of scanning the jungle, his controller orders him to check in with the chief before signing out for the day.

Harrison enters the office and takes the chair indicated to him.

"Harrison, I want to acknowledge what a fine job you're doing," Boyd says in a gruff voice. "And all of us want you to come back."

Harrison stiffens in his chair. "Come back? But my time isn't up yet, sir."

"Well, it seems there's been some variance to the rules. Your Admiral Kachel contacted me this morning and said that anyone who's being reviewed for promotion must be on an active-duty roster. He also said that it would take another week or two before yours is completed. So, you're reinstated to the Wingate for two weeks. I've made all the preparations. You can take the DEA vehicle that's assigned to you—assuming you'll return it in two weeks."

"Of course, sir. Thank you." There's nothing else to be said. Harrison's life has always been controlled by others, and if the admiral ordered him back, back he must go. Maybe the change will help him forget about Sixteen.

"Then it's resolved," Boyd says. "You leave at 1800 tomorrow. That will give you some time to get ready. See you in a couple weeks, Harrison."

Chapter Five

Harrison doesn't know exactly what he should or shouldn't say to Megan, but he does spend most of the day making sure she knows precisely how he feels about her. He believes she's not ready to hear what he has to say, but he has to tell her anyway, and now, this afternoon.

Things don't go well. At the end, Megan is shouting, "Are you only planning to stay if you don't get the promotion? Because if that's all you're concerned about, don't inconvenience yourself by crawling into bed with me! I can't promote you!"

"Look, I don't care about the promotion as much as you seem to think. Even if I get it, I might not re-enlist anyway. But if I'm discharged with the higher rank, I'll maintain the higher pay here. And hey, I have to come back."

When she finally looks up at him, he grins at her. "Even If I stay with the Wingate, I've got to return the DEA vehicle. The chief made it clear, it's settled. I'll be back."

She can feel her defenses withering. She nods and tries to smile, but the smile holds uncertainty. She feels as though she has been betrayed.

He hopes he can try talking with her again when he returns. It's nearly 1800 hours as he approaches his vehicle, duffle bag in hand, stopping momentarily to screen the vehicle's general appearance. The adrenaline starts to flow. The closer he gets, the faster his heart thumps. It's the same every time; this is what he lives for, the speed, the power, the exhilaration. The planet's atmosphere magnifies the sensation of close-surface flying: nothing like the endless boredom of space, where you seemingly stand still for hours at a time. But that freedom is what he needs right now. In space, there are no drug dealers with little white guns, no unhappy women, and no half-breeds freaking out and dying just like that.

Harrison stores his duffle bag behind the pilot's seat and climbs in, then depresses the button to close the shield. The windowless vehicle has been sitting in the hot sun all day, and the sticky leather grabs onto his pilot's suit with every move he makes. But he doesn't really mind; after he straps himself to the thickly cushioned captain's chair and breathes deeply, he can still detect the new smell. This makes him smile. To knock off some of the heat, he activates the climate control, and refreshingly cool air begins blowing on him.

With another glance at the chronometer, Harrison knows he needs to hurry. He has to be in the air by 1800 hours. A test of the command panel and navigational controls, then he grips the half-round solid control wheel encased with thick black rubber. Each flight is like the first; the anticipation of being in control of the powerful vehicle reminds him of feelings he had as a student pilot.

With both feet on the control pedals, he assures himself that everything checks accurate, then he contacts Houston flight control. Flight control has been notified of his planned departure, and assigns him the flight path he needs to rendezvous with the Wingate. Everything in the air above 5,000 meters is under government control, so he's obligated to follow their instructions. This means he has little to do: just set the heading that flight control plotted, and wait for them to notify him when it's time to ascend.

As he heads northwest across the desert, the vehicle continues to accelerate until it reaches its assigned speed and altitude. At first, the desert below appears dead. Out of curiosity, Harrison turns on the high-speed camera just to see what the floor really holds.

The viewer only picks up a blur of brown; the heat rising off the sandy desert floor gives an appearance of motion. However, the high-speed camera is efficient enough to take clear images of any activity below. Harrison occasionally glances at them. There's an abundance of animal life, small buildings partially covered with sand, scarce vegetation, and people. Some of the people are in vehicles. A large area is blank, marked as unusable on most maps, an area that was reserved for government experiments.

"Was" is the operative term, Harrison thinks. From his reading on anti-matter propulsion, he knows it had been used for the development of matter-fusion power plants, where the basis of life itself had been transformed to serve man's needs. Presently, it is nothing more than a waste facility.

After the SJ.26 hits mach three, the sonic boom quickly follows. Its echo ricochets off the canyon walls below. It's just another element for the desert dwellers to contend with in their plight to escape the all-consuming drugs and the violence that seems to be their genetic inheritance.

His communicator squawks; its flight control, giving him his new heading and ascent instructions. He switches the camera off, relishing the thought of putting the SJ.26 to its first real test. His enthusiasm heightens as he increases to nearly full power. He is now 1,400 kilometers northwest of Houston.

As heat waves rising off the dry lake beds hit like solid walls, he pulls back on the control wheel, and with a single voice command the small craft reconfigures for hypersonic speed. The wings mold to the fuselage; rudders and flaps retract into their respective housings, and the hatch-protector covers slide over the entrance lid to protect it from space debris. The electronic force-field extends several hundred meters ahead, absorbing most of the impact from the clear air turbulence. Some, but not all, of the buffeting calms down. It isn't like zero gravity, but the gravity drive deflects the gravitational forces that hold everything in place as the matter-fission power plant propels the SJ.26 into hyper speed.

Once he achieves the proper climb angle, Harrison can set the vehicle on automatic. It takes every ounce of power the small ship can muster to reach this speed and steep-climb angle. The autopilot will not allow this, it must be done manually. Soon the pressure lessens, and the speed levels off. Occasionally, he gazes straight ahead at the blue sky, and at the ground behind. Both can still be seen on either side of the viewer's back portion. Combined with the sensation of flying level, this makes for a strange sight.

The five-hour trip to the Wingate will give Harrison plenty of time to think about what he wants, and what he requires; after all, it is his life — something he didn't fully understand before his encounter with Sixteen. The half-breeds have no choices, but he does. He must. If not, what point is there to life itself?

For the first time, Harrison actually misses life on the planet. It's a strange emotion for him. He obviously never missed what he never had. Although he hasn't been there long enough to call it home, a yearning to return takes over, and the feeling quickly turns into loneliness. As determined as he is, he simply can't think of space in the same way. The loneliness soon surrounds him, like the ship itself ... The ship no longer represents the fortress it once did, but suddenly seems isolated and vulnerable.

Shaking off the uneasiness, Harrison settles back and prepares himself for the long trip. More crucial than speed is the time to think. He begins to codify affairs in his head.

Without realizing it, he nods. Yes, that's probably it. People are made to interact with each other. Maybe that's why the planet has such a drawing effect. It's the one fine thread that binds us together, we're all a part of it and it's a part of us. Everyone has a purpose, everything has a reason. Although most of them don't seem to behave like it. Possibly, they're just too busy worrying about their own life to see what's going on around them. Like that drug dealer. How many times a day is that scene played out ... a hundred? A thousand? How many people get used? How many people like Sixteen die every day, and no one knows or cares, and if that's so, if there's no rational conclusion, then it's simply organized anarchy, but I don't believe that.

Those people on the planet, what more could they want? The planet is such a beautiful place, and all they seem to care about is destroying it. I always felt sorry for them, being stuck down there. But maybe I was wrong. Perhaps I'm the one who doesn't realize what's truly important.

If he doesn't return, Harrison decides, he will miss it. A lot. Especially the sound of a running stream — that's something he'd never heard until his brief assignment on the planet. Or seeing the sunlight shining through the trees. The scents of the flowers. And Megan.

Thinking about Megan distracts him from his confusion about the planet. He looks up just as the vehicle enters a white haze. Harrison looks back at the planet, knowing that all he'll see for a while will be white — the ionosphere protecting the planet's fragile balance also traps in the manmade gases.

In a few minutes he will pass through the inner atmosphere, in less than an hour he will reach its outer edge.

¤ ¤ ¤

Now, bordering the outer edge, he brakes through the white haze and his view changes abruptly to black as he enters the dark side. What looks to be a million stars spread out like the lights of a large city. And suddenly, there it is, concealed in the mother planet's shadow. The Wingate, gallantly protruding from the orbiting space station like a crowning monument to space technology. Definitely one of a kind, a monolith in space travel, renowned by those who built her, and feared by those who oppose it. The station, now in its perigee of orbit, receives shipments of supplies throughout the month and keeps them in storage until the Wingate returns. After being transferred to the Wingate, the supplies are delivered to the manned outposts across the galaxy.

As Harrison closes in on the Wingate, the giant starship takes control. Its security won't allow anything near that isn't one of her own, or that hasn't been scheduled by Houston. Not that a small vehicle like Harrison's SJ.26 could do any real damage to a giant starship; however, this is standard operating procedure.

Long before the Wingate comes into clear view, Harrison hears a familiar friendly voice from the communicator. Although his vehicle number and name are already on the screen, the man asks him to identify himself. It's always the same routine, to see if the pilot is capable of and willing to comply with orders, and to make sure their information is correct.

The fast-talking communications officer asks Harrison, "How did you like your vacation, where did you get that vehicle? I didn't recognize the ID number on screen."

"Oh, just a little something I picked up in Houston."

"Not too bad. Pick me up one next time you're out. How's the woman down there?

"Gorgeous. Not so military, if you know what I mean."

"Can't even imagine it," came the reply. "I'm putting you on the starboard side, first level, Hangar Three. Our orbiting speed is five degrees per min."

Harrison pauses. Hangar one has always been Harrison's location. The senior pilots are first out in an emergency, and the first hangar always goes to the senior pilot on each level. One is also closest to the sleeping quarters.

"Hangar Three?" Harrison replies. "Who's in Hangar One?"

"I'm...not sure. We can't leave open holes, you know."

As Harrison nears the station, the starlight carves a shadowy outline. Soon, an enormous black object ringed in lights flows into view. Its size, at first sight, is forbidding to most. Although it's a familiar one to Harrison, it still amazes him to think that something so large can move at all. Once the Wingate comes into full view, it's easy to see how the massive ship can travel at light speed: Each of its four exhaust portals is several hundred meters across. Each side has four through-and-through landing ports called wings. The top three ports are for designated fighters; the bottom one is reserved for much larger ships, like the supply shuttles. Each wing has massive doors that will seal off the ports in case of attack. Harrison notices they are all open, as are the exhaust portal doors.

Harrison aligns with the first level and contacts the director for permission to enter the landing port. The planet is now rotating behind the Wingate and is moving out of view, but not out of mind. As soon as he receives the director's "Area is clear to enter," Harrison starts in.

Inside, he has less than two kilometers to slow the vehicle and match the Wingate's speed. Only then can he set down. Too fast at set-down, and he will shoot straight through and out the other side; too slow, and the ship will pull away and he'll go back out the entrance. It is all theoretical and has never happened, but it's possible. After matching the Wingate's speed, Harrison is pulled down with a demanding jolt from the artificial gravity. He quickly moves to another line in front of Hangar Three, and prepares to exit the vehicle.

From the huge control room, located near the ceiling and walled with thick protective glass, the director watches everything. Harrison knows that, as each pilot clears the area, the director will summon a large robot on rails to place the vehicle in the proper hangar. Then, the vehicle will be readied for its next flight.

Harrison pressurizes his flight suit and depressurizes the cabin, then slams a fist on each latch at the same time to open the lid. Although he's at Hangar Three, the walk to the thick pressurized doors isn't that far. Or at least, not too far under normal circumstances. After being on the planet for such a long time, the Wingate's artificial gravity feels very odd.

He walks slowly toward the row of individual exit doors; at the end are four huge doors for loading and unloading supplies. He heads for the first open door. Now inside, he depresses the door-closed indicator. The thick doors glide together. Inside, it's a room-size elevator. On his rapid descent to the center of the wing, he can hear and feel the small room pressurize itself. When he arrives at the center floor, the rearward doors open and he's one step from the inside lobby of the ship. Removing his helmet, he walks straight to his first checkpoint, the wing commander.

"Captain Harrison, reporting for duty."

Commander Benson looks up and allows a half-smile to show. "Harrison, I didn't expect to see you again. I thought when you returned from liberty, you'd be promoted out of here."

"I did too, sir. But it seems there's been some kind of alteration to the rules."

"So I heard. I have you back on the active duty roster already. It's not exactly a vacation, but I think I have something you'll find to your liking."

"What's that, sir?" As he speaks, he's seeking his name on one of the many screens displayed on the commander's desk.

Benson smiles tightly. "You'll see. But first, stow your gear. Oh, and one more thing … I'm sorry about your Number One hangar, but I didn't expect you'd be back as a pilot. Number Three is the best I can do on such short notice."

Harrison wheels around. "You mean they didn't tell you that I was coming back as a pilot?"

"Not until this morning. I tried to talk Admiral Kachel out of the entire procedure, but he wouldn't hear of it."

Harrison believes him. Wing Commander Benson has always been fair and easy to get along with. The admiral, on the other hand, gives little weight to the pilots' opinions.

"How is the admiral, anyway?" Harrison asks.

Another half-smile. "Are you sure you want to know?"

"That bad?"

"He still makes the pilots stand at attention in the barracks while he inspects the fighter ships. Do you have any idea how long that takes him?"

Harrison snorts. "I don't have to guess. I remember too well."

"But don't worry, you won't be put through any of that."

Harrison gives Benson a questioning look.

"You won't be around here after tomorrow."

Harrison's helmet slips in his grasp and he tightens his fingers around it. "Where am I going?"

"Well, I have to clear it with Admiral Kachel, but I have a shuttle going into Sector G1Eight. That's a long way off our projected path, and I believe that she should have some protection."

"She, sir? You mean the shuttle?"

Benson's eyes level on Harrison. "No, not the shuttle. I think the pilot's name is Laura."

Harrison fights his gasp of recognition, but is certain Benson saw his reaction. "That sounds fine, but ... what do we own in Sector Eight?"

"There's an outpost established there."

"I didn't know we had anything that far out. What happened to Sector Seven?"

Benson nods slowly. "Yes, I'd forgotten you've been out of touch. The admiral decided to skip Sector Seven and go straight into eight."

Harrison whistles. "That should take the whole week."

"That's the way I figure it, Captain. This way, you can be on duty and still keep away from the admiral."

"After next week, I'm not going to worry about Admiral Kachel anymore."

"What do you mean by that?"

"When my enlistment is up, I'm leaving."

"But what about your promotion? I'm sure you'll get it."

"It doesn't matter. I'm ready for a change."

Benson starts to speak, but hesitates before replying, "Well, for now, you get your things stowed, and I have to get to the helm. The admiral will be docking shortly. We'll talk about this later."

¤ ¤ ¤

It definitely isn't like his place in Houston, but Harrison does get comfortable in the captain's quarters. He feels a little better with the situation knowing it won't be for long. Within the half-hour, he runs down some of his old comrades; they decide to meet in the staff dining room. The other pilots fill Harrison in on everything that has happened during his absence, but only after he tells of his adventures as a DEA agent.

Harrison is enjoying himself and hasn't noticed the time passing — the alarm sounds and a voice comes over the ship's intercom. The polite female voice states, "All Wingate members on five-minute alert."

"Oh, man, I forgot about the time." Harrison leaps to his feet.

The warning is to notify the crew that they have just five minutes to prepare themselves and their belongings for the uneven and at times jerky movements that occur when the Wingate disengages from the orbiting space station. Not to mention the effect it has on the ship's artificial gravity.

Laughing, Harrison and his buddies join the throng of crew members running back and forth with last-minute tasks.

¤ ¤ ¤

The Wingate breaks free of the space station. Harrison, back in the dining room, views the station drifting out of sight. It looks more like a discarded drum with wings as it floats away. After what seems like an eternity, the alarm finally sounds a second time, and the polite female voice returns — this time, to warn everyone that they have just five minutes to prepare themselves for the commanding thrust induced to break the Wingate free of the planet's gravitational pull. Harrison turns his chair around to face forward and straps himself in; he wants to view the panorama screen.

The sound of the four giant reactors powering up resonates through the solid steel walls. No one in the huge dining area says a word. In fact, there's no other sound in the room as they listen to the unbroken roar of the power plants. Everyone, including Harrison, seems to be holding his breath. If anything were to go wrong, it will be during the transformation to light speed.

Harrison senses the vibration, he braces for the sudden weight on his chest, a weight so heavy it feels as if it could suffocate him. Minutes seem like hours as the giant ship strains to achieve its cruising speed. Then just as suddenly as it began, the pressure eases off.

The Wingate breaks orbit. Harrison watches for the longest time as the stars pass, each one a little faster than the one before, until he realizes the excitement has worn off, his enthusiasm is gone. It's time to call it a day.

¤ ¤ ¤

Twelve hours later, it's as if he'd never left. If someone can leave for two months, and when they return nothing of importance has changed, he wonders, how significant is this program anyway? Somehow, the trouble doesn't justify the end. Worse yet, it doesn't even matter who does it.

The thought saddens him deeply, to believe that so many loyal people put everything on the line for nothing. In his mind, the program parallels his life: non-productive. What surprises him even more is, he'd never really thought about the space program's importance before, just that he had a duty to it.

He'd never told Chief Boyd exactly how he brought Radcliff's ship down, knowing he would have disapproved. Actually, he couldn't have explained why he tried such a risky maneuver. It was undoubtedly one of the most important decisions of his life, and he took pride in thinking he was the only one who could have achieved it.

He always strives to be the best; it helps to fill the void in his life, which of late seems to have no real meaning, no beneficial reason for him to exist. Working with the DEA was his first task with merit. Had Radcliff gotten away, Harrison would have labeled himself an undeniable failure.

Commander Benson, who has tried without success to persuade Harrison to stay on, is now briefing him on the new outpost G1 Eight in sector eight. Harrison thinks it ridiculous to have one more meaningless outpost, seemingly leading to nowhere. This, of course, he keeps to himself. Harrison returns to his quarters to just sit all day and night in a holding pattern. After two months of making his own decisions, this waiting around is poisoning him. Harrison's depression sets in like cement; it forms a barrier that threatens to smother him. Finally, the next evening, Benson conveys notice that he has cleared the mission with the admiral, and that Harrison is to prepare to leave. Harrison sighs. That's the admiral for you. Never lets you know anything until the last minute.

But Harrison doesn't really mind the short notice. He's just glad to be going, especially with Laura, on this, his last mission for the Wingate. He's curious about how she feels toward him now. Of course, he doesn't mention this to Benson, or anyone else, but things between him and Laura have been pretty intense in the past. Unlike Megan's goodbye, their parting had been amicable enough. Yet as always, Harrison was left wondering why their relationship didn't go deeper than it did, or mean more to her.

But it doesn't matter; they're both professionals. If Laura does or doesn't hold any lingering feelings for him, either way, they won't let it interfere with the mission, or his decisions.

Chapter Six

When the call ultimately comes, he suits up and is at the shuttle hangar in a matter of minutes. Laura, already inside the shuttle, has everything ready to go, or so she thinks.

Inside the supply shuttle, Harrison meets Jim, the new copilot. While Jim isn't looking, he gives Laura a wink, then waits for her reaction.

She grins and winks right back. "You're going to protect me from the pirates, right? Who's going to protect me from you?"

"Don't worry, you're safe," Harrison smiles. "Maybe. Who else is going?"

"This is it," Laura replies. "The three of us."

Harrison scowls. "Is there pressure in the cargo area?"

"No. Why?"

"Air it up. I want to check the fighter." The small vehicle would never survive the week-long trip by itself; therefore, it's housed inside the shuttle until needed. After the supplies are loaded, the air is removed, and then the fighter is stowed.

Laura looks confused. "The fighter? It's been checked and we're ready to go."

"Oh, no. Until I've checked it, we're not ready to go."

Laura knows Harrison is serious and she doesn't want an argument, especially one she will lose. She turns to Jim and says. "Re-pressurize Cargo Hold Two".

When Harrison returns to the control room, he tells Laura this will be his last mission. "I guess that's why I don't want anything going wrong. This fighter belongs to the DEA. It shouldn't have been assigned a Wingate mission."

Laura's eyes exhibit understanding. "Oh, now I see why you're so touchy about it. I thought it was one of the Wingate's fighters."

Harrison continues to explain the entire situation to her ... with him and the admiral, at least.

"Admiral Kachel isn't that bad," Laura repeats herself. "He's just under a lot of pressure, a lot of pressure."

"Is that what you call it?" Harrison snaps back.

"Come on, you don't really mean that."

"Well, let's see." He tries to hide his growing ire. "I get a five-minute notification that I'm your sole security on a week-long journey, with a fighter that doesn't even belong to him. There should be two other pilots on a mission this remote, and we shouldn't be flying anything but Wingate property." He begins to tell Laura how senseless he believes the entire program is, but suddenly catches himself. "Look, I don't mean to sound so harsh, but ... don't you see what I'm talking about? You can't even discuss it with him. You can no longer reason with the man. I didn't even try this time. He's like this all the time now." He leans back in the chair and looks her in the eye. "After next week, the admiral is your problem."

"You know you're going to miss all this," Laura grins. "You leave? I'll have to see it to believe it."

He doesn't reply. She decides to let the conversation drop there, turns her chair around, and locks herself to the seat.

Harrison's glad she let it go; right now, he's more concerned about going that far out with only one fighter when there should be a squadron of at least three.

But there's no turning back. Harrison locks himself in while Laura obtains permission to exit the port. The craft departs the Wingate and sets course for Sector Eight.

¤ ¤ ¤

At the DEA building in Houston, the new day begins with new issues connected to new problems, which are just beginning to materialize.

One of the many controllers calls over to Megan, "I have another agent down."

Megan nods. "I've already notified Search and Rescue."

A few moments later, Chief Boyd walks into the control room. "Where's he down at?" Then, he turns to Megan. "I wonder how Harrison got so lucky? I've been over and over his recordings, and I still can't figure out how he caught Radcliff asleep when we can't even get close to a major trafficker. I can't see a thing he did different."

"Could it have been luck?" Megan says.

"Maybe." Boyd thought a moment. "Notify all clean-up crews, when we get another minor trafficker, I want him alive for questioning. Their strategy seems to be shifting. They're not running, they're fighting. And they're not doing it by themselves. The drug lords were always hard to expose, but this is absurd. ... They know where our people are before we do."

Megan relays the message to all agents and their clean-up crews. As she is finishing up, Angie enters the room. "Okay, kiddo," Angie smiles. "I'm ready to take over. You look tired."

Megan yawns as she's briefing her, and then says, "It has been a long night. See you tomorrow."

Megan heads straight home, tired and ready for a bath and bed.

As she inserts her key card in the slot, the metal door to her fourteenth floor apartment disappears into the wall like an elevator door sliding open. Her first reaction to what she sees is shock, then outrage. But just as quickly, her anger turns to fear. The larger furniture pieces from the front room have been broken into small pieces and piled in one corner;

the smaller items have simply been tossed to the floor. Even her carefully collected paintings are mutilated.

She immediately shoves the key card back in, making sure the door closes and locks, then races for the security monitor in the hall lobby. The guards respond to her yells promptly.

While they make certain no one is still in the apartment, Megan calls the chief.

"I'm going to send over a couple of agents," Boyd states. "Tell Security to keep a guard on the door until they get there. Do you have someone you can stay with?"

"Uh, yes," Megan replies, thinking. "I can stay with Angie. Please connect me and I'll ask."

"No need. I'll send her over to get you."

¤ ¤ ¤

Seventy-two hours later, near one of the many planets located in Sector Seven, three pirate ships prepare to carry out a well-orchestrated plan.

"The signal from the supply ship is very strong, Captain," says an older man in a timid voice.

"Good, they're on schedule. I estimate them to be in position at 30 degrees, mark it."

He suddenly gives the older man a harsh glare. "You seem unsure. I know this isn't your first dance, so what is it?"

The old guy knows better than to hide anything from Captain Tutelage, or "Captain Careful" as the crew had so justifiably nicknamed him. Tutelage is attuned to everything concerning the ship, and stays that way. Pirating isn't an easy way of life. Let something slip by, and it could cost you everything.

Tutelage stares at the man impatiently.

"Captain, it's just that...this is another government ship, a supply ship. We don't need the government onto us, and we don't need any more of their supplies."

Tutelage turns away. "Open visual communications." Now the captains of the other two ships can see and hear him. "Remember, you two must intercept the supply vessel when it reaches midpoint of the planet. I'll do the rest."

His ship brakes off in the opposite direction, leaving the dirty work to his cohorts.

"What about the fighter?" yells the captain of the smallest ship, the Dollins.

Tutelage scowls. "As soon as it's released, I'll receive the signal. After I calculate its speed and direction, it won't be hard to hit. Remember, this will be the most valuable supply ship yet. Don't miss."

¤ ¤ ¤

Harrison and Laura are just sitting down to eat when Jim calls to her. "You better come and see this".

Laura and Harrison both rush to the pilot's control area.

"What do you make of this?" Jim asks. "Two inbound ships on an interception course."

"Looks to me like we have company," Harrison replies, then starts for the common area to retrieve his helmet.

"What's your big hurry?" Laura follows after him.

"Oh, no real reason," Harrison's face is grim. "When you're the only fighter pilot, you gotta plan ahead. I just thought I should get out in case they decide to blow you up."

"Ha, ha, you're very funny." She turns and calls back, "Jim, open the communication line and we'll see who it is."

When there's no reply after a couple of minutes, she states, "They're getting too close, Jim. Cut the power. Let's get a close-up view on the scanner and compare it with the computer's list to see what type of ships they are."

Before the comparison can be completed, Harrison takes one glance and says, "Those are old military ships. Equipped with military-grade weapons."

"How — how do you know that?" Laura's face reflects her trepidation.

"Don't worry, they're not powerful enough to penetrate the hull at this range," Harrison says as he heads for Cargo Hold Two.

He stops at the doorway just before the airlock. "Look, Laura, I know you're a good pilot...one of the best I've worked with ... but close off the portal doors anyway."

She glares at him. "Yeah, I got it, Captain. Like I've never done this before."

"Hey, don't take it the wrong way, I'm a little nervous too. Just didn't want you to overlook anything."

Without answering, she turns to the instrument panel and taps in the order to start the giant, finger-like doors closing. Half raise up and the other half come down, they then interlock in the middle to seal off the exhaust ports leading to the power plant, which would never withstand a direct hit. When the green display light begins to glow, she looks up. "All right, the exhaust doors are sealed. Feel better?"

He returns her grin, relieved as he starts through the airlock.

With the power plant shut down, the supply ship has already slowed to less than half speed. The two pirate ships are continuing their advance adjacent to the shuttle. Laura and Jim watch their progress, and wait for Harrison's craft to emerge.

¤ ¤ ¤

Once inside the fighter, Harrison punches in the code in order for the power to generate simultaneously with the cabin pressurization. He knows he can't blast off from within the cargo area, but he wants to be ready. The entire time, he's cursing Admiral Kachel for not giving him more fighters to protect the ship. When ready, he notifies Laura.

As Laura opens the outer door, Harrison expels a jet stream of fresh air to propel him out of the cargo hull. Once outside, he gives Laura the "All clear," and waits as the cargo door rolls shut. Harrison releases another jet of air, this time only on the right side, to cause the SJ.26 to rotate.

After he maneuvers the vehicle into position, where the blast from the power plant won't have any effect on the supply shuttle, he punches both throttles all the way down. The white hot exhaust illuminates the entire area, especially reflecting off the rear of the supply ship. The thrust pushes Harrison's body deep into the heavily padded captain's chair as the craft gathers speed rapidly.

¤ ¤ ¤

The captain of the Dollins, the closest pirate ship, yells, "Their fighter ship has just been released from the cargo hull."

"But that can't be," comes the reply from Tutelage, which is now out of sight. "I'm not receiving any signal from the module."

"I'm telling you, it's out!"

¤ ¤ ¤

"Harrison, the scanners just picked up a third ship," Laura yells. "It's coming up from behind us."

"Well, he'll just have to wait his turn." Harrison tries not to show his concern. "I'm already tracking one now, in a minute I'll have him."

Harrison's speed increases, the exhaust stretches out into a long thin line that resembles a gleaming thread, then finally a shooting star — until he swings around and begins his attack on the first pirate.

Both ships are firing frantically at Harrison, but the fighter is moving much too fast for the lasers to lock on. Although they, too, have been quickened by the absence of gravity, they're just making a calculated guess at where he'll be when the lasers reach him.

¤ ¤ ¤

Captain Tutelage yells in a demanding tone, "Why aren't we getting a signal on him?"

"I — I don't know. We've been set up!" the Dollins replies.

"No, you fool! There must be a malfunction. We'll work around it."

The leader's words do nothing to quench the man's panic. "I'm telling you, we've been set up!"

The closest pirate ship, Capetown, reports for the first time. "He's coming in behind me."

"You two start down," Tutelage barks the order. "Lead him around to the other side of the planet."

"What about you?"

"Don't worry about me. I'm not leaving without that supply ship."

"It won't work. We won't make it halfway around and he'll have us," yells a voice from the Dollins. The captain's concern for his smaller ship is well-grounded.

"When you get anchored in the gravitational pull, you can cut power, close the exhaust doors, and orbit the planet. He can't follow you forever. Besides, he won't venture far from the supply ship. Especially when he's the only one they've got." The thought makes him flash a rare smile to the crew.

¤ ¤ ¤

Harrison has already closed in on the first hostile ship with lasers locked. "Hope the next one's this easy," he says as he punches the fire button.

A powerful white blast shoots directly into the Capetown's exhaust port. The ship implodes from its instantly breached matter fission plant, and then explodes. Evidence of the enormous eruption will be obvious for years to come, as it propagates endlessly outward. The blast leaves Harrison momentarily seeing spots, but soon his vision clears and he watches as the smaller pieces die out quickly, the larger ones hurtling out of sight, still on fire.

¤ ¤ ¤

The swollen ball of light blows out, and then fades from the screen. Jim can see that worrying about Captain Harrison has strained Laura emotionally, and with good reason. He still has two ships to subdue, both larger than the first. He knows he should say something to help calm her, but doesn't know what.

"Laura, he's already eliminated one," Jim says. "He's locked on and about to engage the other one. This is what Captain Harrison does, remember?"

"Yeah. Yeah, I know," she replies, but the worry doesn't leave her eyes.

¤ ¤ ¤

Harrison starts in after the Dollins, which has already begun its descent with power off and exhaust doors closed, probably hoping to lock into some form of orbit around the planet.

The old military vessel has several vulnerable points and Harrison has trained extensively on hitting them. But the first thing is to eliminate the lasers. Harrison doesn't like leaving Laura with the third pirate still coming on, but knowing he will return long before the pirates can penetrate the hull of the supply ship helps. Besides, it's standard operating procedure to eliminate the enemy when you have the opportunity. If not, he could easily become trapped between the two.

As they approach the planet their speed increases rapidly, but there's no way the pirate ship can outrun Harrison's fighter. Utilizing the strike-and-run tactic, it doesn't take Harrison long to take out the weapons onboard the old military ship. Now, it's just a matter of hammering away at the vulnerable areas.

¤ ¤ ¤

As the pirate ship continues to founder into the planet's cloudy atmosphere, Harrison soon realizes what they are attempting — to use the planet's gravitational pull to pick up speed, then slingshot out into space. But Harrison doesn't intend to follow it that far. They're nearly halfway to the backside of the planet, on Laura's opposite side — too far from her. Besides, Harrison's smaller ship won't withstand the heat from entering the planet's atmosphere at this speed. He has no alternative but to allow the pirates to go in alone. Harrison quickly calculates, as the Dollins disappears into the thick cloud cover, where it will exit, then continues around to the planet's backside to wait.

¤ ¤ ¤

Like so many best-laid plans, it fails. The Dollins is a no-show. He realizes they must have altered the flight path by staying closer to the surface, which would elongate the ship's exit from the planet. Although at their speed, and with a ship of that size, they may have accelerated too fast to pull out and struck the surface. Finishing his orbit will allow Harrison to search for them, not to mention the fact that Laura should have drifted past the inconsequential planet by now, and this route will be more immediate to reach her. The computer calculates her approximate position and sets the coordinates for the ship. Harrison starts off in her direction.

Plan B also fails. The pirate ship never materializes, nor any heat signature. Harrison concludes that the Dollins has, in fact, made a direct impact with the surface and is now the newest addition to a barren landscape. When he reaches the rendezvous point where Laura and the last pirate ship should be, there is nothing — no Laura, no pirates.

Harrison continues around the planet to search the area where he had left the shuttle. If she isn't there, she and Jim, thinking they must have lost him, very well may have headed back. Either way, he can track them from that point.

It takes an hour at full speed to reach the exact position where they'd been. But once again, he finds nothing in any direction.

"No way," he shouts. "She knows the routine as well as me. She wouldn't have drifted that close to the planet."

Yet the heat scanner reveals no traces of power-plant exhaust, nor do his instruments pick up an ion trail. The impossible has just happened: An entire ship has vanished.

Harrison sends out a communication to the Sector Eight outpost. The outpost is equipped to contact the Wingate. "Tell them what's happening and that the supply ship must be on the planet's surface," he says.

"The Wingate is on its way," Sector Eight replies. "Do not attempt a rescue by yourself."

Harrison hears, understands the message, and elects to ignore it. Even at its best speed, it will take the Wingate a minimum of twenty-four hours to reach Sector Seven, and he isn't continuing on to Sector Eight and leaving Laura behind. Against orders, Harrison heads for the planet — alone.

¤ ¤ ¤

The SJ.26's instruments can't penetrate the gaseous cloud cover that encircles the planet, so Harrison enters the atmosphere cautiously. From his pre-flight briefing, he knows the planet has an atmosphere which helps to moderate the temperature that for the most part goes unchanged year-round. But it's a poisonous atmosphere, consisting mainly of sulfur and ammonia. Without knowing the terrain, he doesn't dare descend any faster than he is.

As he advances beyond the thick cloud cover, visibility clears; the instruments come back on line as well. With a quick glance at the heat scanner, he's gratified to see that the screen has picked up the crash of the Dollins. It's possible they came in too fast, as Harrison had predicted, or had sustained too much damage from his lasers. But that doesn't explain why Laura's ship has disappeared too.

He continues to scan the surface to no avail. Except for the crashed ship, the heat scanner indicates nothing.

After making several near surface passes, he suddenly remembers the vehicle is equipped with a DEA high-speed camera. With a glance, Harrison now gets a clear view of the rugged terrain from several thousand meters. Thanks to the camera, he can now encompass a wider area. After several hours of scanning, he begins to wonder whether he can locate Laura by himself. The SJ.26's heat scanner is accurate, but limited compared to the precision instruments onboard the Wingate, which could have traced the slightest temperature increase to its source — if Harrison hadn't already disturbed the atmosphere.

Harrison takes note of a large flat area inside one of the many craters. It seems clear of debris. He slows a bit. On his second or third pass, he's certain — it doesn't appear to be a natural clearing. Rather, it looks as if someone has cleared and leveled the area for a reason. Tiny beads of sweat form on Harrison's forehead as he tries to imagine every possibility, then the not-so-possible outcome of him landing on it. Harrison thinks what other option do I have? It's either that, or waste even more time going back to the Wingate for help.

Rather than choosing the center, Harrison sets down alongside the cleared area, only to find he's right about its size: The clearing looks to be at least a thousand meters in length and several hundred meters across. He emerges from the safety of his ship for a closer inspection. Upon examination, he notes deep impressions, as if something had been sitting on the cleared section. Something very large and very heavy. Like a supply ship.

Harrison gazes at the clearing, trying to think of a way to make sense of the situation. There's only one place it could have gone from here — straight down beneath the surface. And that's crazy, Harrison, just crazy. What'ya thinking — the whole planet's hollow? But that's the only viable explanation he can come up with.

Okay, okay, if that's it — if they did just sink like a rock — how do I find them?

He looks toward the ship. It's a long shot, but if there's an opening, just maybe the high-speed camera can find it. He maneuvers the vehicle around the area.

The crater is much larger than he first estimated — approximately two thousand meters in diameter and very shallow, maybe eight to ten meters in depth, with an indentation located at one end of the base. Even though it's obscured by heavy dust, which is mostly his own doing, Harrison can distinguish that, masked inside the depression's wall, is an ordinary-looking loading-dock door — one he assumes won't be easily accessed. Instinct tells him there has to be another entrance, that there's always an emergency exit nearby. He continues to check. With a closer examination of the section between the dock door and the cleared strip, he soon unveils it.

He needs both exits to be guarded at the same time. Considering he's alone, he'll have to do both jobs himself, and quickly, assuming those who have Laura, Jim, and the supply ship know he's already here.

Chapter Seven

Harrison returns to the crater wall, positions his vehicle across from the dock door, and activates the lasers. When they build to full power, he directs them at the crater door and sets the computer to fire the weapons on his remote command. Harrison then hastily makes his way back to the emergency exit on foot, knowing that he only has minutes to prepare.

What seems like a short distance in the air is a long trek for Harrison in the bulky pressurized flight suit. He knows he will tire quickly walking over the planet's uneven surface, especially since it's covered with jagged rocks. He also notices that, although it's quite a small planet, it has a very heavy gravitational pull. Climbing the small but rough crater wall takes much longer than he'd expected.

Harrison finally reaches the emergency exit; he fires his laser pistol at the round steel plate covering the portal exit. When that doesn't work. He readies the stinger and manually blasts the steel plate: twelve shots, each several centimeters apart. This will leave a small hole, but one large enough for him to squeeze through.

Accelerated by the alien atmosphere, the stingers waste no time eating through the steel lid. At first, a large thrust of air surges from the small holes. But as Harrison fires at the cover with his hand laser, the entire thing detonates. The eruption blows the steel lid straight up.

As soon as the blast settles, there's a long pause, then a gust of escaping gas, after which Harrison promptly drops through the now open hatch.

Inside, he finds himself at the end of a long hallway. The walls and floor are seamless and appear endless. The smooth walls reflect the red and white emergency lights in the floor, which are flashing in a rapid sequence. He makes his way down the hall, hoping that everyone will be busy trying to repair the pressure loss.

When he reaches the end of the hall, he sees that it leads to another identical one. He peers around the corner to his right; this hall, too, seems to continue forever. To his left, he sees a door slowly closing. But there's no time or reason to wonder why; a man in a pressurized suit is racing down the hall in his direction, pointing a weapon at him.

Harrison aims his laser and fires. The blast hurls the man back several meters. Harrison rushes down the hall, past the still-smoldering body and on to the closed door at the end of the hall.

Depressing the indicator on the wall allows the door to open into what appears to be a small pressurization room. He steps inside, knowing that he has little time to waste; the door closes and the room immediately fills with air. When the meter indicating normal pressure glows, the inner door now opens to reveal what looks to be a warehouse. The warehouse is over half-filled with containers, most covered with government trademarks, supplies stolen from the space program. To his left, at the end of the wall, is a second doorway. Trusting this will take him to the main room and therefore be heavily guarded, he continues on, his awareness heightened.

The display's green light indicates the door isn't sealed, so Harrison lies on the floor and uses the barrel of his laser pistol to reach up and activate the door sensor. As the door begins to open, Harrison takes aim.

A person is standing at what looks to be the control area; several computer screens cover the roughly carved wall. Directly in front of him is an immense open section with several huge steel cylinders that appear to be holding up the ceiling. Laura's ship sits to his immediate right, with the pirate ship beside it.

The person operating the computer looks more like a programmer than a pirate. And that is about all Harrison has time to conclude. The man spies Harrison lying in the doorway and starts to run, but doesn't reach his weapon before Harrison fires.

The blast misses the man and strikes the computer bank where he'd been standing. There's a small explosion, which cause the cylinders to begin to move. The ceiling drops several centimeters; the warming alarm is set off. The green display turns red and the door Harrison's hiding behind begins to close.

Before he is sealed out of the control room, Harrison jumps up and quickly lunges through the now partly closed doorway, then bolts for the supply ship. The man, now hiding behind the computer bank, shoots wildly. Harrison can hear the white-hot blast whistle overhead. He dives behind the ship's front landing gear. The pressurized suit helps to break his fall on the rocky floor.

Harrison crawls to the opposite side of the landing gear, where he has both a clear view and adequate protection. He takes careful aim this time and squeezes off a second shot. It proves fatal for the pirate. The man's torso slams against the wall behind him and ricochets to the floor. Harrison is now alone in the large room. He glances upward toward the front of Laura's ship, noting that the entrance door has been cut open. Activating his helmet's internal communicator proves a waste of time; there's no reply from Laura or Jim. Apparently, the pirates have broken through the pilot's control room door as well.

Harrison hurries to the only other exit in the large room. As soon as the door is open, he witnesses a man backing out of a room approximately halfway down the hall, holding a laser. What surprises him is that the man isn't aiming at him, but back into the room.

The man turns toward Harrison just as he switches the stinger to automatic; the small flash of light carrying the stinger strikes the man in the head, knocking him to the floor without a sound.

Harrison runs to the door and cautiously peers into the room. Laura is sitting in the corner, holding Jim's head off the floor. Blood is pouring from a gaping wound in Jim's chest—a wound no one could have survived.

"Laura, are you all right?" Harrison yells, striding toward her.

But Laura doesn't answer; she just sits cradling Jim.

"Laura, there's nothing you can do for him. Come on, let's get out of here."

"He — he was going to kill me, but Jim pulled me behind him." She turning a vacant expression to Harrison. "He gave his life for mine."

Harrison grabs Laura by the shoulder and shakes her. "Laura, we have to go. Pick up your helmet."

She gazes down at Jim. "Can't we —?"

Harrison shakes his head. "Sorry, but I'm not sure we'll get out of here in one piece, even without Jim. He would understand, Laura."

She gently lowers Jim's head to the floor and reaches for her helmet. Then, unable to take her eyes off his body, she slowly backs out of the room.

"How many men do they have?" Harrison asks.

Her reply is slow. "All I ever saw was four."

"That's all? Four?"

She whirls around. "What did you expect? This is a warehouse, not a fortress. And besides, I haven't seen the whole place. So I'm not sure."

Harrison starts down the hall. Laura puts on her helmet as she runs to keep up.

"One was here when we arrived," she says, as though trying to prove she's over Jim's death. "And there were two in the pirate ship and one in the pursuit vehicle."

Harrison slows down. "What pursuit vehicle?"

"I'll explain later."

Now it's his turn to keep up.

They arrive at the large room. Laura takes one look at the ship, then says, her voice shaking, "Oh, man, look at that! The supply ship isn't going anywhere — all the airtight doors have been cut open."

"That's all right," Harrison states. "The fighter's outside. We can still get out of here."

The only other door leads to the emergency hatch he'd entered through, so he turns back down the hall, passing the room where Jim's body lays in the hope of finding the loading-dock door.

"How do you know which way to go?" Laura asks. She's breathing hard.

"My ship's in this direction. Besides, there's a bad air leak back there, everything is sealed up." Harrison is referring to the emergency hatch he'd cut open.

They were passing through another short hallway, and heading through a second doorway, when suddenly, they hear an explosion.

"What's that?" Laura shouts, slowing briefly until Harrison grabs her arm and pulls her forward.

"Don't worry, we're getting close." Harrison has activated the ship's weapons. It will take two minutes for the power to rebuild and the weapons to reset and fire again.

He follows the echo, knowing it will lead them to the dock door. It's easy to recognize; the ship's lasers have created a large hole through the solid steel door, and the entire hallway is burned black.

"What the hell could have done this?" Laura ask

"Let's just say we don't have much time." Harrison grabs Laura's hand. To her puzzled look, he adds, "I'll explain later." Together they run down the long hallway.

Nearly halfway down, Laura yells, "There's a man following us. It's ... it's the captain of the pirate ship. Tutelage, I think."

Harrison doesn't say a word. He just keeps on running.

"Aren't you going to do something?"

Harrison still says nothing.

Laura is beginning to tire; they pass through what was at one time a bulkhead. Now blown away, it has little resemblance to a barrier of any kind. All that remains to distinguish it is the steel ring that's fastened to the walls.

The glossy finished walls stop abruptly, and the hallway now looks more like a cavern. Harrison turns into an opening in the tunnel wall and pulls Laura in with him, then forces her back against the wall. The opening is very small, Harrison has to keep himself pressed against the wall to stay clear of the tunnel.

Laura leans forward and looks Harrison directly in the eye. "We can't hide here. It's much too small, and besides, he saw us duck in here."

Harrison raises his left arm and holds her securely against the wall.

Their two minutes has elapsed; the SJ.26 lets loose another devastating blast that rips down the tunnel with a loud shriek. The glaring-white flash fills the hallway, nearly blinding both of them as it surges past. They can feel the cavern walls shudder as the blast collides with the end of the hall.

Harrison peers down the hall. There's no sign of Tutelage. But then, he doesn't expect there to be Tutelage has been vaporized by the SJ.26.

"Come on, let's go." He steps into the hall.

Laura jerks him back. "Why didn't you tell me what you were doing?"

"I couldn't talk."

"What?"

"I was counting the seconds. The lasers will fire every two minutes until they're deactivated." Harrison explains

Laura needing no more explanation, she begins running for the opening at the end of the tunnel.

"What's the big hurry?" he calls after her. "We've got a minute and a half."

She doesn't answer, but keeps running.

Once inside the fighter, Laura straps herself into the copilot's seat as Harrison prepares for lift-off. As soon as they break free of the planet's static atmosphere, Harrison contacts outpost G1Eight and notifies them of his position. Even with the SJ.26, the journey from Sector Seven to Sector Eight will take them several hours.

"So Laura, tell me, how did they ever get you to land?"

She laughs bitterly. "That was easy. They just maneuvered overhead and hooked on."

"With what?"

"I don't know. Some kind of an electronic beam."

"Why didn't you just take off when they got overhead?"

"That pursuit vehicle that I told you about?"

He nods.

"It came from inside the pirate ship and stayed behind us. They made sure we were aware of their presence by firing a couple of shots into the exhaust doors."

"I wonder why the instruments didn't pick up the exhaust heat or ion trail?" Harrison asks, not really expecting Laura to know, but wanting to keep her mind off Jim.

"They were moving so fast when they caught on, we didn't need acceleration to reach the planet's outer atmosphere."

"I see. And once in the atmosphere, my instruments were useless." Harrison sighs.

¤ ¤ ¤

Harrison and Laura spend the next twenty hours at the outpost in Sector Eight, awaiting the Wingate. When it arrives, Harrison re-docks the DEA vehicle in Hangar Three. Meanwhile, fresh supplies from the Wingate are transferred to the outpost.

After leaving Sector Eight, they return to the planet in Sector Seven, where Harrison shows the loading crew where the stolen supplies are. It will take several hours for the electricians to repair the damage done to the computer by Harrison's laser. But it has to be done; the computer operates the platform, and that is the only way to get the supply ship out. Once the work is completed, everything from Laura's ship must be reloaded, and the Wingate will be underway.

¤ ¤ ¤

"Chief Boyd, I have a clean-up crew coming in with the secondary trafficker you wanted," Megan calls out.

Boyd, disheartened by the agents' lack of success against the major producers, and a work overload, doesn't want to deal with this matter right now. But deal he must. "Who is it?"

"T487. We don't have a name on him yet."

"Have the men take him straight down for questioning."

"You don't want to see him first?"

"No. They have my permission to proceed with the questioning. Tell them to bring the recorded disc to me immediately."

¤ ¤ ¤

While five floors below they're strapping T487 onto the cart, the drug trafficker looks up at the doctor with an unwarranted pleasant smile and says, "I didn't know the DEA took prisoners. When I saw the clean-up crew come in, I was worried. Thought I was a dead man."

"We don't keep prisoners." In his hand, the doctor holds a hypodermic filled with serum.

"Hey, you don't need that! I'll tell you everything I know."

"Oh, this is just something to make sure you remember everything clearly."

The trafficker relaxes. "Well, I guess that's all right. But one question. If you don't keep prisoners, where will I go when we're finished here?"

The doctor gives him an insolent grin. "Oh, I don't know. To the incinerator, maybe."

The trafficker begins screaming, tossing his head around, and fighting to free himself from the straps securing his arms and legs. Four husky men from the clean-up crew have no trouble restraining him in the end, though.

The doctor forces the man's head down and presses it firmly into the thin padding covering the cart he's strapped to. With his neck exposed, the doctor thrusts the needle deep and releases the serum. He then turns to the nurse seated behind the thick, mirrored window and motions for her to start the recording. With another nod to the clean-up crew, he leaves the room.

In a few of minutes, it's all over. After removing the straps, the doctor lifts both sides of the thin padding hanging over the ends of the cart the trafficker is lying on and throws them on top of the body so they meet in the middle. Starting at the top, he zips the man into the prefab body bag.

Two of the agents grab the bag with the man sealed inside, one at the foot and one at the head. The huge men only need the use of one hand each to carry the body. As they head out, the nurse holds open the thick steel door.

The doctor directs his gaze to the other two men standing nearby — agents of the clean-up crew — and ask, "Is there anything else?"

"The disc." The agents look intimidating in their black suits, black helmets, and weapons hanging on their shoulders.

"The disc?" The doctor pauses. "I—I normally take care of that."

They don't bother to explain that they'd been instructed to deliver the disc in person. They simply repeat, "The disc."

"Didn't you hear me? I said I'd take care of it." The doctor knows he's pushing his luck. It takes a certain type of individual to exterminate people for a living. A person who just follows orders, and doesn't care who he harms in the process.

One of the agents maneuvers for the nurse, who tries desperately to seal the door but isn't quick enough. The agent grabs for the recording instrument panel and nearly destroys it removing the disc. Both men then head for the door, neither bothering to look back. Upon their exit, the good doctor begins to wonder about his position with the DEA. He whispers under his breath. "First the half-breed incident, and now this."

¤ ¤ ¤

On board the Wingate, Wing Commander Benson's communication viewer comes to life. "Yes, Admiral Kachel," he replies to the imposing figure now displayed on the screen.

"Are the reclaimed supplies stowed?"

"Almost, sir. I'm sealing up the last of it now."

"I want Harrison in my office as soon as you get everything closed up."

"I'll do it now, sir. The men can finish up down here."

On the way to the admiral's office, Harrison speaks to Commander Benson. "I wonder what the admiral is going to say?"

Benson's mood darkens. "I don't know. Six months ago, I'd have said that he would probably commend you on a job well done. But now, I can't say. I don't know the admiral anymore. Don't think anyone does."

Harrison glances at the commander, but says no more.

When they arrive at the admiral's office door, the reply is immediate: "Enter."

"You wanted to see me, sir?"

Kachel glowers at Harrison. "You can leave, Commander, and close the door on your way out."

Benson gives Harrison an encouraging look on his way out.

Kachel turns his scowl to Harrison. "Harrison, I'm very disappointed in you. In light of what just happened, I feel it only right to inform you that I can't allow this promotion to go through. Fact is, you'll be lucky not to be demoted."

"What! What are you talking about?" Harrison yells, trying to figure out how rescuing Laura and breaking up a pirating ring could possibly result in a demotion.

"I'll tell you what I'm talking about," Kachel yells back. "You disobeyed orders."

"I—I got the job done."

"All you got was a good pilot killed."

"And you think Laura would be alive now if I hadn't? They would have killed her too, and you know it."

"Did they tell you that?"

Shocked, Harrison is unable to respond to the sarcastic remark.

"We have a book that we follow here, Captain. It has the best approach for these types of situations. It's called operating procedure,

Harrison. Procedures tested over and over again by experts to find the best method for handling every predicament." He sneers at Harrison. "Or maybe you know something we don't? If that's the case, maybe you should rewrite the book."

Before Harrison can reply, Kachel continues. "And what if something had gone wrong with your one-man rescue attempt? We wouldn't have any idea what went on, or where to look for either one of you!"

"I told Sector Eight everything I knew and where I was going." He had to say it, he couldn't hold it in. "Without additional fighters — and I think that's also in the rule book, too — I did the best I could do, sir."

"That doesn't matter now. You disregarded the safety of yourself and two other pilots when you went in alone, and that's not the kind of officer I want under me. For that, you can forget about any promotion around here, and for disobeying a direct order, I'm putting you on report. You're confined to your quarters. Effective immediately. Dismissed!"

Harrison opens his mouth to respond, but can't think of anything appropriate to say. So he turns and leaves the room.

He doesn't bother to tell Commander Benson or Laura what has happened. He knows that they'll find out soon enough through the ship's grapevine.

¤ ¤ ¤

The knock on the inside door of a heavily guarded office building brings a slow response.

"Enter." The man inside looks up at his well-dressed second-in-command. "So, Mr. Pressnell, how's the space program doing?"

"Well sir, not good. There's been an unfortunate development. We lost the supply depot in Sector Seven."

The head councilor's face washes red with anger; Pressnell can see the man's wrath expand to the top of his bald head. "What! How?"

Pressnell thinks the party leader is about to explode. "It's just a temporary setback, sir."

"Do you know what your 'temporary setback' is going to cost us?"

"Sir —"

"Months! Or maybe years. That's what it'll take to replace it. How could you let this happen?"

"I—I'm sorry, sir...its Admiral Kachel. He devised a plan of his own without my permission and without even notifying me, and it simply backfired on him."

The man behind the desk shakes his head, somewhat mollified. "Yes, Admiral Kachel. I might have known it would be him, he doesn't agree with any of this. But do you understand what this means? That was our safety buffer. Not one single delay from now on or we don't meet the deadline."

Pressnell nods. "I understand."

"I hope so." The man leans back against his leather chair.

"What should I do about Kachel?" Pressnell asks.

"See to it that he doesn't ever make another mistake. Replace him ... with someone more responsible."

Pressnell fights to hide his surprise. "Unseat the admiral of the Wingate! How?"

"I don't care how you do it, just do it."

¤ ¤ ¤

Confined to his quarters aboard the Wingate, Harrison is getting some much needed rest. Although he's allowed to leave his closet-sized room, it's only to go to the equally tiny captain's lounge to read or watch an occasional report. And whenever he leaves, he is accompanied by a guard.

Driven by her guilt, Laura comes to visit several times. "After all, it was my rescue that has brought all this trouble on you. Although I would have come to visit you anyway," she tells him.

He returns her smile. "You know, that almost makes this whole thing worth it."

And it's true; Harrison is more than glad to see her. But after a couple of days, even Laura's visits don't help lighten the weight of responsibility he feels for what has happened. As he gazes at the picture of his father on the wall, then at all the medals on the man's chest, he is saddened to think that, very possibly, he has failed his father. He looks at the small metal desk, on which are laid the insignificant number of his own medals, wondering if their only purpose now is to serve as paperweights.

On Laura's last visit, Harrison asked her to find some way to relay a message to the DEA. Laura returns with her answer later that same night.

"Well, what did you find out?" he anxiously states.

"No way, no way at all for now," she replies, sounding discouraged.

Harrison collapses back onto the pillow of his narrow bed. "That's just great!"

"But tomorrow I just might deliver your message myself."

His head shoots up, and he rises from the bed to look into her grinning face; his eyes hold a question.

As Laura explains, her face brightens even more. "Tomorrow we dock, right?"

He nods.

"And they're going to transport most of the recovered weapons back down. So I pleaded with Commander Benson to place me on the supply shuttle pilots' schedule. And he said yes!"

Harrison makes a fist. "Good idea. You can deliver the message to Chief Boyd in person?"

"Yes," Laura says as she pushes him back to the bed. "But it'll cost you. Everything has its price, and I've done a massive amount of pleading on your behalf, Captain Harrison."

He reaches up, grabs her wrists gently to stop her. "This is very important to me. Too important to risk. You know the rules. If you get caught, you'll be piloting nothing for a long to come."

"I'll worry about that later. Right now you've got to pay up, right?"

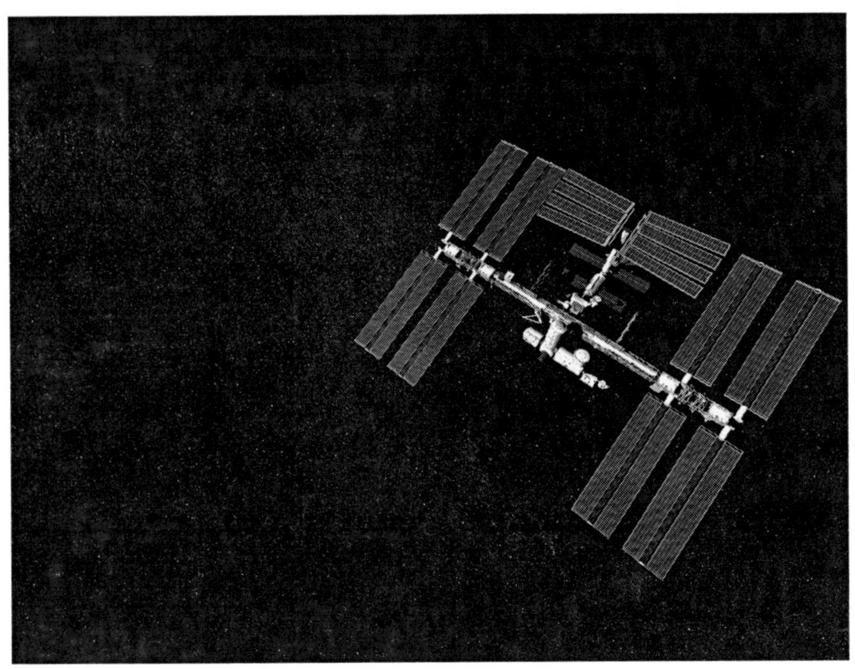

Chapter Eight

After the Wingate's long, slow but successful docking to the orbiting space station the following day, the recovered weapons are packed into the supply shuttles. This takes most of the day, so its late evening before the first shuttle departs for the planet below.

Later, a guard appears at Harrison's door. "Captain Harrison, I've been ordered by the acting judge to read you this decree." He produces a folded paper from his jacket. Unfolding it, he begins to read. "A date and time has been scheduled for your hearing. You'll be confined to quarters until then, and not permitted any visitors." The guard allows the hand holding the paper to drop to his side. "There's more if you care to read it. It's all routine, you understand."

Harrison holds his hand out and the guard passes the document over, and then closes the door.

Now, Harrison's boredom turns to desperation. What if the chief can't help, or doesn't understand the message I'm sending him? He thinks. What if Admiral Kachel is too far gone? What if he can't be reasoned with? The worries become endlessly clotted in his mind.

¤ ¤ ¤

Several hours later, Laura reaches the planet's surface. It's the start of a new day, and Houston flight control is just beginning to energize. Immediately upon landing, she contacts the DEA main office in Houston and asks if Chief Boyd is in yet. The stone-faced woman on the viewer makes it perfectly clear that the chief is much to busy to see anyone.

"Look, it's a matter of life or death," Laura persists. "Tell him...Tell Chief Boyd that it's about Captain Harrison."

The woman's face softens, and moments later, Boyd's face appears on her communicator screen. The huge, white-haired man looks tired. "Boyd here, what's this all about now?"

Laura is cautious. "Well, sir, Captain Harrison won't be coming back."

Boyd's face brightens. "Why? What —?"

"And he won't be returning your vehicle either. He's being held aboard the Wingate, and isn't permitted to contact you in person. In fact, he can't talk to anyone."

"What did he do to deserve all this?"

Laura takes a deep breath. "Harrison let them know that he was going to resign from the space program and sign on with the DEA. And now the admiral won't let him leave. He ordered him...Captain Harrison, that is...to be held in his quarters."

Boyd shakes his head, then casts his eyes away, frowning. "I don't understand how the admiral could do that. Or why he would even want to."

"Sir, I think... I think the admiral is afraid that Harrison will tell."

Boyd's eyes snap back to Laura's. "Tell what?"

"I don't know, sir. They won't let me in to talk to him. But ...I think it's something about the drugs."

Boyd is instantly alert. "Well, I'll talk to him and your admiral too."

It worked. The chief is sufficiently stirred up. "Thank you so much for listening, sir." She makes a point of glancing around her, and then turns back to the screen. "Well, sir, I have to go now before I get caught." She quickly shuts off the viewer before Boyd can ask her name.

¤ ¤ ¤

Well, that should get some response, Laura thinks as the viewer goes black. She's satisfied she's made the right decision. If I'd told that stuff Harrison asked me to tell, this DEA guy would probably have said, "It's none of our business." Besides, it's not all a lie. He is confined to his quarters. She smiles. I'd love to see Admiral Kachel's face when this DEA guy contacts him.

¤ ¤ ¤

"Admiral Kachel, there's a Chief Boyd from the DEA on the communicator, and he wants to talk with Captain Harrison."

The admiral looks up from his desk. "You know Captain Harrison is on report, tell him he can't talk."

"Sir, I told him that already, he said that he would have to talk to you, then."

"Tell him I'm busy."

The communication officer turns around. "Yes, sir," he says.

A minute later, the young officer is back. "Admiral Kachel, sir —"

The admiral looks up. "What is it now?"

"Sir, Chief Boyd said there would be no shuttles returning, and that we should cancel any scheduled departures until further notice ... sir."

The admiral's face turns instantly red. "What? Who does he think he is?" Kachel takes a deep breath and lets it out. "All right, all right! I'll talk to him. Put it through. And close the door and seal it!"

With a nod, the officer does his bidding.

The admiral is yelling a split second before Chief Boyd's face appears. "This is Admiral Kachel here, what's this all about?"

"Didn't the communication officer tell you?" Chief Boyd replies.

"No."

"There will be no shuttles until further notice."

"You can't do that!"

"I already have. I'll be meeting with the head of the space program as well. The Wingate won't be going anywhere for a long time."

Kachel pounds his desk, his computer's voice remote jumps, but Boyd's face never moves. "Boyd, on whose authority are you —?"

"On my authority," comes the quiet answer.

Kachel makes no rebuttal to this; it is a well-known fact the head of the DEA can do pretty much as he pleases. But Boyd isn't off the hook yet. "And what is the charge?" he asks.

"Contraband. Drug smuggling."

Kachel laughs. "My superiors will never believe that! Yours won't either. The Chief Executives aren't that stup —"

Boyd grabs a fistful of computer printouts that are always piled high on his desk and begins waving them at the monitor. "I have here written and signed documents that what I say is true. And if that isn't enough, you are also holding a DEA agent hostage." He stops waving the printouts and peers hard into the screen. "But we will find him, and he better be alive when we do."

Kachel stops laughing. "You mean Harrison?"

"You know who I mean."

"I don't believe you have the authority to stop anything."

Boyd opens his mouth to reply, but the viewer suddenly goes black.

¤ ¤ ¤

A few minutes later, Kachel is still sitting at his desk, questioning if DEA Chief Boyd is indeed powerful enough to make this kind of trouble. If he holds the Wingate, all schedules could be behind, and Kachel knows he will be called to explain why.

The viewer lights up to the face of the communication officer, who is sealed out of the admiral's office, "Admiral, its Councilor Pressnell, sir."

"Put him on."

A split-second later, Pressnell's face appears.

"Hello, Mr. Pressnell, what can I do for —?"

"Kachel, you're an idiot! First the supply depot fiasco, and now you have the DEA after you. What's this about you holding one of Boyd's agents?"

"He — he wants Harrison, but Harrison isn't his. He's ours —"

"I don't care what or who he wants, give it to him!"

Kachel deliberates desperately, unwilling to give up control of the situation. "Can he really hold us past our scheduled departure?"

Pressnell nods; his lip curls up. "He can hold you till hell freezes over. Get this matter cleared up now. We won't tolerate any more setbacks, you hear me?"

As quickly as Pressnell's face disappears, Kachel yells at the communication officer, "Get the Commander-in-Chief of the DEA back on the viewer. Right away."

"Yes sir, Admiral." A moment later, the viewer springs back to life.

"Chief Boyd here."

The admiral tries for a conciliatory look, but fails. "Ah, yes, Chief. It seems I was out of line with you. Now that I've had a chance to think it over, it's really not that definitive. If you want to talk with Harrison, of course you can."

"No, I think it's too late for that, don't you?"

"What — what do you mean?"

"I think you're hiding something. You should have let me talk with Harrison earlier."

"I don't understand," Kachel seems bewildered. "You … you can ask him anything you want."

"Sure I can," Boyd answers, nodding, "now that you've had time to tell him what to say. No thanks."

"You're not implying that I would threaten Captain Harrison, are you?"

There's a long pause. "There will be a team of agents up there by tomorrow morning. We're going to go over the Wingate from top to bottom, and I expect full cooperation from you and your people."

"From top to bottom?" Kachel howls. "That could take weeks with a ship of this size."

"Normally yes, but as understaffed as I am right now, it'll be more like months."

"Wait! There's no need for all of this," Kachel says, hating the pleading tone in his own voice. "What would it take to change your mind?" But before Boyd can reply, Kachel asks, "What if Harrison tells you everything is all right himself … in person?"

Boyd's answer is slow. "I don't know about that."

"Oh, of course I can do that, Chief. I can have him in your office by tomorrow morning. And the charges against him aren't that serious, I could have them dropped, immediately, today. That way, he'd be discharged with full honors. He only has a couple of weeks left anyway. We could cut him loose early. This way, he wouldn't have to return. You can have your agent and your vehicle back on the job, instead of exhausting your valuable time up here."

Boyd considers the proposal. "Well, I'll hold off with the team until I speak to Harrison, but all shuttles are grounded."

"That's ... acceptable."

¤ ¤ ¤

Boyd turns off the viewer and examines the results of the voice analyzer, although he doesn't really need to. It doesn't take a computer to tell him that Admiral Kachel went from bold as brass to terrified in a matter of minutes. And that he is, in fact, hiding something. Something he's desperate to keep under wraps.

Boyd leans back in his leather chair and, rubbing his chin, considers the situation deeply. Does Harrison know something he hasn't yet told me? Considering how he concealed the half-breed, that's possible. Boyd sighs. If he's holding something else back, I might have to give Harrison the kind of discipline I haven't given an agent in a long time. He would have to be made an example of. But on the other hand, if Harrison hasn't told anyone outside the DEA, I might hold off on that. After all, if he knows something about drugs on the Wingate, that would be momentous, to say the least.

Chapter Nine

At three a.m., a security team armed only with long black stun clubs enters Harrison's room.

"Captain Harrison, pack your gear."

Harrison wipes the sleep from his eyes and looks over at the chronometer. When he sees the hour, his gut tightens. "Where's the admiral sending me — a penal colony on some unknown asteroid?"

The two men burst out laughing. "By the looks of these papers, I'd say you're about to go anywhere you want," the taller one states as he retrieves a large envelope from the pocket of his dark blue jumpsuit and hands it to Harrison.

Harrison sits on the edge of the bed and opens the envelope. "What's this? My discharge papers? And they're postdated for the remainder of my enlistment." Harrison continues riffling through the envelope. "Hmm. Look at this. He's got me leaving as a captain with full honors." When he reads over the papers, he allows himself to believe that Laura has truly come through for him.

"You can read them again later, Captain," the shorter man says, and taps Harrison's leg with the nightstick. "You have one hour to be at Hangar Three. You're scheduled to depart for Houston at 0400."

Harrison looks up at them, blinking. "What about the hearing?"

The taller one shakes his head. "What hearing? That's all been omitted. It seems the admiral had a change of heart." They head for the door. "No need for an escort. You know your way out of here. Oh, one more thing. You're supposed to contact the head of the DEA as soon as you land."

¤ ¤ ¤

The hour passes quickly as Harrison gathers his few belongings and packs them into his duffle bag. Mostly, his thoughts are of Laura Renee.

She hasn't yet returned from the planet, so he leaves her a video message on the viewer: "Hey, I can't talk now, but I can tell you I'm getting out of here. Contact me in Houston. I'll fill you in then. And, thanks, I owe you." He can't resist adding with a grin, "Guess you proved you do have your own way of getting what you want."

It feels strange to be able to leave his quarters; he blinks and glances around several times on the trip down the hallway. On impulse, he decides to see Wing Commander Benson on his way out.

¤ ¤ ¤

"I'm sorry to see you go, Harrison."

"Well, Commander, if things were different ..." He stops. As long as Admiral Kachel is in command, he knows things won't change.

Benson nods, as though reading his thoughts.

"Well, I better get to the hangar. I wouldn't want to be late."

Harrison turns and slowly walks down the long hall leading to the pressurized elevator that will return him to Level One, duffle bag over his shoulder, helmet in hand. He turns to take one last look back. "Take care of yourself, Commander," he yells

Benson nods. "You, too."

¤ ¤ ¤

When the pressurized doors open at Level One, Harrison stops. There's someone watching him from the director's window, and it isn't the director. Only one man wears a blue cap with wide gold bars.

Harrison stares back, but Kachel doesn't flinch. The blank look reflects the admiral's emptiness; like a plastic mold, he has no expression. Harrison sees no reason to acknowledge the man who tried to take away his honor, his self-respect, his very freedom. He passes by, on his way to Hangar Three. Still, he can't shake the thought: Why would the admiral wake at four a.m. just to watch me leave? Could he be that anxious to see me go?

¤ ¤ ¤

The minute he receives his departure clearance code, Harrison sets a course for Houston, with the intent of arriving at ten a.m. His emotions are mixed. He's glad to be going back to the planet, to his own place, and most of all back to Megan, whom he'd missed more then he realized. Still, he has a bad taste in his mouth about the Wingate. Something is definitely wrong with the admiral, and it isn't just the pressure of being the ship's commander.

Harrison lands at Houston, and endures the formality that everyone goes through when they re-enter the atmosphere. The experts will go over the ship to make sure he isn't bringing in anything illegal or deadly.

Harrison doesn't want to wait until after the hunt is over to voice his concerns; he contacts Chief Boyd from the re-entry checkpoint.

"Harrison, what's going on with the Wingate?"

"Well, sir, I don't know for sure."

"The girl who contacted me yesterday said you knew something about drugs on the Wingate."

Harrison sucks in a startled breath. "What? Who said that? You said it's a girl?"

"She wouldn't give a name … highly irregular. But we did find out that she contacted us from the shuttle pilots' waiting area here in Houston."

That had to be Laura. But why would she say a crazy thing like that? Thinking fast, Harrison responds, "Ah, that's not entirely true, sir. But there is something wrong up there. When you first said 'a girl,' I thought you meant the shuttle pilot — Laura Renee. But her shuttle never returned, and I have no idea where she is."

"None of the shuttles returned, Captain. I'm detaining them and holding the Wingate. I was waiting on your report before I sent the agents to investigate."

"I don't think you'll find any drugs onboard the Wingate."

"I was afraid you would say that," Boyd murmured. "I'll admit I gave Admiral Kachel a hard time. But I couldn't figure out why they were holding you, so the girl's story held weight on that basis alone." He sighs. "Just as well. I don't have a team to spare anyway."

"Sir, no matter what the reason, I'm glad you got me out of there." Harrison is talking fast. "And I hope this doesn't cause you any grief with the council."

"I don't know what to make of it," Boyd says. "I don't expect you in today, after the long flight and considering everything you've been through. But report for the evening shift tomorrow, and come in early. I want a detailed account of everything you suspect is going on up there. We'll keep the Wingate and her shuttles on hold for now."

Harrison ends the call wondering if Laura's well-intended ploy hasn't opened up yet another hornet's nest.

Chapter Ten

Considering he's been designated for night surveillance, Harrison knows he should hit the sack the minute he gets back to his place — to get acquainted with sleeping days — but he's more excited than tired. After spending three days and nights confined to his quarters onboard the Wingate, this place seems spacious enough, but still he needs to get out.

He's skeptical about contacting Megan. She worked all night, and would undoubtedly be asleep. After pondering the subject, he scrambles to the viewer and punches in her number. There's no answer. She's probably sleeping, he thinks, and leaves a message when the recorder allows for it.

To his surprise, he's despondent. He needs her reassurance that he has made the right decision. His enthusiasm vanishes; he can't consider enjoying himself without seeing Megan first.

"Well, now what do I do?" he whispers as he slides open the balcony door. Explore the complex? Check out the local cuisine? Yeah. Maybe I'll find someplace nice to take her ... then he remembered the outcome of their last day together ... if she returns my message, that is.

As he stands on the balcony, the warm sunlight feels exceptionally good, and the sweet-scented air makes him think back. "Admiral Kachel doesn't realize it, but he's done me a service. I can't imagine how I could have spent my entire existence in space." It's the start of a new day. Beyond that, the beginning of a new way of life for him, and he wants badly to share it with Megan.

He looks down several hundred meters to the ground below, and the sight reminds him of Sixteen's curiosity about the desert floor. "I wonder what's down there myself," he says. "That's what I need to do."

Harrison hasn't actually been on the ground since his return, and he's anxious to get out. He slides the balcony door shut and grabs up his jacket on the way to the front door. But before the door shuts, he holds his hand out to stop it, and stepping back in, he heads for the bedroom to find his shoulder holster. Sure, it's optional — he isn't yet officially back on duty — but having a weapon handy in an unknown area never hurts.

After securing the holster straps across his back, he finally slips in the laser pistol and puts his jacket on over the top. Standing in front of the mirror, he notices that the barrel peeks out from beneath his jacket when he lifts his arm. He adjusts the holster one last time and heads for the door.

The elevator transports him to the first floor, but this still leaves him twenty meters aboveground. He searches and soon locates the exit door that leads to the stairwell. Every support column under the complex harbors stairwells for emergency use, and by the looks of the rusty, dirt-covered door, they don't have many emergencies.

Harrison heads down the spiraling steps; the darkness increases as he descends within the giant tube. At the base of the stairs stands yet another rusty metal door. This one, he quickly realizes, has been secured from the inside. The door's narrow slit, near the center, allows only a small amount of light to enter the stairwell. While faint, the light reveals the four metal handles sealing the door. Harrison doesn't recognize anything on the outside through the small opening, but the extra light helps him to locate a hollow metal bar that just fits the handles. Not by accident: It's clear that the bar is designed to unseal the door.

Now on the ground, he heads straight for the center of the huge complex. Harrison snakes between the gray, waist-high pylons standing ready to protect the support column against all intrusions. From here, it looks as though the darkness extends for an eternity, he can't see the other support columns holding up the complex. The ground under his shoes feels dry and hard; there isn't a single blade of grass or plant of any kind to be found. Not even a weed, he thinks with an inquisitive smile. But what does he know; maybe this is how it's supposed to be.

He hears sounds echoing out from the heart of the complex. The anemic looking lights attached to the underside of the complex are pointing every which way, they're so high overhead that only a modest amount of light reaches the ground. Also half of them aren't operating.

As Harrison presses on, he begins to feel that this isn't such a good idea after all. But it's too late to retreat; his curiosity has gotten the best of him. Besides, this might be his only chance to wander around and learn firsthand before he goes back on duty.

After a short hike, he spots several buildings in the distance, ones that wasn't visible from the doorway. The structures are curiously short, only about chest-high. As he gets closer, he sees that they look abandoned. In that case, he thinks, no one will mind me taking a look inside.

He had imagined the buildings being used for storage, but realizes now they've been hastily pieced together with scrap wood. Some debris is lying about inside ... and beds. "They're homes," Harrison shouts with a start, curious as to where the ex-occupants are.

He quickly continues on, aiming toward the center of the complex. The air now has a heavy metal taste about it, as if you could develop lead poisoning simply from breathing it.

His awareness is heightened by the ever-increasing darkness. Suddenly, he begins to suspect that he's being watched. Although he can't actually see anyone, even though his eyes have adjusted to the dim light. Maybe it's just shadows, he muses. After years of flight, Harrison has learned to rely on fact, not feelings.

Keeping the support column that he'd exited from in sight, he walks on, noting that the terrain is getting rougher. But he soon reaches a smooth cement pad, which enables him to speed up. Several minutes into the accelerated pace, he hears a noise from behind. He whirls around; hand already perched on his shoulder holster, he sees something coming beyond the light.

At first, he thinks it's just a wooden cart — he can't see the wheels on the wooden board, but knows it's moving toward him. As it draws near, it looks as if someone is sitting on it.

Harrison holds his breath, waiting for whoever or whatever it is to catch up. But as it moves closer, others come into view, and they continue to multiply until they're too numerous to count. The situation makes Harrison very uncomfortable, but he can't go back; the carts have separated him from the stairwell. Then, just as he drags his laser pistol out, they stop advancing.

Harrison waits for them to make their next move. Nothing happens. He slowly turns and begins to walk away, just to see what they will do. He senses them moving after him, matching his pace, as it were. When he pauses a second time, they too stop.

Harrison turns and walks toward them; no one moves, they all stay frozen in place. All but one. The biggest (a definite leader) pushes his board-cart to the front, as if to face off with Harrison.

Harrison draws near enough to see clearly in the dim light. What he sees gives him the shock of his life. All of them look exactly like Sixteen! None of them has legs!

As he edges closer, he realizes that even their faces look identical to Sixteen's, right down to their sunken eyes with large dark circles and short black hair. Even in the weak light, he can see that they all have the same yellowish tan. He also notes that they have unusually thin arms, and their hands are rough and calloused. Try as he might, he can't remember what Sixteen's arms and hands looked like.

But one thing he is sure of: He's outnumbered. There are at least thirty-five, maybe forty of them.

"Who are you?" he yells. "Do you live down here?"

He waits but gets no reply. He stifles a laugh; he has to admit it's a strange sight indeed. The micro-army of half-breeds looks as though they're sitting on giant skateboards.

"Why are you following me? Is there something I can do?"

He waits, but again, no one volunteers any information.

He remembers how proud Sixteen was of his intelligence, and how anxious he was to prove it to Harrison.

"Didn't anyone teach you to talk?" he asks, hoping this will coerce them into saying something.

It doesn't work. They just sit there looking at him with big dark eyes. It's a look of enduring pain, Harrison thinks ... agony from a life that no one would want. He disputes the overwhelming urge to help them. How can he? He couldn't even help *one* of these unfortunates, and there are perhaps hundreds of them down here. His rational mind tells him: The best thing for me to do is just leave. How do I know they're like Sixteen, anyway? They might not be all that harmless.

He isn't about to press his luck and push through their midst, so he turns and once again heads for the center of the complex. As he walks away, the half-breeds follow. Harrison accelerates his pace; likewise, they too pick up speed.

While the half-breeds hold their distance, he can't help thinking about what he'll do if they advance on him. He doesn't want to shoot anyone, especially considering all of them resemble Sixteen. Is their silence some form of aggression? He wonders. Maybe it's the way they communicate. If so, for the life of him, he can't understand it.

Up ahead is a cement wall about one-and-a-half meters in height, with what appear to be several small holes at the bottom. Drain holes, most likely. Harrison hastens to the wall, and quickly scales it. Landing on the other side, he thinks this wall may not stop them, but it will surely slow them down.

Harrison continues at a hearty pace, stopping only long enough to look back, but no one follows. Maybe that's their boundary, and they won't cross it. The thought gives him hope.

After a short distance, Harrison slows. The smooth cement floor ends abruptly, and once again he is navigating the rocky terrain. Ahead is what looks to be an old maintenance building; beyond, several large fires blaze, their light reflecting off the steel underside of the enormous complex above and casting a red glow over the entire area. In the distance, between him and the fires, in what looks like a formation around another building, he can see numerous buildings — a makeshift city. "Well," he mutters, "maybe there's people after all."

He can hear a clamor coming from within the maintenance building, a large structure with openings on all four sides. Harrison cautiously moves into one doorway and peers around the corner.

The building is simply one large dark and smoky room, its gloom relieved by a few flickering candles. The thick air has a heavy odor, a strangely balmy stench that he cannot quite place. Suddenly, he realizes what is going on, and dares not venture any further inside. Curious, Harrison watches from the doorway as some sort of strange ritual is enacted.

A small but equal mix of normal-looking men and women, faces cast in icy aspect, sit in a circle. In the middle of the circle is a woman tied with a heavy rope. The rope stretches around her ankles and travels up her back to bind her wrists, then around her body just under the arms, and from there to the ceiling. There is a sizeable block of wood under her feet, but the rope does not permit her to stand firmly upon it. She is suspended from the ceiling by the rope, trying desperately to hold to the block of wood with her toes, but cannot help herself from slipping off. She drops off the block of wood and swings backward. Fighting violently, she attempts to re-establish a foothold on the block. Except for the towel wrapped around her head, perhaps to keep the others from seeing her agony, she wears no other garment.

Harrison can almost feel the woman's pain as she stumbles from the block and the rope tightens under her arms. He can hear her gasp for air every time she slips off.

A clear tube protrudes from the right side of her neck. It has been strapped to her collarbone, likely to keep it from coming out. Harrison can see blood as it trickles down inside the tube and into a glass bottle that waits on the floor. There are several full bottles of blood sitting alongside.

She couldn't have much left, Harrison thinks, considering that she is equivalent in size to a half-starved child. A plan of rescue is formulating in his mind, when he suddenly recalls the lesson he learned with Sixteen. Even if he was not outnumbered, he was not about to repeat that mistake. Whatever was going on, he would not — could not — get involved. Harrison backs out the door and slips unnoticed into the murky darkness outside.

Why would anyone want her blood? He wonders as he feels the hair on the back of his neck rising. What will they do with it? Perhaps a religious cult of some kind? He can't recall Sixteen mentioning religion in their short time together.

He looks around to assure himself that no one has followed him out, then continues walking away, wondering what the woman has done to deserve such an agonizing death.

There's a slight downgrade between him and the remaining buildings, which makes the long walk somewhat easier. When he finally reaches the buildings, he feels just as confused as he'd been at the beginning of his journey. The little village looks old and extremely rundown, much more than he had theorized. Smoke from the fire lingers above, blackening the underside of the complex. Harrison doesn't know what they found to burn, but it lets off a sickening smell that makes his eyes water. The buildings don't look any more livable than the first ones. However, these are occupied. Some of the shanties gape open in front; others simply have no doors. Inside one of the first shacks he passes, he distinguishes a body lying in the corner, covered with rags. Harrison doesn't know whether the person is dead or alive. He can't see legs, but at this point doesn't want to know if they're present or not.

The shacks are everywhere, though randomly placed, not in any type of order. Harrison walks by one and notices a woman and three children sitting inside. He stops to look around. No one moves, no one says a word. All four appear virtually dead — motionless, as if waiting for him to leave.

Harrison decides to do just that; he's seen all he can bear.

Just as he turns to begin the long walk back to the stairwell, an ear-piercing scream resounds as through an unbalanced siren. A second screaming siren immediately joins in, and together the sound echoes throughout the shanty town. The noise level is so loud that Harrison has to cover his ears. However, the deafening sound doesn't seem to bother anyone else; rather, they begin exiting the shanties, moving in the direction of the noise. With a finger in each ear, Harrison questionably follows them.

As they near the source of the noise, he recognizes two flashing red lights just beneath the ceiling, striving to pierce the smoky haze. People are converging from every direction, and a large crowd has already gathered around a massive steel box. As best as he can tell, the box is the size of a small building — about twenty meters wide and a hundred meters long, with three-meter-high sides. His curiosity draws him nearer the box. Edging closer, he notices several rows of small holes in the walls of the box, about five centimeters in diameter, with a small lip around each hole. Harrison cannot imagine why the people are congregating around the box, but as quickly as they began the screaming sirens cease — although, like the persistent ringing in Harrison's ears, the red lights continue to flash through the haze.

He tries to be inconspicuous as possible, just peering around a metal pole, but no one seems to be paying attention to him anyway. The walls of the box are so high, Harrison can't see what's inside. At one end of the box is a small building, no openings except for a steel arm extending out from the center of one side, which connects to one side of the large box. At the other end is a building so huge it touches the ceiling. Several pipes stretch out from the top and connect to the complex above.

The lights catch Harrison's eye again; they seem to be getting brighter. As he watches, he notices they're mounted on a steel plate, and the entire thing is coming down on top of the box. Only now does he realize what it is.

It's a giant dumpster! He's certain. It must be full of rubbish from the complex above. The horns are a warning that the trash is going to be dumped. Then the top plate comes down and compacts it.

Since most waste on the planet is recycled, Harrison assumes the trash must be used for the complex's electricity and or heat. From the outside, the thing is rather amazing. It looks to be fully automatic and constructed to last indefinitely.

As the massive stainless steel lid gets dangerously close to the container, people begin climbing out. This must be their only source of food, Harrison thinks, eating out of the garbage bin.

Some are carting out discarded pieces of wood and plastic, probably to construct more shacks. A few stragglers work their way over the wall just as the steel cover comes within two or three meters of sealing off their only means of escape. Suddenly, several men on the ground begin shoving them back into the box, either pushing them back in with their hands or using long staffs. The captives quickly flee to the opposite side, but are unfortunately met with the same inhumane treatment there.

Harrison is astonished. The horde has gathered around the box so tightly, pushing and shoving, there's obviously no way the ones stranded inside can climb out.

It takes the massive lid only seconds to move directly overhead. One man's effort at a last-minute dive for freedom proves inadequate. His escape is cut short by the thick steel cover that shows no mercy: It cleaves his body at the waist and continues down into the box to compact his remains, along with the rest of the unfortunates inside.

Harrison can hear the victims screaming through the drain holes. But they aren't yelling for help; they undoubtedly know there's no stopping it now. The walls are filled with people clinging onto them, watching intense through the holes. As the thick steel lid continues descending, they follow it downward, hole by hole, until the final scream is heard and the occupants inside are crushed.

A short moment later, the spectators jump back as blood begins to overrun the drain holes. Once again the crowd goes wild, fighting over the holes that have the blood oozing from them. Some are trying to capture it in containers, but most simply frame their mouths over the drain holes.

Harrison can only look on in amazement. His nausea alternates with a hollow feeling in the pit of his stomach and a lump in his throat. He can't move, or even turn away, although he knows if he watches any longer, he's going to be sick. It's the worst thing he has ever seen, or imagined. Does everyone know what goes on down here? Everyone but me? He thinks. We have gone from the highest form of life to this?

Humans may shape their own destiny, but obviously man isn't in control after all, he thinks while watching some of the crowd siphon the last of the blood with makeshift straws. Others are licking up what is still running out of the holes.

Maybe we just believe we have control, when actually, who knows what will evolve in the end? When there's too many inhabitants, they die off from sickness and disease, or simply kill each other. But ... this must be the sickest society yet, living off human blood like some form of parasite.

Maybe we're not as intelligent as we believe, he thinks.

Chapter Eleven

The horrible display over, the crowd begins to break up. Harrison needs to sit badly, but won't risk lingering. Instinct tells him that if he does, there is a good chance he'll end up like the captured woman. As quickly as his stomach allows, he turns to head back, then instinctively grabs for his weapon.

He's been so engrossed by the bloody executions in front of him; he hasn't noticed the crowd gathering behind him. Now, the path leading out of the city is blocked, he's trapped, and there are more locals accumulating by the minute.

He knows there's no reason trying to communicate with these people. Attempting to convince them he means no harm would be a waste of time. As he pulls his laser pistol and readies it to fire, a man suddenly steps out from the crowd and approaches him.

With his noticeable amount of gray hair and ragged clothes, the man is undeniably the oldest of the group. "Did you enjoy the show?" he asks, tauntingly. "You see now what you'll do if you get hungry enough." He looks around at the tightly packed crowd. "You shouldn't have come alone. If the government wants to know what we're doing, I'll tell you. We're all playing a game. It's just a game." He looks down at the weapon. "Do you think we're afraid of that?" he laughs. "No, we're only afraid of one thing, and dying is not it?" After the speech, an ominous silence surrounds them, the crowd makes no moves.

If the man is being honest, Harrison has a serious problem. The fear of death is the only thing Harrison has in his favor, and that has just been diminished.

The man reaches out and grabs Harrison's arm. For what seems to be the longest moment of his life, Harrison watches as the red blinking lights, now down to eye level, flash across the hollow gaze of the crowd. Their eyes, with an eerie reflective quality, show no compassion. They appear not to notice the light, nor the earthy stench emanating from the mass.

But the man's words do convince Harrison that deadly force is his only option of getting out alive. He squeezes the trigger. The blast propels the man's blazing body back several meters, where it lands with a gruesome thud at the mob's feet. Those nearest him gather around the body to gape at the blackened remains, and then suddenly start for Harrison. Harrison knows he can't kill them all, but he'll die trying.

The man nearest Harrison lunges at him with a handmade weapon, but before he can accomplish his task, Harrison shoots. A third man emerges from the group, swinging a machete. Harrison prepares to fire, but holds back when he sees a thin green light strike the right side of the man's throat and dart around to the back of his neck.

Harrison has no idea what it is, but makes a good guess when the man clutches his neck, and the blood begins to run between his fingers, then down his shoulder. The light has opened his neck deeper than any surgeon's scalpel could.

Several from the crowd lunge, knocking the man to the ground. He's immediately covered with people swarming over him. The narrow green light strikes again. This time, it slashes the back of a distracted assailant. The light cuts to the bone; almost instantly, the bottom portion of his shirt is drenched in blood. As with the first man, several from the crowd ravage him.

Harrison finally sees where the light is coming from: a sizeable fellow standing behind the crowd, towering a half-meter or more above everyone else. The man is wounding everyone who comes close to Harrison, leaving the crowd distracted with their frenzied bloodbath. He's wearing a DEA uniform.

The man's actions have created an opening for Harrison's escape. When he reaches his rescuer, both waste no time fleeing on the path Harrison had originally come down from.

Once outside the makeshift city and atop the slight grade, they slow their pace. As soon as Harrison is sure no one has followed them, he says, "Who are you?"

The burly man in the DEA uniform smiles, still breathing heavily from the run.

"Winston ... from Search and Rescue," he says.

Harrison recalls the voice. "Yeah, I remember you, from the jungle. Thanks, but let's don't make a habit out of this."

"Don't feel too bad," Winston replies. "I'd do it again, and again. It's my job."

"Well, thanks anyway. But how did you know where I was?"

"Megan couldn't get hold of you, so she sent me to investigate. I found your vehicle still on the roof, so I asked around. One of the guards said that a man fitting your description was spotted on their monitor when the door alarm went off. After you leave the confines of the complex, you're pretty much on your own."

Although he's not surprised they had monitored him, Harrison is shocked at what is allowed to take place under their complex. "What form of weapon did you use back there? I've never seen one like that," he says.

Winston raises up his laser pistol and grins. "This? I just power it down a little. That's why all the agents carry the smaller pistols, unlike that cannon you got." He glances around. "Let's get out of here."

Harrison follows Winston's gaze, then says, "Wait a minute, there's something I need to see."

Winston laughs sarcastically. "Haven't you seen enough for one day?"

"No, it's not that. It's ... Oh, just come with me. I'll explain once we're inside."

Harrison starts toward the old maintenance building. Inside, they're met with absolute silence; except for the woman, everyone is gone. The four candles are still giving off smoldering fumes as they burn. The woman remains bound by the rope, but the wooden block has been removed and she's dangling freely now.

Knowing she's dead, Harrison reaches out to stop the body from swaying. Her skin feels cold and rubbery. The tube has been removed from her neck; there's no sign of blood anywhere. After seeing what has taken place at the trash compactor, Harrison understands why they wanted her.

"They don't waste a drop," he says.

Winston comes up from behind. "Who's this ... another one of your old friends?"

Harrison knows Winston is referring to Sixteen. Everyone in the department must know by now, but he doesn't want to talk about it.

"Come on, Harrison," Winston urges. "We don't have time for this. Let's get back to the stairwell, all right?"

Harrison stays silent.

When they overtake the wall where he had left the half-breeds earlier, there's no one in sight. They move through the area vigilant and on to the emergency exit.

Entering the stairwell, Winston watches impatiently as Harrison reseals the door. Then both men begin their long ascent up the steep, winding stairs single file.

Halfway up, Harrison stops climbing. He looks up. "Tell me, Winston, how is it people become that demented? It's ... it's as though they'd adopted blood as their food source."

"You mean you don't know?"

More smart remarks, Harrison thinks. "No, I don't know. That's why I asked."

"Well, why don't you ask Megan? Or better yet, ask the government."

"Because I'm asking you."

Winston thinks for a moment, and Harrison presumes he's working on his next smart-as remark. Winston's attitude is sarcastic , "All right,

I'll tell you, but we'll have to keep moving. The guards are timing me, and I don't want them storming down here for no reason."

Harrison nods, and they continue climbing as Winston talks. "You've had the two-week crash course, so you already know how people used to shoot drugs into their bodies."

"Yeah," Harrison says. "They'd stick the needle in their vein and release the drug, then pull blood back into the needle, then pass the needle on to the next person."

"That's right. The drug, mixed with someone's blood, would enhance the effect. After several generations of this, the offspring of heavy drug abusers are born with large amounts of amphetamines in their bodies, and an even larger dependency on drugs. Over time, their blood became an effective substance itself. That's why they call them 'druggies,' even though it's not just drugs they're hooked on now. But druggies are the same as drug addicts. Maybe worse. When the druggies run out of money, they simply sell some blood. But you can only sell so much blood. And they still require drugs, or someone's blood. But it can't be from the same bloodline. It has to be from outside the family. It can't be from a regular person, either. It has to be from another druggie.

"When they become completely out of touch with reality and they need blood or something all the time, they end up in the old city ... or a place like this." Winston stops and points behind him, and then looks straight at him as if Harrison were to blame.

Harrison ignores the gesture. "Well, why doesn't the government help stop it?"

Winston spins around, then pushes Harrison against the dirty steel wall. Pressing his forearm against Harrison's neck, Winston leans down and sticks his huge head in Harrison's face. "Listen, man, the government stopped helping these people a long time ago. You see, while you're up there flying around in your priceless starship, the rest of us are down here living with the problem. The only thing the government's worried about is how much money they can steal for their precious space program.

"That's why they take care of you fighter pilots so well. You protect their investments. Handpicked from the best, with all your education and training. Like hell. They only want one thing from you. To do their dirty work."

He releases Harrison and slowly pulls away from him. "It's all government brainwashing. They don't care about us or how we get the job done, or how many we have to exterminate. Just so the druggies don't interfere with their plans."

"What plans?" Harrison asks, taking a badly needed swallow and rubbing his throat.

Winston storms back up the steps, but Harrison just stands catching his breath. Winston leans over the steel rail and yells down at him, "Plans? You tell me." He takes a few more steps, and then sighs heavily. "If I brought back a crew and they cleaned this place out, do you know how long it would take before it looked like this again? I'll tell you ... a month. Go ask your government if they'll do anything about it. Like they give a damn." He turns and starts up the stairs again.

Looking up, Harrison wonders why, if Winston really feels this way, he'd even bothered coming to find him. But still, he owes him. "Thanks for your help anyway," he calls up.

"Don't thank me, thank the government," comes the echoing reply.

¤ ¤ ¤

Harrison waits for Winston to get most of the way up before he starts climbing the stairs again. He isn't afraid of him, but he doesn't want any more surprises. Harrison has a lot to think about, and Winston's personal issues aren't included on the list.

A flashing image of the drained woman hanging in the maintenance building haunts him. The way she looked and felt; the hole in her neck. How pale she had been.

Suddenly, the other thing that has been tormenting him finally comes to light. Sixteen had been hanging from a viewer cord that cut deep into his neck, but there was no blood ... just like the woman in the maintenance building.

Two-thirds up the winding stairs, he stops to rest and think, leaning against the wall. Winston's explanation seems too easy, too pat. What he's just seen needs some kind of order and perspective, to give some meaning to Sixteen's death.

He hears the faint noise of a door shutting; Winston must have already reached the top and gone out. One less thing to worry about, he thinks as he slowly slides down the curved wall and sits on the step.

Considering that it was an effective drug in itself, almost anyone could have wanted Sixteen's blood. He knows that now. But who knew he was in my apartment, and how did they get in? They didn't break in, and Sixteen wouldn't have opened the door for just anyone.

Harrison has never been convinced it was burglars; nothing was missing, and everything of value was thoroughly destroyed, not riffled through as though someone was looking for valuables. But what if somebody was looking for money, and discovered Sixteen instead? Or maybe they just wanted it to look like that? That would explain why everything was ravaged. Of course, that must be it.

Harrison knows most of the unresolved questions won't be answered sitting on a dirty stairwell, although one thing is certain: Sixteen was telling the truth about not needing drugs, and he didn't kill himself. Harrison regrets not believing in him in the first place now, and is saddened to think of how painful his death must have been. Trying to shake those thoughts, Harrison rises and continues up the winding steps.

He finally reaches the top, and heads straight to the first elevator that returns him to Level 30. Immediately upon arriving at his apartment, he rushes directly to the viewer. Megan's picture is on the screen, and the message light is blinking. A push of the button brings her face to life.

The recording begins to speak. "Harrison, I — I'm staying at a friend's house, I'll explain later. I've been looking for you all day. We're starting to worry. Here's my temporary number. ... Contact me ASAP."

There is no mention of how angry she'd been when he left for his final assignment with the space program. That's good. Feeling safe, he punches in the number she left. But Angie's face appears on the screen instead of Megan's.

"Is Megan there?"

Before Angie can reply, Megan appears.

"It's all right, Angie," Megan says, "its Harrison. Harrison, where have you been? I've checked everywhere. I sent Winston to find you. Hope you don't mind."

"No, not at all. Megan, I need to see you tonight, before you go to work. I've been doing some investigating, and I found out a couple things. And well ... I really want to see you."

Megan nods and gives a sideways glance off-screen. "I want to see you too. How about dinner?"

"All right. I found a nice place in my complex."

"Good, I'll be over in about an hour."

Megan suddenly looks down, then quickly back up. "Uh, oh, Angie's got a call. Gotta go."

Harrison knows he needs time to get cleaned up. After being down below, his skin feels as if it's crawling.

The hour passes quickly; before he's ready, Megan is knocking on the door. When the door slides open, there she stands wearing her DEA uniform and a nervous smile. She's pleased to see him but unsure of his emotions. He had forgotten how shiny her blue eyes look against the background of her dark, curly hair. As always, her beauty has left him at a loss for words.

"Well, can I come in?"

Harrison can only nod and whisper, "I missed you."

Megan steps through the doorway as he holds out his arms.

"I missed you too," she replies as the long hug ends. "I was hoping you weren't mad at me for sending Winston to look for you."

"It's a good thing you did. Do you know what goes on down there?"

She nods against his shoulder. "I've heard."

"Speaking of Winston ... He said something I didn't understand."

"What was that?" She pulls away a bit.

"Well, he told me if they sent a clean-up crew down there, that in one month, it would look the same. I thought the clean-up crews' only duty is to destroy the plants and drug labs the agents find."

"Yes," she replies, wide eyes glancing away from him. "The agents locate the drug traffickers, and the clean-up crews eliminate them."

"Then why would he say a thing like that?"

She keeps her gaze over his shoulder. "Well ... the clean-up crews' second priority is to keep the, ah ... drug population down."

"You mean they exterminate the people down there?" Harrison points at the floor.

As though it hurts, she turns her head to meet his eyes and gives a careful smile. "Look, why don't we go inside? Better to talk there than in the hall."

"Oh, sorry," he says, flushed. "Guess I'm not much of a host." He leads her into the living room and, before they know it, they're sitting on the sofa with coffee, dinner forgotten for now.

"Now, about your question," she states. "I guess they didn't mention that in your training because ..." she smiles, "they probably never thought you'd poke around down there. But they're never sent, the crews that is, under the complexes — there's no real reason for it — only to the old city."

Harrison reflects. "I've never been inside the old city of Houston, but I've flown over it. I'm certain there's a lot of people there but —"

"Over six million druggies crowded into seven hundred square kilometers. And I've never been there either. Nobody goes in the old city except the clean-up crews."

Harrison's eyes narrow. "Nobody? What about the city police?"

Megan shakes her head. "Actually, it's no longer a city. When the druggies first became aggressive, everyone began moving into complexes like this one, outside the city limits. And when the people moved outside the city, the factories did, too. So when the businesses left and stores closed up, tax money stopped coming into the city. They abolished the council and disbanded the police force. It's now unincorporated."

Harrison sets his coffee cup on the table in front of them. "Wait a minute. You mean there's no one to keep order or maintain the old city?"

Megan shrugs. "Just the clean-up crew. In the beginning, most of them were from the police force. That's how the crews got started."

He leans forward and places his elbows on his knees, trying to take it all in. "Megan, why do they live under here? There's nothing for them down there."

She takes a long sip from her cup before answering. "They stay down there with the hope that someone from the complex will take them in."

He twists his head to look back at her. "And do they?"

"Of course. For payment. In blood."

"You mean ...?"

"You got it. Like a never-ending cycle."

Harrison now realizes what the half-breeds had expected from him. "So ... they haven't lost their minds. They wanted me to keep them in return for blood?"

Another nod, but her face looks more anguished than he'd ever seen before. "Unfortunately, when they bring the female druggies up, they use more than just their blood," she finally answers.

Harrison considers the implications, remembering what Winston had said. "What would happen if no one thinned out the drug population?"

"The government doesn't want to find out."

Harrison leans back on the sofa. "Let me see if I got this straight. The old city is completely inhabited by druggies, and the government has the clean-up crews go in and thin them out." He gives Megan a questioning look. "How often do they do that?"

She suddenly looks away. "You'll learn all about it at the academy."

Harrison stares for so long she finally sighs and turns back to him. "All right. We only have twelve crews, and our office has several thousand square kilometers to cover. That's a lot of old cities. The crews go from sunup to sundown every day."

"They just go from one city to another?" he asks. "Like, randomly?"

"No, not quite. We have satellite surveillance cameras and people inside that keep us informed. They let us know when an area's getting out of hand or banding together."

"What do you mean, 'out of hand'?"

"You know ... rebellious. Druggies are a lot more aggressive than half-breeds or drudges." Megan's face is more shielded than before.

"Yeah, I figured that out. But who would they rebel against? Us?"

She nods. "Or maybe the government, or the people themselves. We don't know what they'd do, because we've never let them get that strong." She drains her cup and stands, stretching. "How about that dinner you promised me?"

"Oh yeah, right," he says. Harrison intends to pump her for more information later. In his entire life, he'd never thought about "us against them," with the exception of the drug traffickers. Now, he's learning something about his government he never knew before. Something sinister. Something that he never imagined possible.

Chapter Twelve

As Mr. Pressnell's viewer blinks to life, he stops reading, but doesn't inconvenience himself by looking up from the old rare book. "What is it, Lisa?"

"Mr. Pressnell, its Admiral Kachel from the Wingate."

"I don't want to see him. Convey the message." He continues to turn the pages.

"He said it's urgent, he must speak to you, in private."

Pressnell lays his head back against the chair in pure disgust. "All right, put him on."

A moment later, while relaxing his tie, "Talk fast, Kachel, I'm extremely busy with damage control, trying to prove our sanity to the Council. They want to know why I kept the weapon hijacks classified. I also have my hands full suppressing the rumors and speculations on why the pirates were warehousing them. And you know who I have to thank for all this embarrassment — that fighter pilot that you were supposed to restrain."

"Yes, I know," Kachel is puzzled. "I still can't fathom what went wrong. Don't know exactly what transpired yet, sir. But the reason I contacted you is to determine whether I can leave as scheduled, or is the DEA going to continue interfering with my assignments."

"I don't know. I'm not getting anywhere with Chief Boyd. He's always out when I contact his office. Boyd's a hard man to deal with anyway."

"What about Harrison?" Kachel asks.

"He's down here now, and that makes him my problem, doesn't it?"

"Yes, sir."

"Then I'll handle him. Besides, he doesn't know anything."

"But he suspects something," the admiral hastily replies. "And I know Harrison. He won't stop until he gets all the answers. There's only one way to stop Harrison —"

"That's real shrewd, Kachel. We take him out now, and we'll have agents coming out of the cracks, looking behind every door and on every ship trying to find out why."

Kachel sighs. "There could be an accident."

"It's too late for that. Boyd's aware of your little imprisonment ploy. You shouldn't have failed."

"Then what?"

"I said I would handle it. Good day." Pressnell swats the viewer's sensor light off. Thinking about Kachel's words of wisdom, he combs down his salt-and-pepper hair and straightens his custom-tailored suit jacket. Harrison won't stop until he gets all the answers? Maybe I'll just provide some of my own answers. Give him a little decoy. Turn this situation to my advantage. Just because the head councilor said not to touch him, doesn't mean I can't try to stop him, he thinks.

He reaches out and touches the viewer. "Lisa, get me Advanced Technology. I want to speak to Mr. Solomon."

The viewer comes back to life momentarily.

"Mr. Pressnell, what can I do for you?"

"I need your assistance on a personal project."

"No problem, Mr. Pressnell. You know, we at Advanced are always willing to work with the government in any capacity."

"Good. I'm glad to hear you say that. But it's not Advanced that I need. This is ... of a bit more personal nature. We've worked on special projects before and, well, this is one of those personal favors."

"I fully understand, Mr. Pressnell. All you need is to say the word and I'll take it from there."

Solomon's round face is radiant. Pressnell can see by the man's wide smile that he's more than happy to do the government's dirty work and prove his worth, not to mention preserving his company's contracts. Pressnell only wishes he had more like him to call on. "I don't know precisely when or how, but someone from the DEA is going to pay you a … a visit," he tells Solomon. "He'll be looking for answers concerning the modules. Allow him access; let him find his answers before you … discover him. Then call me"

"Whatever you say, Mr. Pressnell. No problem sir."

¤ ¤ ¤

Megan and Harrison have arrived at the new but quaint restaurant. The dining room is quite small, as is the table that they're finally seated at, but Harrison doesn't mind, as he's so close to Megan.

"So, tell me, how have things been since I left?"

"Not so good." She fiddles with her empty glass. "The Rescue teams can barely keep up. We're losing more agents all the time."

"Really?" Harrison says in a bitter voice. "Then why doesn't the government just eliminate the old city altogether?"

Megan gives him a funny look, and takes a bite of her smoked salmon appetizer. "And start a war? Remember, there are more of them than there are of us. Besides, that would just drive them into the country. Then we wouldn't be able to go outside. We'd be prisoners on our own planet. No, it's better this way. They stay in the city, and we stay out."

Harrison realizes that he sounds harsh, uncaring. But he doesn't think it wise to show much sympathy for the residents below the complex. He can sense Megan isn't compassionate to their plight, and if he appears too concerned, Megan might talk to the wrong people. "You don't understand," he says. "I don't mean just forcing them to leave the old city. I was thinking more of going in and eliminating all of them and just being done with it before it's too late."

Her drink has just arrived and she waits for the server to leave. "What do you mean 'before it's too late'?"

"Look, I've been in the service most of my life, and I've seen various conflicts. It's old history, many times over."

"I was never good at history. You'll have to explain."

"I know this might sound harsh, but ... a small number of the planet's population is enjoying life in this high-rise paradise, while the majority risk their neck to rescue scraps from a trash compactor. How long do you think it will take them to realize all of this is here," he raises his arms to indicate the clean, orderly restaurant, "and challenge the system, knowing we have everything readily available — including drugs?"

Megan shakes her head. "Harrison, they already know what's here. That's why we have to keep them down. But you'll never eliminate all of them, unless you stop it at the source."

"Which is?" Harrison takes a drink and shifts his seat around.

"You seem overly concerned," Megan says, "and that's dangerous. Agents don't usually get this involved with ... those people."

Harrison waits. He's sure Megan would prefer to change the subject, but he has no intention of permitting her an easy out this time.

After a long pause, Megan finally answers. "Look around you. We are the source. It only takes five or six generations of drug users. And from then on, as you say, the rest is history."

"What's so remarkable about drugs that everyone has to get involved?" Harrison asks, not caring how much his frustration shows. "I mean, what could justify this burden?"

Megan sighs. "With drugs, people can obtain the level of ... efficiency they think they should have. Their lives can be improved in any way they need ... or so they seem to think. You see, constant improvement has become a way of life here. 'Good' isn't good enough. You have to continuously improve if you wish to maintain this lifestyle. If you're not growing, improving at what you do, you'll be replaced." Her voice is becoming louder and more nervous as she talks. "But for most people ... the only way they know how to improve is with enhancement drugs. Some stay on them for decades."

Harrison leans back in his chair. "It appears to me they — I mean we, the people here — already have everything we could want. How much better could it get?"

"Yes, possibly. But inside, I think a lot of people up here are seriously troubled. You see, the improvement is short-lived, so they need more when the effects wear off."

"So drugs are the answer to all their limitations?"

She sighs again. "Harrison, you'll get most of this in your training, but ... no. Actually, enhancement just helps them with their personal problems, and makes the unsolvable ones more tolerable. Besides, without it, they'd have to face an undistorted world of harsh realities, and ... just be themselves." She catches herself and looks away. "Of course, that's just my own opinion."

"So what you're saying is, if we're not careful, our great-great-grandchildren could be druggies?"

Megan forces a smile and turns back to him. "Let's change the subject."

Harrison knows he's pushed as far as he can go without raising suspicion. "All right."

She thinks for a moment. "What do you miss most about the space program?"

He pretends to entertain the question, and then sighs dramatically. "Oh, I think the thing I miss most is waking up to the sound of the life-support malfunction warning horn."

She laughs. "Oh yeah, I'd miss that too. Come on, seriously."

Harrison hesitates, then says, "Several years ago, I was patrolling a shuttle route in Sector Three when a meteor shower passed within a few kilometers of a small planet that was just ahead. Each time a meteor hit the atmosphere, the entire planet burst into an array filled with every color you could imagine."

"Oh! That must have been so very beautiful."

Harrison nods, then quickly changes the topic. "Why is it taking so long to get your place back in order?"

Megan glances around, then turns back to him. "It's not. I didn't want to say anything back at Angie's, but the chief assigned a couple of agents to stay there. He thinks that whoever came in will be back."

Harrison's eyes narrow. With this information, his theory about the trashing of his own place doesn't seem nearly as ill-formed. "Why?" His voice sinks. "Why does he think they'll come back?"

"They didn't take anything, just trashed the place. Like they were looking for something in particular."

"Like ... drugs?"

Megan shakes her head. "No, I don't think so. Everyone in the complex knows I'm with the DEA. My place would be the last one for drugs."

Harrison nods without speaking.

"You should have seen it. It looked like your home after that half-breed decorated it."

Harrison now is certain he has no intention of telling Megan what he has figured out about Sixteen's death.

"What do you think they were after, then?" he whispers. "You, maybe?"

"We're not sure." Megan avoids his eyes. "But I'm going to stay with Angie for a while and see what develops."

Megan is nearly finished with her meal, and gives Harrison a Why aren't you eating? look. He knows what she's thinking, because he's thinking it, too. He has missed her, missed her a lot. But there's more on his mind. What Megan said about her place ... He tries to remember exactly how everything looked the night Sixteen was killed.

"What's the matter," Megan asks. "Don't you like it?"

"What?"

"Your food. Is something wrong with it? You haven't eaten much."

"No, it's just fine. I'm not that hungry." No sense pretending any longer; he drops his fork and slides the plate away.

"Is it something I said?"

"No, of course not."

"Well, I'm finished. We can leave anytime you're ready."

¤ ¤ ¤

On their way back, they pass a fruit market, and Harrison stops.

"Something appeals to you?" Megan smiles.

There's a long pause before Harrison replies. "I was supposed to pick up some fruit for Sixteen and ... a plug-in for the computer," he says.

"What? Look, I know you're still probably upset about his death, but —"

"That's it."

"What?" Megan says. "That's what?"

"Come on." Harrison whirls around and rushes toward the elevator.

She's slow to react, and has to run to catch up. "Where are we going?"

"My place."

They must race to catch the elevator doors that are already sliding closed. Megan asks what is going on several times, but Harrison won't talk about it in the crowded elevator. All he will say is, "I just remembered something, and I'm going to check it out."

As soon as the elevator doors reopen at the thirtieth level, he's out and practically running down the hall to his place, with Megan walking fast but far behind. Harrison holds the door and waits for her to catch up.

"Come on in."

"Now will you tell me what's going on?" she pants.

Not answering right away, he leads Megan to the computer. "This is what's going on. I found a module at Radcliff's hideout. Sixteen was going to use the computer to figure out what it corresponded with. That's what they were looking for when they broke in. It has to be. I was convinced he was murdered for his blood, but that's what they wanted me to think."

Blue eyes wide with confusion, Megan asks, "How do you know all that, and who's 'they'?"

"Never mind, just hang on." Harrison turns on his computer and punches in the command to summon up the last entry, but nothing happens. "Well, I don't know. Maybe he didn't get in, I guess."

"If it's a module, why don't you try that as a search term?"

"Good thinking." Harrison types in the word "module," and the screen comes to life with a 3D drawing of the module.

"What does that mean?" Megan says. "It's just a model of it."

"I don't know." Harrison presses the key for the next page and a wiring diagram appears. He presses it again, and the list of frequencies for modules scrolls across the screen. A place for remarks and the trademark "A-T" appears at the bottom of the screen.

"Look here," he yells, his voice rising with excitement. "The remarks are from Sixteen, he did get into it. He left a note. It says that the blue module corresponds with the SJ.26. Also that the modules must be replaced every time it's re-pressurized."

"They simply unplug the old module and plug in the new one," Megan whispers, amazed. "With this technology, the drug lords could calculate the location of every agent."

"That's the way it looks." Harrison stands quietly for some time.

"So where's the thing at?"

"I don't know, but one thing's for sure. It's not here."

Megan stops to think. "Maybe he threw it in the trash."

Harrison gives her a long, hard look. "If there's one place on this planet I'm never going again, it's the trash compactor."

"Well, it's definitely not here." She returns the same look.

He turns to the screen. "I was right. They only wanted the module, but they killed Sixteen as a cover-up. I gave them the alibi they needed. How stupid could I be? I brought him here to live and, and now look ... He said that he would die here, he was right."

Megan lays her hand on his shoulder. "You didn't kill him."

"He's dead because of me. Is there a difference?"

Megan sighs. "Look, you can't bring him back. And I'm very sorry about that. The only thing we can do is not let his death be in vain. Obviously someone wanted the module back before we discovered their operation, and they covered it up by killing Sixteen. What we must do now is find out who."

"Yeah, you're right," Unfortunately, Harrison doesn't know who to trust, especially at the DEA. But to accomplish what he is planning, he has to rely on someone ... and Megan's place was destroyed. Unless the cover-up is far more elaborate than he can imagine, he deems she's the one to trust.

He turns to confront her. "You're going to work tonight, right?"

"Well ... Yeah."

"I want you to go in early."

"Wait a minute," she expels a deep breath. "You think that it's someone at DEA headquarters?"

"It has to be, Megan. Who else would have access to the SJ.26? The place is too tight. And the modules must be replaced constantly. Has to be someone inside." He looks at her, searching her face. "So, are you willing to help me find out who the traitor is?"

At first she doesn't say anything while she digests the situation. Then she aggressively looks at him. "I — I'll do whatever you want, but you'll plainly see that you're wrong. You don't know the people I work with. … None of them would ever do something like this."

Harrison's chest heaves. "Look, I hope I am wrong, but I don't think so. And if I'm right, someone inside the DEA is leading a lot of agents to their deaths. Your agents, and one little half-breed who didn't get to see the sunshine until the day he died."

Harrison shakes off the thought and turns to Megan. "And they'll keep doing it until we stop them. Here's the plan: I have an SJ.26 that should need the module replaced — it's been re-pressurized. As soon as you get to headquarters, tell the chief what's going on. You'll need to convince him to put my ship under surveillance. When we catch this lowlife, he'll tell us where he gets these modules."

The still-doubtful Megan leaves for DEA headquarters, while Harrison puts into motion his plan to catch the traitor.

¤ ¤ ¤

Without stopping to talk to anyone, Megan marches straight to Chief Boyd's office. Boyd looks up from his paper-filled desk. "Yes, Megan, what is it?"

She shuts the door behind her, making sure it's closed tight. "It's Harrison, Chief. He's got this crazy idea that someone in our own department is sabotaging the SJ.26."

"What? You're right, he is crazy." The slightly overweight chief shoves his worn leather chair away from the desk. "You tell Harrison that there's nothing wrong with the SJ model. You hear me?"

"It's not like equipment sabotage," Megan explains. "He believes that the drug lords have installed a tracking module inside the agents' vehicles."

Boyd shakes his head. "Yeah, right. Security in this building is airtight."

"Chief, I know it seems impossible, but I think Harrison's onto something," Megan persists. "I've seen the module. And you've said it yourself. The drug lords seem to know where our agents are before we do —"

"Just how stupid do I look," Boyd snaps back. "Don't you think I have a contingency plan for just such a plot? We monitor every signal from those vehicles, coming and going. And if one of them lands anywhere but this roof, Walter goes over it nose-to-tail with a fine-tooth comb. And no one gets past these guards." He points up toward the rooftop landing pad.

"And how well do we know these guards? As you'll recall, the last ones came straight over from Capitol City — recruited, authorized, and trained." Megan protests.

He leans forward and places both hands on the desk. "Megan, I've seen their background checks, their records, reports, everything."

She takes a deep breath. "I don't mean any disrespect, but think about it, sir. ... Everything you've just referred to came from only one place — the capital."

The blood seems to drain from his face. "You're talking about a national conspiracy here. Is that what he thinks?"

Megan is confident in defending Harrison. "You can ask him yourself. He's on his way over right now, and this is what he has planned, if you agree ..."

¤ ¤ ¤

Harrison suits up, checks his laser pistol, and heads for his vehicle, which is parked on the rooftop landing port. From his complex, it's an extremely short flight to headquarters.

When he receives the clearance signal to land, he intentionally sets the vehicle down in a dark, secluded area that's out of sight from the main entrance. His intent: to make it appealing for someone to tamper with. Exiting the vehicle, he heads for the elevator. Guarding the outer entrance is Richard, polite as ever, greeting Harrison while opening the door. "Good to see you again, Captain Harrison," he says.

"Thank you, it's good to be back, Richard."

Harrison enters the first security door and states his name to the computer, which analyzes his voice, then quickly opens the elevator doors. Richard watches Harrison step onto the elevator, then turns and closes the door.

Harrison says "fifth floor" and slips off the elevator just before the doors close. Staying constricted against the wall, he waits, hoping the guard won't take a second look.

¤ ¤ ¤

The empty elevator makes its first stop at the DEA fifth floor. Standing outside Chief Boyd's office, Megan watches as the elevator lights pause and the doors open. As soon as she sees the lift is empty, she turns and says, "Chief, Captain Harrison is ready."

Boyd looks over at the three heavily armed men, hand-picked volunteers from the clean-up crew, and nods.

The three huge men just barely fit into the elevator. As the last one enters, he presses the button to return the elevator to the rooftop.

¤ ¤ ¤

Harrison cracks the outer door just enough to peek out. Seeing Richard nowhere in sight, he slides out, keeping his body pressed firmly against the small brick building in the center of the rooftop landing port. Clinging to the wall like some type of unwanted vine, he silently inches to the rear of the building, and then cautiously peers around the corner at the line of vehicles parked against the rear barrier.

A small sigh escapes from his lips as he pulls his weapon; the guard stands to the right front of his vehicle, looking around unafraid. Harrison suspects the guard will be proven as the guilty party. Either way, there's no turning back now. Moving as quickly and quietly as he can, he makes his way across the open area between him and the vehicles.

¤ ¤ ¤

Richard, with his back to Harrison, frantically removes the cowling cover from the nose of Harrison's vehicle and reaches into the eye-level electronics compartment with his left arm. Harrison isn't halfway across when Richard somehow senses him coming. He spins around and grabs for his pistol, but Harrison fires first. The blast, striking the guard in the chest and engulfing his upper torso, knocks him to the ground. With his eyes boring into Harrison, his suit smoking, the edges still yet smoldering, he fights violently to maintain an upright position.

Harrison recognizes the sleek metal chest plate now exposed by the laser, he knows immediately what he's confronting. At this range, the laser would have terminated a human and left few remains. But this is no human.

Chapter Thirteen

The android's face is so mutilated, it can't see. Its eyes are fixed on the last position it saw. Nevertheless, it's transmitting a high-pitched frequency in the hope of pinpointing Harrison's location. Finding success, it quickly raises its left arm in his direction. Before Harrison can squeeze off a second shot in defense against the android's weapon embedded in its arm, several bursts of a much-larger caliber erupt from behind. Harrison dives for cover and the android is engulfed in flames.

After the inferno subsides, Harrison walks to where the three men are standing, looking down at the smoldering remains.

"You didn't leave much to go on," Harrison states. "I'd like to have found out where this thing came from."

"It doesn't matter," one of them replies.

"What do you mean, 'It doesn't matter'?" Harrison chides. "I think —"

"Once disabled, androids are programmed for self-destruct."

Everyone turns to the sound of numerous footsteps. Men are overflowing the modest building, racing across the landing pad with fire extinguishers in hand, and Chief Boyd close behind.

"Well, congratulations, Harrison. How did you know?"

"It was just a hunch, sir." Harrison reaches into the open compartment of his vehicle and extracts the module. then hands it to boyd "Here, you'll undoubtedly find one of these in every SJ.26."

Boyd looks at him hard. "You're going to tell me everything, Harrison." He clutches the module tightly in his left hand, trying to cover up his look of embarrassment with pain.

Although Harrison knows what's going through Boyd's mind, he doesn't respect it. How could he let a thing like this happen? He tries to envision it. Is he incompetent, or just outdated? Looking at his boss, whose face now shows how overworked and fatigued he is, he believes his fears may be well-founded.

Boyd finally speaks. "Harrison, I want to see you in my office, now." Turning to the clean-up crew, "You three take this ... this thing down to the lab." Without looking back again, Boyd starts for the elevator.

As the chief enters the main office with Harrison close behind, Megan looks up from her control panel. "What happened up there?" she asks. "Every warning signal in the place was going — "

"Just bring me the file on that guard, and tell the lab I want their report as soon as possible."

Eyebrows raised, she immediately gets to work.

Boyd sits down in the chair behind his desk and turns to face Harrison. "Now let's have it. How did you know?"

"Well, sir, I found one of those modules at Radcliff's hideout. We didn't know what its function was at first."

Boyd scowls. "You said 'we'?"

"Yes, me ... and the half-breed."

"The mutant you turned loose in your home? The same one that trashed it before he killed himself?"

"He didn't destroy my place, sir. That was done by the person or persons looking for the module. When they didn't find what they were after, they headed for Megan's place. They were trying to retrieve it before we discovered its purpose. And I believe they killed ... the half-breed to cover up their investigation, and probably to keep him from talking."

Boyd, with a sweep of his hand, invites Harrison to sit. "Its purpose? And that is?"

"It transmits a signal that tells direction and speed of the vehicle it's designed for. In this case, the SJ.26."

Boyd is deeply amazed; his shoulders drop and he falls back into his chair. "Why didn't we pick up the signal?"

"They have to be activated. When the signal is turned off, they turn off."

Boyd nods. "That answers a lot of questions."

"It also explains why I took Radcliff by surprise."

"Of course. You had that old JT.24 that came out of storage." Boyd activates his viewer. "Megan, find Walter and tell him to set up a schedule to inspect every vehicle."

"What should I tell him to inspect for?"

Boyd glances at Harrison. "Harrison will show him what he's looking for." Boyd cuts the connection and turns to Harrison. "How did you know it was Richard?"

"Well, I didn't know at first. But that doctor from the infirmary and this guard were the only two that I came in contact with. They were the only two that noticed me exiting with Sixteen — er, the half-breed. And the guard seemed curious to me. For one thing, he shouldn't have allowed me to leave with the half-breed alive, but he did. I've worked with androids before; they're always overly polite when it comes to humans. Like holding the door for you. An android would have been programmed to identify the damaged modules and replace them. He could have very easily detected the module in my pocket."

They both turn as Megan knocks. She enters the office and places a file folder in front of the chief. "Here's the file on the guard."

Boyd grabs the file and begins leafing through the recycled paper that is stuck together. "Liquid paper, modules, androids, where does it end?" He gives Megan a glance. "I know you've read this. When was his last examination?"

"Six months ago, sir. It's on the second page."

"Well, we know that he was, ah ... replaced within the last six months." Boyd looks at the ceiling. "How could I have allowed an android in here for six months and not detected it?"

Megan gasps. "That's about the same time we began receiving the new vehicles, wasn't it, Chief?"

The viewer begins to blink, Boyd pushes the screen on. "We have the preliminary findings on the android," says the soft female voice.

"Yes, bring it in."

The woman enters right away and hands Chief Boyd the file. "Not much here, sir. The thing was pretty well destroyed. But we do know that it was a newer model created by Advanced Technology."

Harrison stiffens. "That's the same company that fabricates the SJ.26!"

"You're right, Harrison." Boyd nods as he looks the file over. "They're a very prominent company that somehow acquires the majority of government contracts."

"Sir, I'd like to proceed with this."

"You've been a big help, but —" Boyd stops long enough to dismiss the woman, and then returns his gaze to Harrison. "All right. You might as well. You're already involved. But this is much too crucial for one man, and a new one at that. I'm putting my best agents on this."

Harrison nods. "I'd like to question the people at Advanced Technology."

"No. Not until we have more to go on. Just because they developed the android doesn't mean they programmed it."

"One way to find out," Harrison says.

Breathing heavily, Boyd closes the file and lays it on the desk; then he reaches up to rub his forehead. "And if you're wrong, the Senior Council would have the justification they've been looking for."

"I — I don't understand."

Megan turns to him. "Rod, some of the head Council members have been trying desperately to eliminate the Commander-in-Chief's position for years. So they can control the DEA directly. If they could prove we've been misusing authority — for example, if you question Advanced Technology and it backfires — that would be all they need. And with a big company like Advanced — "

"It's getting late," Boyd interrupts. "The only thing you can do now is check out the guard's residence — although you won't likely find him there ... alive, at least. Also, make sure you show Walter what he's looking for with the vehicle inspections. Maybe tomorrow the lab will have more on this android."

Boyd hands over the guard's file. "We'll get a fresh start in the morning."

Megan and Harrison leave the office, stopping at her desk in the control room. There, he stands tapping the file on its corner.

"You have another plan, don't you, Rod?"

He looks over at her, half-smiling. "Well, I guess I better see Walter before I check out the guard's place."

"That wasn't an answer."

"I'll stop back later tonight."

"Okay, okay," Megan says. "I'll call down and tell Walter you're on the way. And ... be careful. You and I still have some things to discuss ... about us."

¤ ¤ ¤

While Harrison indicates to Walter where the modules plug-in, Walter assigns one of his men to replace the cowling cover on Harrison's vehicle. Harrison quickly obtains directions from flight control to the guard's place of residence, and it isn't long before he's approaching a curiously solitary building whose landing port hasn't been used in months. Harrison exits the ship.

He slips inside the building — there's a lock on the rooftop entrance, but it isn't engaged — and takes the first stairway down, only to find that the entire building is empty, and has been for quite some time.

"Well, it doesn't look as if I'm going to find much here," he mutters, continuing downward as he quickly checks each floor with the hope of finding a lead. But he's really expecting a body.

When Harrison finally reaches the guard's apartment, he stumbles onto a notice attached to the open door: It's an order to vacate the premises. The same is on every door, unsigned except for the initials "A-T" in the lower right-hand corner. With his pistol drawn, he enters the dark room. Only a faint light from the hallway leaks into the living room, making it look as though the guard's living quarters have been untouched, not at all like the previous floors. Those had been emptied of furniture and fixtures.

After as thorough as an investigation can possibly be made in the dark apartment, he concludes that the guard had left suddenly, before the evacuation notice. But with no neighbors or security personnel to question, he leaves knowing little more than when he arrived.

On the way back, he can't help wondering why anyone would vacate an entire building. He needs to question someone who lived here. But the notice reveals little information, except the initials "A-T."

He freezes in the middle of the landing port, just now realizing where he'd seen the letters before.

"Advanced Technology," he whispers. "They must own the building. That means they make the SJ.26, and the module, and the android who installed it." He cringes. "Whether the chief wants to admit it or not, A-T is behind this in some capacity." Harrison knows that it's time to investigate Advanced Technology.

He pauses a moment, considering the risks. He's still technically a fighter pilot — actually, a discharged fighter pilot — not yet a full-fledged DEA agent. At least he could take a look around, even if he doesn't get in. How much trouble can he bring down on the DEA for just checking the place out?

Deciding it doesn't really matter at this point — his curiosity is burning a hole in his brain — he obtains the location and heading for Advanced Technology from flight control.

"It's located at Annapolis," the controller states. "That's a three-hour flight at normal speed. Shall I file it?"

"Negative," Harrison replies. "Cancel." A flight plan would just serve as a warning to whoever is monitoring incoming flights, notifying them that he's on his way. Rather, Harrison starts in the opposite direction. When he clears Houston's control, he quickly alters his heading for Annapolis. He's careful to stay clear of Houston's control area as he launches out across the desert. The normal three-hour flight time can be cut in half with the SJ.26 at full power. The SJ.26 isn't your normal vehicle; Advanced Technology has outdone themselves with their SJ model. He can thank them for that, at least.

Harrison knows he will arrive at four a.m. — an appropriate time for an uninvited sightseeing tour of the premises, and possibly the best way to avoid all those silly personal questions guards are trained to ask.

¤ ¤ ¤

Megan pounds on the control room keyboard as though she's trying to beat something into it. A moment later, the chief's face appears on her screen, and by his tone she knows he's just woken up.

"Yes, Megan, what's wrong?"

"We had an assault on one of our agents, sir. Just minutes ago."

"Yes ...?"

"It was ... from within the city."

"What? Is the agent down?"

"Yes."

"What hit him?"

"High-tech, heavy bore. Military grade. That's all we know for sure. I need your permission to send in Search and Rescue after dark."

"Yes, of course. But first, get a clean-up crew together."

"I already have one standing by. He went down over Sector 23. We should have no trouble finding him."

Boyd thinks a moment, rubbing the grizzle on his chin. "Don't we have people in Sector 23?"

"Yes."

"Send them a communiqué. I want their report first thing. I need to know where the druggies acquired something that effective. And have a second crew standing by. Begin cleaning out the entire sector as soon as it's light enough."

"Yes sir, but the entire sector will probably take more than two crews."

Sector 23 is particularly heavy with abandoned superstructures. Most of them are equipped with landing ports, but the majority is unusable.

"I don't care how many clean-up crews it takes," Boyd states. "Whatever that weapon is, I want it out of their hands."

¤ ¤ ¤

Harrison arrives at A-T Corporation close to four a.m., as planned. There's a guard at each entrance, but oddly, that seems to be it for security. It would be relatively simple for anyone to gain entry into the large single-story building.

Harrison flies inconspicuously overhead and continues until he's out of sight, then brings the vehicle back around to the south side of the building, where there are no guards. He lands in a field consisting of tall weeds and a few scarce trees.

It's a tedious hike to the lengthy building, but with Harrison's black flight suit and the help of an occasional tree to break up the monotony and hide him, he makes it undetected. Upon reaching the rear of the building, he discovers why there are so few guards: a thick metal wall surrounds the complex. After examining the back section of the barrier, he decides the only way in is to scale the wall.

Several of the metal plates that make up the wall have developed small openings at the seams with age and lack of maintenance. Harrison is able to slip a hand into each opening, grab hold of the plate, and use it as a handhold to pull himself up the wall, a few centimeters at a time, until finally he reaches the top. From the top of the wall, it's a long jump to the roof. He lands with a loud thud — too loud — and fights to maintain his awkward position, legs dangling over the edge, hoping he hasn't alarmed the guards or set off a sensor. When nothing happens, he slowly pulls himself up the slightly angled roof.

At the top, he finds a closed vent and tries with no luck to open it; the louvers on the vent are much too thick to crimp. Harrison knows the laser would be far too noisy; he must use the inaudible shoulder weapon to penetrate the bars that hold the louvers in place. It takes only seconds for the stinger to eat through. Now, Harrison can remove as much of the vent as he needs. He suddenly stops as guilt washes over him.

"I'm breaking in like some kind of common criminal," he says. He quickly brushes it off. Although the chief would never agree to his method of doing things, A-T is guilty of manufacturing the modules that have gotten several agents killed. Harrison has the right, no, the obligation to stop them.

Using the camera-like sights on his laser pistol to see inside, he realizes he's directly above some type of machine shop. Its equivalent to a small factory blended within a large one; he can smell the cutting oil from the machines below. It isn't where he wants to begin the investigation — he'd hoped for offices. But they would likely have alarms, so this will have to do.

Harrison spies a long chain dangling from the ceiling. Following it up, he can see that it goes through a pulley, then back down to the floor. Apparently, it's used to open and shut the roof vent. He uses the barrel of his pistol to bring the chain within reach. A hard tug on the chain assures him that it will hold his weight. He looks down at the long drop to the machinery below, and knows he's betting his life on that assumption.

Holding tight to both chains, he quietly slips into the opening. The chain swings him back and forth a couple of times before he's able to start down, but it does hold.

Once safely on the floor, Harrison can hardly budge. He's landed in a jungle of robotic arms and conveyer belts. The machines, totally automated, leave no room for humans to walk around.

After untangling himself, and traversing through the maze of cables, belts and giant arms that seem to have been frozen in time, he eventually comes upon a path just wide enough to ease through, which ends at a small shanty. It appears similar to several such buildings he'd seen from the roof. After a quick examination of the one-man building, he whispers, "All right, so this is where the computer operator programs the machines." The screens inside the room show a list of jobs and their start-times; apparently, the machines begin work without an operator.

Harrison snakes down the path in the opposite direction, which guides him out of the production area and into what looks to be a shipping dock. Several crates sit on the dock floor, boxed up, ready for loading. From the labels on each crate, they state they contain standard types of electronics. Harrison glances only briefly at the crates as he moves quietly through the aisles, noticing nothing out of the ordinary until he reaches the opposite end of the dock. In front of one loading-dock door are several medium-sized boxes waiting to be shipped, with the name "Wingate" stamped across the front.

Until then, Harrison hadn't planned to linger.

He sets one of the many boxes on the floor and reads the label. "FRAGILE: KEEP IN PRESSURIZED AREA" is stamped on it; the top is sealed with a strip that reads, "ADMIRAL KACHEL ONLY."

"What the hell?" he whispers. After a quick glance around to ensure he's alone, he quickly breaks the seal and opens the box. He has to choke back his gasp; the box is completely full of modules, hundreds of blue modules just like the one Sixteen had identified as belonging to the SJ.26 — the vehicle the DEA now has ... the same vehicle that the fighter pilots aboard the Wingate depend on in combat.

Harrison stands, rubbing his chin, looking back at all the boxes. There must be thousands here. Thousands, he thinks.

Harrison picks up one of the modules, looks it over, and then slips it into his pocket.

I knew there was something wrong with Kachel, but what would the admiral have to gain from installing them in the fighters? Harrison wonders. That would explain why the pirates have been so precise with their attacks lately. Why they showed so little fear in attacking Laura's ship. The modules would give them the ability to know exactly how many fighters are escorting a supply ship, and track their position at all times. But working with the drug traffickers too? Chief Boyd's got to see this.

He hears a noise from somewhere in the darkness. Before he can even turn, he feels a heavy thud from behind, his vision blurs, everything goes black as he crumbles forward. He tries unsuccessfully to open his eyes; the last thing Harrison remembers is his body falling over the box and the modules dumping onto the floor.

Chapter Fourteen

Harrison is awakened by several harsh slaps to his already aching head. A sharp pain is throbbing at the back of his skull, which feels like someone has just stuck a hot knife in it, and his face burns from being smacked. He tries instinctively to check the damage to the back of his head, but is unable to move his arms. He hears voices, though, and someone says, "He's coming around."

But try as he might, he can't break the grip of unconsciousness holding him in limbo. Several moments later, he's finally able to open his eyes, but the blinding light issues a new kind of pain. His chin drops to his chest as he gasps for air; only now does he realize that someone has been holding his head up. Slowly, he opens his eyes again; now, he's able to focus.

He's sitting with both arms tied securely to a heavy metal chair. Water is running down his chest and between his legs. He can't feel the cold water through the thick pilot's suit, but knows his hair is soaked, and can sense water dripping off his chin. Fear is the only thing keeping him conscious. He eases his throbbing head upright. The light becomes brighter, telling him it's directly overhead. In front of him is a solid brick wall.

A man steps forward and blocks his view. Now, his eyes have something to focus on. He attempts a look up, to see if he recognizes the man, but the light only shines chest-high, and Harrison can't see the man's face in the dark.

Harrison hears voices. At least two others. One with a very heavy accent. He distinguishes an exit door to his far left. Adjacent to the door stands another man, much larger than the one in front of him.

The man moves toward him. Harrison's first instinct is to reach for his laser, but he quickly realizes there's nothing to be gained by pulling on the straps binding his arms, as he looks down to find his holster empty.

The well-dressed man standing in front of Harrison holds out his right hand. Seemingly from nowhere, his laser pistol appears.

"Looking for this? Now tell us ... who are you?"

Harrison doesn't know if he should answer, but he isn't given long to think about it. The huge man now standing beside Harrison grabs him by the hair and pulls his head back. "He's just another thief," he says to the man in front. "Let me take him to the incinerator."

The man in front snaps his fingers, and the big man reluctantly lets Harrison's hair slip from his hand.

"This is government issue," the man holding the laser pistol states. "Very nice. Where did you get it?"

Again, the big man answers for Harrison. "He stole it. He's just a thief. Let me take him to the incinerator."

The man in front ignores his plea. "That uniform you're wearing ... do you work for the government, or did you steal that, too?"

Harrison glares.

The big man grunts, "I'll make him talk." And before the others can stop him, he pulls back his right arm and let's loose with a crunching blow to the left side of Harrison's face.

Something cracks as the big fist connects. His vision blurs, at the same time his back teeth feel as if they no longer line up with his jaw. It takes a moment for the pain to begin, but when it does, it quickly becomes a throbbing anguish. He can feel the left side of his face swelling. Moving his jaw is painful, but he doesn't think it's broken, just out of place. Or at least, he hopes so.

"Now, I ask you again, who do you work for?"

Harrison, knowing it would be safer to be behind bars than to answer, replies, "What if I am a thief?" Blood spatters onto his lap as he speaks. "Are you going to turn me in?" He's trying to sound braver than he feels.

"That depends on what you know. You see, once you've acquired our technology secrets ... well, we could notify the government, but they'd just sentence you to a penal colony. Even that doesn't guarantee that you won't sell the technology, now does it? To separate and delete an internal memory download is very troublesome. No, we have a more conclusive solution — though unpleasant for you, simple for us."

The big man smiles down at Harrison. "We're not going to turn you in to the government. We're going to turn you into ashes."

With difficulty, Harrison forces his head back toward the man in front.

"Don't look so surprised," he states. "We don't need to turn you in to the authorities. You see we do a lot of confidential work for the government. And they don't appreciate their objectives becoming common knowledge. We have a mutual agreement: They tell us what they want, and we create it without question. And when it comes to our security, they don't inquire. Now, what's your name?"

"Harrison. Just like it says on the suit."

The big man asks rather brassily, "Shall I start the incinerator for Harrison?"

The man in front nods. "Yes. It hasn't been used for quite some time. You see, Mr. Harrison ... if that's your name ... we assumed every thief knew our policy by now."

Harrison knows he has only one chance: When they untie him and start for the incinerator, hopefully he'll have time to activate the stinger.

"Now, who do you work for?"

"The government."

The big man hasn't yet left Harrison's side to begin the job he so dearly loves. "Why would the government want to break in here?" he states. His befuddlement seems genuine.

Harrison doesn't know who to trust, so he doesn't know if he should answer. He chooses not to say anything. Once again, the big man rears back and let's go. This time, the huge fist lands high on Harrison's left cheek. The pain spreads from the top of his head all the way down his neck. He doesn't know the immediate damage to his left eye, but closes both and braces himself for the third blow. It never comes.

If I get out of this, I'm going to kill that big moron, he thinks. But at the same time, he dares not let revenge cloud his thinking. The second blow has him convinced that no matter what his answers are, these people don't intend to let him live. In order to keep any hope of escape alive, he knows he must stay alert.

Another person enters the room; Harrison struggles desperately to open his eyes. The swollen left one is slower to focus, and everything appears darker through it. He senses the blood flowing from above it; his entire face feels tortured. The blood burns his eye to the point that it's nearly impossible to hold open.

He hears the big man say, "He's ready to talk now."

"Get out," demands the newcomer.

The big man hustles from the room without a word, leaving the two men standing in front of Harrison. They talk in a much lower tone, but Harrison can still hear the new man say, "I contacted Mr. Solomon and told him that we had a break-in."

"Did you tell him his name?" The man in front looks toward Harrison.

"Yes, everything."

"What did he say?"

"He's coming over, and we should do nothing until he gets here. He wants to find out who this guy works for first."

The man in front stiffens. "The boss is coming down here, tonight?"

"Yes, he should be here any time."

After the conversation, the well-dressed man checks Harrison's straps. When Harrison winces, he says, "Just want to make sure you're still here when I get back." Then both captors leave.

¤ ¤ ¤

Harrison can only distinguish a small slit of light as it tries to squeeze through the badly swollen eye. His face has stopped bleeding, but he still has the taste of blood in his mouth.

Looking about the small, windowless room, he sees there's no means of escape. If only they had taken him to the incinerator! There he could have tried to activate the stinger. Now, he's stuck. Even if he can free himself from the straps, it's a sure guess that the only exit will be heavily guarded. He has already made one serious mistake, underestimating their security. His only alternative now is to wait.

Sometime later, Harrison still clinging to the faint hope of escape, a man enters the room, stopping just inside the doorway. Harrison looks up, but can see only a long black dress coat and shoes.

"Well, well ... is it Captain Harrison the fighter pilot, or is it Mr. Harrison the DEA agent?"

This must be Mr. Solomon, Harrison speculates. If so, he has an excellent source to have found out so much in so little time.

The man walks over and lifts Harrison's head by his chin. Looking into his face, he says, "Looks like you've had an accident. Didn't anyone ever tell you that it's unhealthy to wander around in the dark?"

Harrison doesn't respond; he just takes a good look at the man, Mr. Solomon turns loose of his chin and steps back.

Solomon glances at the two men who have just entered the room and says, "Untie him."

Harrison takes a deep breath and waits as the two men untie the straps. But before he can get up, Solomon snarls, "Give Mr. Harrison his weapon and escort him to his vehicle."

Certain it's a trap; Harrison looks around for the big man. But he's nowhere to be found.

One of the guards thrusts Harrison's laser deep into its holster, then says, "Follow me."

The three of them walk past Solomon, who falls in line and follows them out the door. "You should have that eye looked at, Harrison,"

Solomon says, but it's clear he doesn't really care. At that moment, Harrison allows himself to hate the man who appears to be directing the malevolent exhibit he is forced to be a part of.

Harrison follows the man ten meters down the hall when Solomon calls out, "Trevor."

The man in front stops. "Yes, sir."

"Double the guards. Tell them, shoot to kill."

Trevor nods, and then continues down the hall.

At first, Harrison thinks Solomon gave the order as a warning for him not to return. But now he's almost as sure that the order is actually a code to kill him before they reach his vehicle.

Solomon looks over at the big man standing in the shadows and barks, "Make sure Mr. Harrison is taken care of, and when you return, remove that shipment of modules from the dock and restock them in the warehouse."

The man leading Harrison walks at a normal pace, but Harrison falls far behind, partially because of the trauma to his head, but also he's making mental notes in the event he gets the chance to return with reinforcements. At the same time, he wonders why they're taking him outside to kill him and not to the incinerator.

A racket comes from behind. He attempts to turn, but someone shoves on his right shoulder, nearly knocking him to the floor. "Come on, thief, we don't have all night."

Another punishing thrust and Harrison is several meters ahead, but the big man is closing in fast. Harrison knows immediately who it is; his heart hammers, ready to explode. He wants this guy bad, but is he up to it? He thinks. This witless thug won't hesitate to kill me now. Using my laser inside the building would inevitably alert all the guards. Still, the thought of reducing the man to a prominent pile of smoldering ash is tempting.

Trevor has just gone through an open door that closes immediately behind him. As they near the solid steel door, Harrison intentionally slows again. He allows the big man a third shove, but Harrison is anticipating it this time.

"Move it," yells the man beside him as he raises his left hand.

Just as the big thug shoves at his right shoulder, Harrison unexpectedly leans to the left and the man careens off-balance. Harrison grabs him by the shoulder and lower back, and with a commanding shove, he pushes the already unstable man into the closed door. The big man slams hard against the unyielding steel, but quickly comes back. Harrison is ready. As the man turns roughly with a smile, Harrison lets lose a grueling punch square in the mouth that quickly wipes it off.

This time, the back of the man's head collides with the steel door, he buckles to his knees. His eyes roll up and Harrison can see blood flow from his mouth. Everything has gone as planned. Still, it hasn't done as much damage as Harrison hoped.

Putting all his weight on both hands, the big man struggles to his feet. Starting with his left foot, Harrison quickly takes one long step toward the man and brings his right foot up. There's a loud crack as the heavy black boot catches under the man's chin.

The man tries to rise, but collapses to the floor. His huge body jerks several times as he exhales his last breath. Harrison looks around. The man now lies still on the smooth cement floor; the peculiar position of his head tells Harrison that he's broken the man's neck.

Reaching for his laser, he pushes the button that opens the steel door. Surprisingly, there are no guards on the other side, just an empty hall turning sharply to the left. Trevor, now waiting at the end of the hall, is trying to look behind Harrison as he walks down the hall. Harrison answers the question before it's asked: "He forgot something and had to go back."

"We're not waiting for him," Trevor replies. "Come on, I'll take you back to your vehicle."

Harrison, still wary, follows until they finally exit the building. Out front is a short but curious-looking truck with eight large tires. Harrison climbs in on the passenger side, and the two of them drive around back to his ship. He soon realizes why it needs eight tires: The small vehicle rides surprisingly well considering the rough, muddy terrain. Trevor occasionally glances at Harrison, but never speaks. Harrison keeps one hand on his laser pistol, waiting for someone to find the big man's body before they reach their destination. He has no plans of returning to the plant, even if it means terminating Trevor. Fortunately for him, the communicator never activates.

After they reach Harrison's vehicle, Trevor watches as Harrison lumbers up the four steps, across the wing and into the cockpit, then turns on the lights. Once inside, he closes the lid, moaning the entire time. The bright ring of lights disappears into the fuselage as the heavy lid seals itself to the hull. He checks the instrument panel in preparation for takeoff, watching to make sure the eight-wheeled vehicle, now turning the corner, goes away. Every glance makes his head pulsate with a new kind of anguish.

His instrument panel is quick to indicate adequate power; Harrison attempts to put his helmet on, but straightaway realizes how much pain that will inflict. He lets it roll off his shoulder and fall back into its compartment. As he lifts off, he whispers, "Thank God for autopilot," he sets the course for Houston. Whether he can see or not, there are a few things he has to get to the bottom of.

¤ ¤ ¤

"Mr. Pressnell, I'm sorry to wake you, but I thought you would want to know, Captain Harrison has just departed the plant."

"That's all right, Solomon. Did everything go as planned?"

Solomon nods. "Exactly as planned."

"Remember, this must be kept between us."

"The entire incident is forgotten."

"Good." Pressnell grins. "That's why I like doing business with A-T."

"Yes, sir. And after bidding for the new contracts next month, I hope we'll still be working together."

"What? Has it been a year already?"

"Yes. I'm afraid it's that time again."

"Well, Mr. Solomon, you submit your proposals, and I'll do the rest."

"Yes sir, and thank you. Our government contracts mean a lot to us here at A-T."

"The government needs people like you. But for now, let me suggest that you take a short leave. I think that would be the best thing for both of us. Possibly your place in the country? Just until this thing is resolved."

"I'll take that under advisement," Solomon assures him. "And thank you again, sir. We'll look forward to working with you again. Goodbye."

¤ ¤ ¤

Megan hasn't been asleep long when the door alarm buzzes. She jerks herself awake and is instantly on alert. It hasn't been easy to return to her apartment, but after the damage was repaired, there was little reason for her to put off coming back. For the first time, she regrets refusing the temporary guard Chief Boyd had offered.

"It must be Harrison." Her teeth are chattering. "It's got to be. Of course it is." Harrison had told her he'd check back that evening, but he never did. That was it; he's simply running late.

She forces herself to grab a robe and head for the door.

When she activates the door monitor, she sees Harrison leaning against the wall to the left of the door. She can't see his face. Why is he trying to hide from me? She thinks, and pushes the button to open the door.

The heavy security door slides open and Megan waits, but Harrison never comes around. Megan steps out into the hall. "What are you — oh, no?"

She helps him in, slamming her hand on the button to close and lock the door. With some difficulty, she gets him to the couch, then kneels beside him and takes a good look at his face. With panic-wet eyes she asks, "What happened?"

His garbled answer is slow to come. "I was looking around ... in the dark, it's not healthy."

Without replying, she runs to get a towel and some water. On the way back, she stops to activate the emergency button on the viewer. When she returns, Harrison is moving about.

"Lay still," she pleads, and begins gently cleaning some dried blood from around his swollen eyes. "Where did you go last night?"

"A-T," he replies.

She stops wiping for a moment. "Did they do this to you?"

"I'll be all right. ... It was worth it," he says, mangling his words. To reassure her, he reaches for her hand and gives it a half-hearted squeeze.

But Megan isn't convinced of either. Not after watching Harrison's left eye that's out of sync with the right, and blood red.

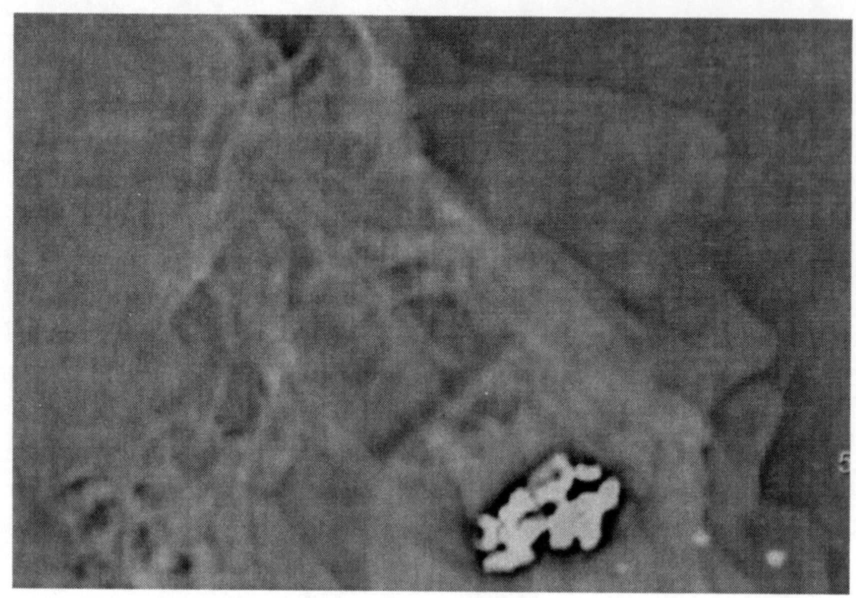

Chapter Fifteen

Megan's nearly finished cleaning his wounds when the doorbell chimes out, "Med-Vac is here."

"Well it's about time, let them enter." She stands.

"Who?" Harrison replies in a slurred voice.

"The medical evacuation people."

"I — I'm not going anywhere."

"No, you're not going anywhere. I called them to look at that eye."

Megan meets them at the door and points at Harrison. "Over here."

Two serious-faced, uniformed men enter the room. One of them places a metal case on the table and opens it. Arranged inside are several small monitors, meters, and dials. He adjusts two dials and a man's face appears on the screen. The apprentice then passes a headset to his partner.

"The man you see onscreen is the doctor. He'll do the examination and determine the damage. He may want to ask you some questions," the apprentice says to Megan.

The medic inspects Harrison's eye, then asks him to open his mouth.

"Well, how is he?" Megan asks impatiently.

"I'm not finished with the examination yet. How did this happen?" He peers at the lump on the back of Harrison's head.

"I ... I'm not sure," Megan replies.

"We'll need an echoencephalogram. Just to check for any skull fractures or brain damage."

As they speak, the apprentice is placing a thin metal band, which has several wires attached to either side, around Harrison's head. He then plugs it into the case and turns to Megan. "He is going to experience a small vibration. Don't be alarmed."

Megan bites back a grin. At this point, very little could alarm her.

A moment later, the apprentice removes the metal band, and then listens through his headset for a moment.

"Well, what did he say?" Megan asks.

He holds up one hand for silence, but after listening for a second, he looks up with a smile. "He says, and I quote, 'Your boyfriend is lucky, he has a thick head.' His jaw's dislocated, that shouldn't be a problem. Also, his back teeth are loose, but they should tighten up in a few days if he doesn't put pressure on them. But he does have some pretty serious eye damage. That will have to be repaired, now."

He pulls a hypo gun from the case and gives Harrison a shot in the neck. Under the remote doctor's supervision, the operation proceeds, surprisingly fast, but no one knows how successful. The medic, as he's packing up to leave, turns to Megan. "When he comes to, he'll have some pain, but that's to be expected. Immediately after he wakes, take him down to the doctor. Meanwhile, keep the bandage on. Oh, and no solid food until those back teeth tighten up."

¤ ¤ ¤

Soon as the men leave, Megan is careful to cover Harrison with a blanket, and then heads to the viewer. After punching in the control room's direct line, she speaks. "Angie, is the chief in?"

"Just a minute."

Boyd's face appears on the viewer right away. "I'm glad you contacted me, I want you to come in early, Megan."

"Chief, I can't. I called to tell you that I'm not coming in tonight. Harrison showed up early this morning, and he's been badly beaten. He needs someone to be here with him."

"What? Beaten by who?"

"I don't know," she replies, tears of frustration welling in her eyes. "He was so out of it. All I could make out was that he went to A-T last night."

Boyd pauses, thinking, then says, "Megan, we need to follow up on that, but there's no time right now. I really need you here. How bad is he?"

"They had to operate on his eye. He'll be under sedation until late tonight and when he comes to, he has to see a doctor right away."

"We can monitor his recovery here. When he comes around, bring him in and we'll have the doctor in the infirmary check him out."

Megan recognizes an edge in Boyd's voice. "What's going on, Chief?"

"We're about to commence a major strike, and I want every available agent in the air tonight."

"Is everyone in now?"

Boyd nods. "Yes, except the clean-up crews. I'll bring them in later today."

Megan pauses. "You're going to keep them working all day and night?"

"They'll get a break, while their ships are being re-supplied. I kept the crews on duty so no one would suspect what we're doing. I was afraid their absence would be too noticeable, and I would like to keep the element of surprise. Besides, the population should be thinned out before we interrupt the flow of drugs. ... I really need your help in coordinating this."

Megan glances at the viewer's chronometer. "What time?"

"I want everything ready to go by dusk. Walter still has his people working to remove those modules."

She nods. "I see. Hit the traffickers before they can mobilize their mercenaries."

"Yes, or execute a backup plan. Their guards won't be a problem for a change. With the modules removed, the agents can get in and identify lab locations. Without interference from the mercenaries, it won't take the crews long to clean up."

"What sectors are we going to strike?"

"Just the primary locations. But I want confirmation on all small operators for later termination."

Megan glances over at the sleeping Harrison. "Chief, you know there'll be turmoil in the old city when this leaks out."

"Don't worry. I have plans in place to handle that. It'll take a couple of days for the shock wave to hit the city. By then, we'll be ready."

Megan sighs. "Sounds like I should get some rest while I still can. This could take days."

"Good idea. But remember, don't trust anyone until we find out who Harrison's new enemy is. They may come back to finish the job."

She smiles bitterly. "Thanks for the cheerful thought. I'll keep the door locked. We'll be in as soon as Harrison's able."

Megan shuts off the viewer and turns to kiss Harrison on the cheek. "You're nothing but trouble, Rod Harrison, but I think I love you anyway."

There's no reply, but she doesn't expect one. She rechecks the door monitor and heads for bed.

¤ ¤ ¤

Pressnell knocks on the heavy wooden door to the party leader's chambers.

The head councilor delivers a hearty grin. "I'm glad you're here. I'd like to commend you on the smoothing over of Admiral Kachel's monumental blunder."

"Well, thank you, sir." It is rare for him, but Pressnell blushes.

"Now, should I commend you on the other issue we discussed?"

"The problem is being remedied as we speak, sir. I won't annoy you with the details, but soon, Admiral Kachel will be out, and the DEA will have no reason to suspect the space program or further hamper our mission."

The Head Councilor nods. "Good. I knew I could depend on you. What about the recovered supplies?"

"More good news, sir. We've established a new, ah, domicile en route to Sector Eight, and we'll begin restocking it as soon as the DEA releases the shuttles. I also have Admiral Kachel's replacement in the cultivating stage now."

"Will he be ready in time?"

Pressnell answers immediately. "Unfortunately, no. The wing commander will have to assume the admiral's duties for the first mission."

The head councilor scowls. "I ... don't understand. We can't resume the operation with the commander in charge. He doesn't know the project, and wouldn't go along with it if he did."

Pressnell leans forward, virtually out of his chair. "Yes we can. He doesn't have to know. I'll have him ship the supplies to the outpost in Sector Six, and let them shuttle it to Sector Eight. Without the protection of the Wingate, it can be intercepted en route."

The head councilor nods. "Good thinking. With that, we can restore our margin of safety." He gives Pressnell an approving look. "It seems as if everything is under control again. You've done better than expected, Mr. Pressnell. But I want to meet Kachel's replacement before he's commissioned to the Wingate."

"Of course. Will that be all?"

"Yes, for now. But until this transfer of power is complete, you're on twenty-four-hour watch."

¤ ¤ ¤

"Captain Harrison and Megan have arrived, Chief."

"Thank you, Angie. Send them in as soon as they come down."

The door opens. Boyd recognizes Megan, but not the person with her. Harrison doesn't look anything like the fighter pilot he remembers. His face is swollen and bruised, bandages cover his left eye. Even so, he fights to stand at attention as he speaks.

"Megan informs me that you're going to launch a major offensive against the traffickers tonight, Chief." With the injury to his jaw, Harrison's words are muffled.

Boyd nods. "Yes. But I see you aren't going to be part of it. I want you in the infirmary. But first," he turns to Megan, "I want you in the control room. We have everything ready to go. I thought, considering that we have more agents than clean-up crews, we'll assign the extra agents to squads. This way, they'll be sure to locate the key players and get out quick. We must dispose of them before they have time to notify their comrades. You know how news travels. Soon as the agents pull out, the clean-up can begin."

Harrison asks, "Can't we just hit every drug location?"

"Well, I would love to," Boyd laughs, showing uncharacteristic humor. "But no, they have to either be manufacturing drugs, or a known drug trafficker must be present. It's not illegal to grow plants, not even coca trees or any of the other plants. So we have to choose our targets carefully."

"I'll get started right away, Chief." Megan stands.

"Remember, we need evidence first — recordings and air samples — before you send in the clean-up crews." Boyd's words are firm, in case Harrison's rebel-like thinking has influenced Megan.

"Of course," Megan replies, and starts for the door just as Angie's voice comes through the speaker to announce the doctor's arrival.

"Tell him to wait a minute," Boyd barks, and clicks off the viewer. Then he turns to Harrison. "Before you accompany the doctor to the infirmary, I want to know ... what exactly did you see at A-T that got you in this condition?"

"I obtained the proof we needed from A-T; I found out who's behind the modules."

The chief raises his eyebrows. "Who?"

"Our very own Admiral Kachel."

"Can you prove that?"

"I've seen the modules, thousands of them." Harrison presents the module he'd put into his pocket prior to being hit over the head. "A-T ships the modules to Admiral Kachel."

Boyd thinks for a moment. "But ...if Kachel's the one, how would he distribute them to the traffickers?"

"I have a theory about that."

Boyd points to a chair. "I'm listening."

Harrison eases into the chair while speaking. "He stores the modules onboard the supply ships that the pirates are sure to seize. This way, the pirates get the supplies, and they can distribute the modules for him. It keeps him out of the loop."

"I knew there was something wrong with the admiral after our first conversation," Boyd muses. "But to prove that Kachel is an accomplice to drug traffickers and pirates ... I don't know. He may just be using the modules to keep track of his own people"

"You wanted to send a team of agents to the Wingate, didn't you? Isn't that still an option?"

Boyd nods. "I had pulled back on the idea, but it's definitely still open. However, if he suspects we're after him, we'll never get near the Wingate."

"I've worked out a plan to get us onboard."

"Not now. You're in no shape for it. Besides, I don't have the manpower available. We'll talk later." Boyd clicks on his viewer and summons the doctor.

"Hello again, Captain." The doctor smiles at Harrison. "Looks like you've had quite a day. Med-Vac briefed me on it. Let's go to the infirmary. I want to examine that eye."

"It's been operated on once today," Harrison snaps.

The doctor looks stern. "Perhaps that's so, but that eye should be examined by a professional."

Boyd looks at Harrison with an unwavering glare and says, "Goodbye, Captain."

Harrison doesn't argue. He turns and heads for the door with the arrogant doctor as his escort.

"Harrison, we'll keep you informed on our progress," Boyd calls after him.

Harrison stops just long enough to nod in appreciation.

¤ ¤ ¤

In the jungle, things are heating up. With the modules removed, the traffickers have no forewarning. The agents now have the upper hand for the first time in nearly a year. The traffickers have become over-reliant on their electronic edge, too comfortable with their year-long forewarning. They've forgotten how to evade the DEA. The agents easily locate and penetrate strongholds. It's truly the break the DEA so desperately needed. Even so, coordinators like Megan have no way of knowing the outcome of each encounter. Contacting agents could give away their positions. Only contact with the clean-up crews is possible, and they come in only after the agents have left.

Boyd checks in with Megan, who is watching and listening to the clean-up activities from the small viewer on her desk. "How many agents have we lost?" he asks.

"Seven confirmed by the clean-up crews. I have Winston looking for two others. Clean-up reports vehicles down in Subdivision Three and Four."

"How is clean-up holding out?"

"Fine, considering this is the fifth location for this crew. The other eleven crews haven't been doing quite as well."

"Put it on the big screen."

Megan hesitates. The chief has never done this before, knowing it would distract the other coordinators. For the most part, they are merely office personnel, and have never observed the actual clean-up activities. But she decides not to challenge him. She posts the picture and sound on the large wall screen.

The clean-up ship has knocked out two large cannons, and is now moving in to release the battle cage containing the crewmen. The cage is kept inside the belly of the ship. Now released it begins a slow decent but picks up speed rapidly on its ten meter drop. A mountain of dirt explodes into the air as the weighty container hits the ground. The walls fall outward, creating ramps for the men to run down. Now the real battle begins, guards with handheld lasers commence firing, but there are no mercenaries present. Although very effective against the small vehicles used by the agents, the guards haven't been a match for the clean-up crew's artillery.

With a combination of intense lights from the ship and the burning of several small wooden structures, the area remains well lit. Everyone in the control room can witness the workers hiding in the fields as the crew liquidates the guards and continues into the main building, only to find and remove the drug trafficker that the agents had left behind.

The captain of the clean-up crew's deep voice fills the office as he assigns orders to his subordinates. "Divert power for the particle beam. ... Take confirmation. ... I want the most populated field extinguished first, no one gets out." The captain looks at his screen; he knows Chief Boyd is monitoring his every move. "With your permission sir, we'll begin the clean up." The aggressive look that's normally on Chief Boyd's face turns calm. He states "Clean it up."

All eyes are fixed on the large screen as the particle beam passes several times over the thick green fields, leaving little more than blackened earth in its path. The people hiding in the fields have little to no warning of the eradication taking place. The poisonous crop that once flourished with its addictive properties suddenly vanishes, along with the ones who harvested it.

While the clean-up crew below is assembling the remaining drudges from inside the buildings, several guards escape to the thick forest surrounding the compound. They are promptly eliminated from the air. Numerous clean-up men detain the prisoners while the others continue throughout the buildings, carrying with them mutilated bodies. Collecting severed arms, legs, and other body parts appears routine to these huge men.

With the area cleared, the big ship sets down in one of the now-desolate fields. The captain gives the order to open the immense outer doors. The heavily armed men with their dark-shield helmets and solid black suits begin to coerce the remaining drudges up the ramp and into the ship, forcing them to carry with them the remains of the dead that have been gathered up.

Killers have always been placed in categories, such as those who kill for financial gain and those who kill for pleasure. The clean-up crew is neither. They swiftly and proficiently terminate drudges as if they are a disease — one that must be eradicated before it can afflict another person. This thought, combined with knowing their job and doing it well, makes them virtually unstoppable.

Uncertain of their fate, most of the captives are unwilling to move up the ramp and into the ship; the clean-up men begin firing into the crowd. The drudges run for the safety of the ship. Now, with the captives inside the huge blackened hull, the solid steel doors slowly close and the ramp lifts to seal off any hope of escape.

With the carnage over, Chief Boyd points to Megan. "Turn off the viewer. They've seen enough."

One of the pale-faced coordinators asks, "What ... what will happen to the prisoners?"

"As you all know, the DEA doesn't take prisoners. In the hull of the ship is an incinerator, fueled by the power plant. In a matter of seconds, the ship will lift off and they'll be immediately reduced to little more than exhaust." He pauses before saying, "Now you know. Everyone back to work." Boyd turns and heads for his office.

No one moves.

"If you wish to mourn for someone, mourn for the ones who died from drugs. Mourn for the seven agents we lost today." He looks at Megan again. "Get them back to work. I'll check with you later." He starts again for the door but turns around. "Call me as soon as you hear from Winston. I want those agents and their vehicles recovered."

Megan nods. After what she's just seen, that shared goal will be the only thing that keeps her going.

Chapter Sixteen

The battle continues throughout the night. The agents move fast without warning; collecting only evidence, leaving decontamination to the clean-up crew.

By morning, the crews are growing fatigued and unable to keep up. The agents, on the other hand, are still going strong, fueled by anger and revenge, not to mention the bonus money usually accompanying the traffickers' eradication. It's dirty, deadly work that rewards well.

Late the third evening, most of the agents have returned. The clandestine assault is over, the word is out, and the remaining traffickers have stopped production and gone into hiding. Megan arrives early to be with Harrison, but doesn't find him in the infirmary where she'd left him that morning. After asking one of the medical staff, she learns he's in Chief Boyd's office.

She enters the office just as Boyd says, "I'll release the shuttles at 0600 tomorrow, be ready to go."

"Go?" Megan's voice is annoying and loud. "Go where?"

Harrison turns to her. "The chief and I have mapped out a plan to get us aboard the Wingate."

"You can't go. … You're not ready. The medics said —"

"I was released from the infirmary earlier today." Harrison glances at the chief, then back at her. "Megan, I have to go. I'm the only one that can get us aboard the Wingate. And … after what I saw at A-T, I'm convinced that we have to get onboard. I explained it to the chief, and he agrees. You'll just have to trust me."

Boyd looks at Megan. "Megan, I'm sure he'll be fine. It's been four days. He looks great, don't you think?"

It's true that Harrison looks better than before. In fact, he's almost healed. His eye is no longer bandaged, and the swelling and bruising are almost gone. But still … the slightest scratch would be too much for her at this moment. "I don't know, Chief —"

"Megan, we really don't have time to waste," Boyd says, his voice kind but firm, then turns his attention to Harrison. "I'll have the shuttle loaded and cleared. Megan, at the start of your shift, I want you to call in four crews. They're to be rested and ready to go by six a.m. I'm going to load two crews in the shuttle with Harrison. The other two will need their ships. See that they're re-supplied and ready to go."

"But … that will only leave me six crews. Remember? Two of them are tied up cleaning out Sector 23 of the old city. I don't think —"

"Six will be enough to finish up."

Megan sighs. "Yes sir," she turns and leaves.

¤ ¤ ¤

At 5:45 the next morning, Harrison boards the shuttle at Houston flight control. Two clean-up crews and several agents are already onboard. One twenty-man crew is situated in each cargo hold. This isn't the first time Harrison has met the men from clean-up; he'd encountered three on the rooftop landing port at DEA headquarters. Somehow, they seem more intimidating now. Perhaps it's a result of the entire crew being present, fully equipped with combat gear, but he wouldn't have believed that only twenty men would fill the ship's forward cargo hull.

He struggles to make his way through to the pilot's control area. Once inside, he finds Laura nervously seated at the ship's controls. "Am I glad to see you!" she yells. "What's going on?"

"I'll explain everything on the way up."

"Up where?"

"Didn't they tell you anything?"

Laura snorts. "Yeah, they said departure time zero six hundred. That's what they said. What about our supplies? And why are all those goons back there?"

"No time to explain now." Harrison keeps his voice low. "Turn on the communicator, it's time to leave."

Laura's eyes narrow, but she decides to go along. She engages the power plants and warms up the communicator with a quick audiovisual test while Houston plots their course.

Once underway, Harrison explains why they're invading the Wingate. Laura sits staring at the screen in front of her.

"Kachel has betrayed his authority," Harrison finishes. "He's a traitor. Haven't you noticed the way he's been acting? There's no doubt in my mind, and Chief Boyd agrees with me. He has to be removed."

Laura turns to him with wide eyes. "You mean you're going to provide those guys access to the Wingate? Those goons? Harrison, there's got to be a better way!"

"I'll be with them for the entire mission."

"Well, I don't want any part of this, and you know I have the right to refuse any mission I judge as —"

"Laura, I asked for you because you're the only one I can trust."

Laura's eyes lock once again on the screen, and for a long moment, neither speaks. At last, she replies, "Can you prove any of this?"

Harrison nods and reaches into his pocket. He brings out one of the blue modules. "I was the one who discovered the operation." He holds it out for her.

"What is it?"

"It's a location module. You know, to relay information like position, direction, and speed. The drug traffickers had these installed in the DEA vehicles."

Laura glares at the module, considers the implications, then looks up at him. "So what does this have to do with the admiral?"

"Kachel has the modules made up and shipped to the Wingate. He then loads them on the supply shuttles that will be seized by pirates. From there, they go straight to the traffickers."

Her eyes remain on the scene in front of her, but Harrison can see her facial expressions as they soften. "How does he know which shuttles the pirates will strike?"

"This module is designed for the SJ.26 — the same vehicle as the fighters on the Wingate. We also removed modules from the shuttles in Houston. The pirates don't strike at random, Laura. They know exactly when and where to hit."

"That explains why they've been so successful lately," she admits. "But there is one hole in your theory."

"What's that?"

"Why didn't the pirates vaporize you on our last mission? I mean, if they knew your speed and direction, they couldn't have missed. So how do you account for that?"

Harrison leans back in his seat. "That did occur to me. It took me a while to figure it out. But you see, the modules can't be re-pressurized once the air's been evacuated without damaging them. When I inspected the vehicle inside the cargo hull, the air had already been evacuated."

Finally, Laura turns to him. Harrison is surprised to see her eyes shining. "So when I ordered Jim to air up the cargo hull, it damaged the module."

"Exactly. They hadn't counted on me inspecting the vehicle after it was loaded."

She sits quietly. "Seems you were very lucky," she says.

Harrison unbuckles himself and stands before answering. "Yes, and I hope my luck holds out."

She looks up at him. "What do you mean?"

"I need the help of those goons, as you call them. But if anything happens to the admiral, I'll have no way of proving my allegations, and we'll never know who else is involved."

"Is the drug problem really that serious down there?" Laura asks.

Harrison nods as he remembers the man with the hypo gun full of drugs, the half-breeds whose entire existence sprang from the drug trade, and the drudges who would live and ultimately die for it.

"It's more widespread than I ever knew," he tells her. "More than you or I would know. More than anyone who spent most of their life in space could possibly know. It's global. It's as if there's some type of conspiracy propelling it." He sighs, then says, "I'm going to check on our passengers. Are you with me?"

She looks at the module in her hand, then up at him. "We've been through a lot, haven't we? And we've always watched each other's backs."

He nods.

Laura hands the module back to him. "Yeah, I'm in."

¤ ¤ ¤

Harrison finds that the men in the cargo hull are taking advantage of their idle time by catching up on some badly needed rest. The cargo hulls are designed for freight, not people, so the men have only the hard floor to lie on. But that doesn't seem to matter to them; some of them are lying on their backs and using their helmets for pillows, some are sitting, but most all are asleep. Their handheld weapons are stored in the corner with their shields, along with some other weapons of a much larger caliber. Their captain appears to be the only one awake; he's sitting at a desk they'd brought aboard, doing some reports.

"How is everything, sir?" Harrison asks.

The captain looks up. "The men will be just fine," he snaps, and immediately goes back to his work.

Harrison continues on to the second cargo area, which is exactly like the first, except for the large, ominous-looking box sitting in the back corner. As tall as Harrison and twice as wide, the black box has only one door with a small window.

Harrison thinks about asking what it is, but decides to investigate on his own.

Although the box isn't much to look at, what he does see disturbs him. The interior of the thick steel box is badly cracked and peeling from what looks to be a tremendous amount of heat. Just as Harrison wonders what kind of blast could generate this type of meltdown, he hears a noise from behind and reels around, expecting a dressing-down from the captain. Instead, he finds a tall, thin lieutenant from the second crew directly behind him, clearing his throat.

"Is there something I can do for you, officer?"

Harrison looks at the box, then back to the lieutenant, now scowls.

"Yes ... Yes, there is. What is this thing?"

"An incinerator. All of our ships are equipped with them. They're much larger, of course. In this case, we brought the portable unit."

"Excuse me?" At this very moment, as the incinerator's purpose comes to him, Harrison storms back into the first cargo hull. The lieutenant is trailing closely.

The captain looks up as Harrison barks, "Captain, I want to know why you brought an incinerator aboard this ship. Do you think this is just another one of your clean-up jobs?"

The captain straightens in his chair, but only so he can raise his arms into a long, lazy stretch. With a yawn, he replies, "Look, we don't know what we're up against, Harrison. Based on the briefing, your admiral is a known accomplice with drug traffickers. They control him, and he controls the Wingate. That makes everyone onboard a suspect."

Harrison is livid.

"These people aren't drug traffickers," he yells. "They're shuttle pilots, scientists and engineers, and most of them are my friends. I won't allow you to go in there and simply wipe them out like an infection!"

The captain's relaxed demeanor disappears. "Listen, Harrison, we've got a job to do, and you're not going to stop us. My men are exhausted. They've been going night and day. The sooner we acquire the admiral, the sooner we go home, that's all."

"You'll never reach the Wingate. I'll turn this ship around."

"No. You know I can't allow that."

"I might not be able to stop you, but you'll never find the admiral without me." Harrison hopes this will soften the captain up.

The captain glares. "I expected as much from you." Keeping his eyes on Harrison, he probes through an open desk drawer on his lower right-hand side, then slowly brings out a large disc binder and lays it on the desktop. The captain carefully unfolds the binder, Harrison peers over the desk. It reads "Wingate designs."

Dismissing Harrison, the captain turns to the lieutenant. "As I interpret it, there are three main arteries to the helm. I want you to divide the men into three squads. At least one of us will get through. Once we've reached the helm, we'll have control of the ship. It won't be a problem pinpointing the admiral's position from there. Terminate everyone you come into contact with. We can't risk a confrontation on their ground."

Visions of the impending massacre flash through Harrison's mind — a team of heavily armed killers shooting innocent people in the halls, stumbling into the cafeteria and blasting away, leaving a trail of mutilated bodies behind ... and it will be his fault.

"All right. All right!" Harrison says as he searches for the captain's nametag. "I'll show you the way, Captain Raynor. But you'll go my way." When Raynor's look turns inquisitive, he adds, "It's more time-consuming, but there won't be any people."

"What about surveillance?"

"I'll take care of that," Harrison replies.

"I thought you'd see things my way," Raynor shoots back. His face has turned unreadable. He yawns one more time, then adds, "Well, that's about it for now. Go back and fill in your pilot. I'll take care of my people."

As Harrison makes his way back to the pilot's control area, he must fight his rage at Captain Raynor's obvious disregard for the innocents aboard the ship. But, there's really nothing more he can do ... just go along for now. If he fails to lead them to Admiral Kachel, his fellow pilots and other crew members will become fair game.

¤ ¤ ¤

The moment Harrison is out of earshot, Raynor turns to his second-in-command. "Lieutenant, I still want three squads. I'll lead the first team. Wait ten minutes, then send the second squad out. Once inside the ship, you'll find that security is rather lax. But just in case Harrison has a plan of his own, I want your team to secure the hangar area. Terminate everyone ... except the director. I'm sure the admiral doesn't load the shuttles himself. The director must be part of the operation. We may need him if something happens to the admiral. You'll want to interrogate him first. Also, clear an area for the other two crews to land. The outer doors can be operated from the helm, so they'll have to be disabled in the open position almost immediately."

"Should the exit doors also be secured, Captain?"

Raynor points at the lieutenant. "That won't be necessary. If we fail, our probability of outrunning the Wingate's firepower is absolute zero."

The lieutenant nods back as if to say, I understand the seriousness of the situation. The obedient man is optimistic of someday being the captain of his own crew. He's a good officer, one who enjoys his work, and the type of person who thoroughly values pissing off people he deems subordinate. He has no intention of allowing this to be his last mission.

¤ ¤ ¤

As Harrison enters the pilots' control area, Laura asks, "What's wrong? You look worried."

"In the words of the captain, the men will be fine," Harrison replies, mocking Captain Raynor's deep voice.

"Men? You mean they're human?" Laura jokes.

"They must be, they're resting."

"Maybe they're recharging."

Harrison laughs.

"So, you never did tell me what happened to your eye," Laura says, chuckling. "Did you get caught with your pants down?"

"I'll have you know I was tied to a chair."

"Hey! That sounds like fun."

"Believe me, it wasn't." Harrison sits down and lays the back of his seat down. "Wake me when we get home."

When she doesn't answer, he glances over to see her smiling at him sadly. He understands. That was something Harrison had always said to Laura when they were returning home from a shuttle mission. The happy memory is quickly repressed by the reality of the situation. Space is no longer his home, and they aren't heading back to their friends and the safety of the Wingate. Those days were forever gone.

¤ ¤ ¤

Angie's working the main desk when Chief Boyd marches into the room and heads straight for her. "Angie, do we still have two crews in Sector 23 of the city?"

"Yes," she answers, noticing his graver-than-usual expression.

"How much longer will they be tied up?"

"The operation is nearly finished, sir."

"Did they identify the weapon?"

She nods. "They have it with them. Do you want me to contact them on the communicator?"

"No. Summon them in. Have them take the weapon down to the lab, re-supply the ships, and be ready to go as soon as possible."

After only a slight pause, she replies, "Yes, sir."

Boyd gives the control room an once-over, and storms out the door to the sound of Angie telling the two crew leaders to abort and return to base.

¤ ¤ ¤

Laura and Harrison are nearing the Wingate. As the giant ship comes into view, a voice snaps over the intercom: "Identify yourself."

Laura turns on the viewing screen and gives the Wingate's communication officer her name, rank, and the shuttle's assigned number.

"It's good to see you, Laura." The voice relaxes. "We've missed you."

"How has everything been up here?" Laura asks.

"All right. Well, fact is, it's been slow since you left. No one's been in or out."

Harrison, trying to stay clear of the viewer screens motions for her to keep talking. "Find out where the admiral is," he mouths.

"Nobody in or out?" Laura continues. "What's going on?"

"Well, they haven't told us anything, but the rumor's going around that the government's put the entire space program on hold."

"Really?" Laura tries to look surprised. "I haven't heard that, but I'm sure Admiral Kachel will straighten that out when he returns."

"Doubt they'd make something like that too easy to hear, but I can tell you this, the admiral has never left the helm," the officer says. "So, what have you been doing on your little vacation?"

"Mostly being bored. They confined us to the pilots' waiting area the whole time."

"Well that doesn't —" He stops suddenly, now listening, then says, "You just got clearance from the director. Starboard side, bottom portal, Shuttle Hangar One."

Laura nods. "All right, I'll talk to you later."

"One more thing, Laura."

Her heart races as she involuntarily holds her breath. The officer begins reading from a screen she can't see. "There's a communiqué for inbound shuttles. You are to be advised that there are three squads of fighters on maneuvers in the area."

She exhales and covers by rolling her eyes. "Oh, no. You mean nine trigger-happy cadets?"

The officer grins. "I just know what the message says."

Soon as the viewer goes black, Harrison picks up the intercom. "Prepare for docking."

"I hope we're doing the right thing."

He looks at the cargo hull door. "We're doing the right thing. I just hope we're doing it the right way."

The docking is flawless; Laura always brings the shuttle in with the expertise of the seasoned professional that she is. But Harrison doesn't wait for the vessel to come to a complete stop before he's up and bounding for the cargo area.

¤ ¤ ¤

The clean-up crew stands in two lines, fitted in their heavy black suits. Few have shields; most carry weapons — much larger than Harrison is familiar with. They wait as the enclosed walkway slowly moves adjacent to the shuttle and encircles the outer door. When the air pressure inside equalizes, it emits a green light. Harrison, now wondering if he's up to the task, hesitates to press the button to open the outer door.

Glaring at him, Captain Raynor quickly motions to the lieutenant, who is standing directly behind Harrison, to do the honors. Against Harrison's secret desire that it won't work, the door opens. Now, there is definitely no turning back. He has the same sinking feeling in the pit of his stomach as he did when he'd watched the people dying in the compactor. Even though Raynor has implied that as long as Harrison leads them to Kachel no one else will be harmed, he has the sneaking feeling that trusting Raynor is like trusting a snake.

As Harrison leads the men down the long hall and through the archway that embarks the main section of the starboard wing, he begins to feel differently about the mission. I didn't have control over what happened at the compactor, he thinks, but that's not the case now. Harrison knows this ship backward and forward, and if Raynor turns out to be a liar, he knows he does have a number of options.

Chapter Seventeen

Wing Commander Benson finishes signing the virtual document's display from his assistant's expresser, then he removes his headset. He turns to see Harrison walking toward him, coming down the long empty hall, and shouts his name.

The four men directly behind Harrison are partially covered by shields. Standing side-by-side, they occupy most of the hall. The remaining crew is shielded in the safety of the heavy armor. It looks as if a solid wall is moving in behind him.

Seeing this, Commander Benson considers running, but his feet won't cooperate, probably because he's never run from anything or anyone in his life. He collects himself and calls out, "What's the meaning of this, Harrison? And who are these men?"

When they reach the end of the hall, Benson is still waiting for his answer. "I said, what is the meaning of this?"

Captain Raynor steps out in front. "We're with the Drug Enforcement Administration. Where might your admiral be located?"

"Why do you want the admiral?"

Raynor doesn't reply. He only restates his demand. "Where's the admiral?"

"Until I know what you're doing here, I'm not answering any of your questions," Benson states. "I'm calling security."

It's obvious that Benson is as unaware of DEA procedure as Harrison once was. But even Harrison only has a mere intimation of just how battle-hardened Raynor is. Suddenly one of the clean-up men steps out of formation and points his weapon at the commander. Harrison jumps between them. "No. Wait," he shouts. "It's all right, Commander. We know the admiral is at the helm. Let them in."

Raynor speaks. "Move aside, Harrison. We can't leave him."

"We'll take him with us."

"No."

"I'm not going to let you kill him."

Captain Raynor has already grown weary of Harrison's meddling and begins looking around. "All right, Harrison, you win." He grabs Benson by the arm and steers him down the hall, stopping at the first door they come to. "What's in here?"

"My office," Benson says.

"Good enough. Open the door."

When the door opens, Raynor shoves Benson in, then points at the first man. "You watch him. If he makes any attempt to contact the admiral, terminate him."

The huge man packing a laser weapon steps in and closes the door. Raynor turns back to Harrison.

"Now to the helm."

Harrison precedes the men down the long, dimly lit hall, through a door and down a secondary hallway. At the end of the second hall is a steep ramp. At the end of the ramp there's five steps leading to a massive platform. Harrison arrives first, and then waits for the entire group to assemble.

Raynor is the last man up, but when Harrison does a quick headcount, he notices some of the men are missing. Turning to Raynor, he asks, "Where's the rest of them?"

"They're securing the shuttle," Raynor says, giving the men a warning look just as Harrison turns away.

Harrison shoves the up-indicator and the platform begins to rise — slowly. He turns to Raynor with a sheepish grin. "The elevator was originally designed to move freight from one level to another. Guess speed isn't one of its greatest assets."

Raynor has nothing to say for the longest time, as they continue up.

"Harrison, how much longer?" he finally ask.

Harrison turns around. "We're almost there, Captain." As if to prove his words, when the platform reaches the first level past the halfway mark, Harrison stops the lift and turns to Raynor. "This is it."

Raynor looks dubious. "Where are we?"

"The center of the ship, Captain." Harrison points down one of the corridors leading off the platform. "No one has any reason to use these inner corridors unless the other levels are blocked, or the outer corridors have been sealed off due to a pressure leak. Taking this route, we won't be noticed."

Raynor glares at Harrison, wondering if he's telling the truth. When he's satisfied, he waves his men forward.

As the men exit the platform, Harrison notices two of them pushing a large box on wheels. The box is outfitted with a short barrel mounted on one side and a tee handle for steering on the other. The peculiar box appears very heavy, but after the men maneuver it back onto the floor, it begins to follow behind unattended. "Which way?" the handler asks.

Harrison starts in the direction of the ship's helm. Once again, Raynor drops into place at the end of the line, but not before depressing the down button on the platform. As the men advance through the empty hall, their footsteps echo, covering up the sound of the lift returning to the first level.

When Harrison reaches the solid steel door at the end of the hall, he stops. On the wall to the right is a round keypad. He punches in a number and the panel replies in kind. Only when he types in a second set of numbers does the door slide open. Inside is another corridor that extends several meters, then makes a sharp right turn. Everyone moves through the open door, but Harrison stops again.

"Now what?" Raynor asks.

"There'll be security cameras and sensors from here on."

"And?"

"There's a guard monitoring everything from a room located at the end of that hall."

Raynor stops. "Harrison, you get behind. We'll have to move fast, and I don't want you hit."

"You can't move that fast. You'll never get down that hall in time. Security will seal you in."

"We have no alternative."

"Yes, you do. Let me go. Alone. I'll take care of security."

Resigned, Raynor pulls the closest man out of line. "You can go, but not alone. He goes with you."

Harrison had hoped to handle it alone, but now realizes that thought was foolish. With no choice, he starts down the empty hall to his right, with one solitary clean-up man close behind.

¤ ¤ ¤

The second lieutenant has secured the Level One landing area and disabled the portal doors. Except for the director, everyone in the area has been terminated. The lieutenant, with three of his men, is now in the director's office which overlooks the entire landing area. Two of the men have the director pinned against the wall, each holding onto an arm as if to pull him apart. The man who at one time controlled everything coming and going aboard the Wingate now resembles a wet washcloth, unable to stand on his own two feet. The third man, armed with a laser, stands directly in front of him.

"Tell me about the modules," the lieutenant demands.

"I — I don't know anything about modules."

"You're wasting my time, Director."

The trio gives the command to their helmet shields, which protect their eyes from the bright laser flash, now suddenly darken.

The director has witnessed the clean-up crew's devastation of the other workers, and knows that the rock-faced lieutenant won't hesitate to terminate him as well.

"All right, I'll tell you this much."

"No," yells the lieutenant. "You'll start at the beginning, and you'll tell me everything."

The director glances at the others. "If I tell everything, they'll kill me."

"If you don't, I'll kill you."

"All right." The director stares out the window as he speaks. "The modules are stored in an empty hangar. Hangar Seven. The admiral tells me which shuttle to stow them on. After the loading crew is finished in the cargo hold, I evacuate the air and authorize the robot to load them."

The lieutenant nods. "Good, that's how they get shipped. Now, how are they installed?"

The director stares in surprise. "If I cooperate and tell you everything, you'll let me go, right?"

"That's not my decision. I don't know what Captain Raynor will do with you if you talk, but I know what I'll do with you if you don't."

"If the old modules are damaged, I have the robot replace them before the vehicles are moved into the hangars."

"How?"

"Through the control panel," he jerked his head to the side, "over there, by the window."

The lieutenant contacts Raynor by means of the communicator inside his helmet. He gives his report, then listens a moment before responding, "Yes sir, everything has been recorded."

The director holds his breath, waiting, knowing that the balance between life and death hinges on what the voice on the other end dictates.

The lieutenant turns to the man holding the weapon and with the same uncaring attitude mouths, "Terminate him."

The director begins to slide toward the floor, but the two hulking men holding him up easily keep him from hitting the deck. The lieutenant turns his back on the director to avoid the blinding flash. The man flaunting the weapon is mercifully quick. A brilliant burst from behind casts the lieutenant's distorted shadow across the docking area.

Turning around, he sees the smoldering remains of the director being collected for the incinerator.

¤ ¤ ¤

Harrison reaches the security office and peers through the thick protective window. He motions for the officer to open the door.

The external speaker comes on. "Who is it?"

"Captain Harrison, open the door."

He knows the officer won't disobey a direct order from a captain; the door opens and Harrison, along with his escort, steps into a large single-room office. "I want you to deactivate the security system for this corridor," Harrison says.

The officer hesitates only a second before he seats himself at the control panel and begins switching the cameras off.

"The sensors, too," Harrison adds. "And the detainment area."

The officer turns to Harrison. "I have to contact the wing commander first."

"No. Just switch it off."

"Sir, I can't turn off security to the helm without Commander Benson's —"

With one hand, the clean-up man grabs the back of the chair and violently jerks him away from the control panel before the guard can touch anything else. The chair rolls across the floor and comes to rest in the center of the room with the guard still in it. "He's no longer useful to us," the man states, his words muffled under the helmet.

The officer thinks the man is speaking to him and agrees. "That's right, Captain Harrison. There's nothing more I can do, I don't have the authority."

The clean-up man is facing Harrison with the barrel of his weapon pointed at the officer. Through his helmet communicator he receives the order from Raynor. "Termination agreed?" he states.

"What do you mean 'termination agreed'?" Harrison shouts. "By whose authority?"

While the two argue, the officer jumps to his feet and attempts to pull his pistol. He doesn't know that behind the dark face shield, the clean-up man is still watching him. The clean-up man doesn't make a move until the officer's pistol has cleared its holster. Then, he simply squeezes the trigger.

Harrison, with no eye protection, is temporarily blinded by the flash of light. Blinking rapidly, he looks around the room, but finds no recognizable parts of the officer. The back of his chair as well as most of the officer himself has been reduced to little more than badly burned fragments, several of which are fused to the burn spot on the back wall with crystallized particles clinging to it.

Heat from the flash has set off several alarms. The damage is done and Harrison can do nothing more; he motions to the clean-up man and they both race for the door.

As he enters the hall, he catches the clean-up crew coming down the corridor. The group has doubled in number. It looks as if the second crew has joined them. Harrison wonders how the second crew found its way. It suddenly makes sense. The clean-up crews must be in constant communication, continuously tracking each other. That would provide for Raynor's strict control. That explains why he always hangs back, Harrison realizes. He's directing the other crew.

Raynor is the first to reach Harrison.

"It was you," Harrison yells. "You're the one that gave the go-ahead to terminate the officer."

"Listen, Harrison, you saw what happened. My man had no alternative. He was protecting himself as well as you. Now, which way to the helm?"

Harrison wants to kill Captain Raynor. However, after seeing what they're capable of — what his people wouldn't hesitate to do to the rest of the Wingate's occupants if Harrison doesn't comply — he bites his lip and ushers the captain and both crews down the hall to a large empty room.

The men carrying protective shields are the first to enter. Once inside, they form two orderly lines; the remaining men stay tucked behind the ones with shields. Across the room is one double door flanked by two small doors.

Harrison points to the center door. "The helm is through there."

Two men, escorted by several shield bearers, roll the curious-looking box into the center of the room and aim it at the double doors. Suddenly, the small doors on either side of the room open and a halo of laser fire covers the room. The ship's security people have apparently reacted quickly to the alarms; they've set a trap for the intruders. But the intruders immediately return fire. Harrison's heart twists in his chest.

The battle lasts several minutes. The clean-up crew's larger weapons return a wave of laser fire threatening to engulf the ship's internal defenses. It's obvious who will come out on top. Harrison knows most of the security people personally, and hopes they will quickly realize this is a battle they can't win.

Finally, security retreats and the doors promptly close. The clean-up crew has sustained few casualties, but the room, because it has absorbed most of the laser fire, has now heated to a dangerous level. Harrison notices the ceiling vents are pushing cold air into the room — he can see a stream of vapor with each gust.

Raynor, confident the ship's security has been adequately subdued, walks to the center of the room to examine the box. It's taken several deliberate assaults but remains intact. He reaches under the protective steel plating and depresses a small button.

Harrison listens as the odd-shaped weapon begins a low, constant hum. As it continues building power, the noise grows violent. Suddenly it begins to bombard the door with hundreds of needle-size white beams. The cutting beams aren't random; their path forms a complete circle approximately two meters in diameter. It continues clockwise around the circle following in the same orbit. The rays penetrate deeper into the door with each pass.

Just as Raynor maneuvers into position, the outer door through which they'd entered earlier closes without warning, trapping Harrison, the captain, and a dozen men inside. Harrison looks up and notices the air vents have been shut down. The wall lights near the ceiling turn off, leaving everything dark except the box weapon and the bright red display light indicating that the door is now sealed. The ship's security is more formidable than first thought.

Raynor turns to Harrison, scowling. "What's going on?"

Harrison's face is blank. "They're evacuating the air from this room, sir," he says.

Raynor gasps. "How long do we have?"

"Less than a minute," Harrison replies, looking at the box. "Will that thing finish in time?"

"I ... don't know. It will continue cutting until it penetrates the door."

"How long will it take?" Harrison yells.

"Depends on how thick the door is." The captain's eyes widen as he shouts commands at the man now operating the box. The sight of Captain Raynor ruffled makes Harrison proud.

A minute later, Harrison is paying the price for not having brought the helmet to his pressurized suit. He's lying on the floor; eyes fixed on the door, helplessly trying to catch what might very well be his last breath as the air is sucked out of the room.

As the first rays pierce the door, the oxygen streaming into the room is quickly ignited as it passes through the hot steel. The flame advances several meters and continues to grow until the weapon finishes cutting the circle. By the time it finishes and automatically shuts down, the door has a perfect ring of fire exploding from it.

The men stand and begin blasting away at the circle, causing the thick steel cutout to fall inward. Raynor motions for the men with shields to move through the two-meter hole first. Harrison, gasping, is grateful he's able to breathe. But suddenly, as he had dreaded, the Wingate's helm is breached.

Inside, they find no admiral and no security as expected, just a skeleton crew. The helm consists of one main control room, with smaller rooms on either side. Harrison takes off in search of Admiral Kachel. Meanwhile, Raynor talks to the first officer, who is now standing in a lineup, awaiting his fate.

"Open the outer detainment doorway," Raynor barks. This will allow the entire crew access to the helm.

The first officer silently refuses.

Raynor moves to the second officer and repeats his command. The second officer takes his cue from the first and makes no attempt to open the outer doors.

Raynor yells at the first clean-up man guarding them. "Terminate him." He points at the officer.

"Wait."

Raynor whirls around.

"Don't," the second officer yells. "I'll open the door."

The captain nods and holds off the clean-up crew with a wave of the hand. "Now, where is your admiral?"

No one volunteers the information. Raynor turns to his men and barks. "Terminate them all."

Harrison comes running at full stride to the helm, panting. "I've located the admiral. He's on his way to communications."

Raynor turns to his men. "Three of you stay here, the rest follow me." Harrison points Raynor to the emergency exit, and then falls in line far behind the last man.

As they near the end of the hall, the door automatically opens and Raynor steps into a large corridor extending in several directions. Engraved on the wall is a sign pointing to the communication area.

By the time Harrison arrives, the clean-up crew is already blasting away at the sealed door.

Harrison looks on as the men labor to open it. Soon as he's sure they're appropriately distracted with their task, he slips away. Knowing there's an emergency exit for the communication room and anticipating the admiral's next move, Harrison heads for the escape route with the hope of apprehending the admiral before the clean-up crewmen open the door and realizes they've been tricked.

¤ ¤ ¤

Inside the room, the communications officer turns to the man standing behind him. "Admiral, there are two unannounced ships approaching. They've had two warnings, and are now nearing the end of our safety zone. They keep repeating that they're DEA and insist on landing. Should I activate the ship's outer defense?"

"No," Kachel replies. "Are the portal doors operational?"

"Not yet, sir. We can't get anyone in there."

"I don't want any more DEA onboard. Are the fighters still on maneuvers?"

"Yes sir. Three squads. Do you want the ships destroyed?"

"No, just keep them from landing."

Kachel heads for the emergency exit, and then suddenly turns back. "They're getting dangerously close to penetrating that door. After you've instructed the fighters, you'd better leave also."

Kachel makes his way down the empty corridor. Approaching the end, he's astonished to see Harrison in pursuit. The admiral launches himself down the second corridor as fast as any first-rate sprinter. Harrison doesn't even try to catch him.

He hears someone coming up from behind and turns to see Raynor accompanied by two clean-up crewmen. He has undoubtedly figured out what Harrison is up to. Raynor races forward and shouts, "Where's the admiral?"

"Don't worry, he won't get away," Harrison replies as he points down the hall. "This corridor ends at an exit door."

"Then let's get him."

"No. I'll go alone. Maybe I can talk him out without a fight."

"I don't care if he puts up a fight. Gives up peacefully, or saves us all a lot of trouble. This thing is finished, now."

"No, no it's not. Let me talk to him. He can't escape what the hell?"

Raynor responds. "All right. You've got five minutes."

At the end of the hall, Harrison peers through the small portal of the pressurized room leading to the outer door that keeps the ship's air from being sucked out when the outer door is opened. Admiral Kachel has sealed himself inside.

Harrison shakes his head and chuckles. The one person who should have known every minute detail of this ship has chosen the worst possible hiding place.

Harrison activates the intercom. "Admiral, you don't have a suit. Even if you did, how far would you get?"

The startled admiral whirls around, now standing straight, the tall man with thick, white hair stares with eyes wide.

He doesn't realize what's happening, Harrison thinks, then reaches over and strikes the door opener.

The door doesn't open.

Looking up for the first time, he sees an iridescent light indicating oxygen is being sucked from the small room in preparation for the outer door opening. Harrison activates the ship's communicator and shouts, "Emergency! Shut off Exit Door 32."

The emergency operator asks, "What is the nature of the emergency?"

"Someone's in the air lock without a suit!" Harrison yells.

"We can't comply," the operator bellows back. "The air-evacuate control has been switched to manual."

So he does know what he's doing, after all, Harrison thinks, his heart sinking. Cursing, he goes back to the intercom. "Admiral, it doesn't have to end this way."

"Yes, it does."

"I don't understand."

The admiral's face falls. "You will in time, Harrison."

He's lost his mind. Harrison's keen intellect scrambles for the right thing to say. "Listen ... sir ... It's not that serious a crime," he lies. "You're giving up too much! You don't realize what you're doing!"

"Oh, but I do, Harrison" Kachel replies. His breathing is becoming strenuous. "It's more disastrous than you can imagine." The admiral's blue-tingly face squints. Harrison catches a tear in the man's eye as he moans.

Just as the small, box-like room is stripped of air, the admiral forces his last words out. "Harrison, why couldn't you have stayed put? None of this would have happened."

"You can stop it before it's too late!"

"It's already too late, Harrison."

"What in the hell are you talking about?" He yells. The admiral collapses to the floor, and then glares up at the tiny window and gasps, "Go back to the space program. ... You'll be safe there —"

The admiral's chest flattens, and then dips into a concave shape as the last of the oxygen is drawn from his lungs. A trickle of blood snakes down his left ear and onto the floor. The green display above the outer door gleams, and the door promptly opens. As the remaining air surges out, Kachel's body begins a slow drift for the door. Harrison can only stand and watch as the freeze-dried corpse moves through the airlock and into the black emptiness of space.

It's already too late, Harrison.

As he thinks of the admiral's last words, Harrison can only assume that, whatever he was referring to, he'd chosen to die rather than face it. Or them.

Hearing footsteps from behind, Harrison turns to see Raynor accompanied by several of his men. Raynor looks through the tiny glass window. "I guess it's over now, Harrison."

"Are you sure?"

The captain's eyes whip to Harrison. "What do you mean by that? Did he say something?"

"It's not what he said, it's the way he said it." Replies Harrison

Raynor gives Harrison a curious look, but as he begins to speak, his communicator flares to life: "Sir, the other two clean-up crews are under attack by fighters."

"Bring the wing commander to the communications area, now," Raynor barks. "I'll meet you there." He turns to the crewmen. "You men retrieve the admiral's body and return to the shuttle. Only one crew will remain behind, the rest of you are finished up here."

As Raynor races down the corridor, Harrison hears him shout, "I'm not through with you, Harrison. We'll talk later."

¤ ¤ ¤

Pressnell is sitting at his desk in Capitol City when the explosion hits. He jumps to his feet just as the thick steel door leading to the outer lobby is badly bent and springs off its hinges at the top. Before he can move any further, there's a second hit. This one brings the door down with a crash. Two heavily armed men in black suits rush in and plant themselves on either side of the now-wasted door. Pressnell immediately recognizes them as part of a clean-up crew, and knows better than to make any sudden movements. He stands motionless with his hands raised, wondering not if, but when they're going to terminate him. When the tall, thin-haired, slightly overweight man wearing a suit treads in, Pressnell drops his hands.

"Chief Boyd, I'll have your ass for this."

"I already have yours."

Boyd holds out a document. Pressnell leans forward with both hands on the desk.

"What is this?" Pressnell asks as he slowly moves his right hand toward the alarm button.

"Don't bother," Boyd smiles. "I gave your security the rest of the day off, with pay, and this document I'm holding is a warrant."

"A warrant! A warrant for what?"

Boyd lets the long paper unfold. "Where should I start? Drug trafficking? Attempted murder of an agent? Or how about misappropriation of government funds? The list goes on. And your Operation Flashback has been cancelled."

"Let me see that."

Boyd holds the warrant out to Pressnell, but when Pressnell makes no attempt to accept it, Boyd thrust it in his face, shoving so hard Pressnell stumbles back into his chair. The chair slams against the wall behind him. Pressnell quickly recovers. Straining to reach the opening on the right side of his file cabinet, he promptly produces a laser pistol. Boyd drops to the floor as the clean-up men open fire.

Boyd reluctantly rises to his feet, waving away the stench-laden smoke that now fills the room. He looks disappointedly at the crewmen. "Clean this mess up and return to the ship. I have to inform the head councilor that Mr. Pressnell is no longer with us."

¤ ¤ ¤

Later that same night, Boyd summons Megan and Harrison to his Houston office.

Megan speaks first. "Chief, how did you know that Pressnell was the main conspirator?"

"Well, to begin with, the way Harrison found those modules. There's no way he could have gained entry into A-T unless someone wanted him to, not to mention leaving. That's when I was certain someone was using Harrison to implicate Admiral Kachel."

Harrison looks up, curious. "How did you know it was Pressnell?"

"We didn't at first," Boyd replies. "I had agents watching the head administrator of A-T. The man who met Harrison at the plant that night, that was Mr. Solomon. But he made an unexpected move and eluded my men. Our agents located his place in the country, and that's where we found him … or should I say, what was left of him. Those high-caliber lasers don't leave much. But finding him led us to Pressnell. Pressnell knew that after we found the modules, we'd trace them back to him. So he authorized this Mr. Solomon to set up Admiral Kachel, who was already in over his head, and we played directly into his hands by eliminating him ourselves."

Boyd leans back in his chair. "Pressnell was cunning. He delegated Kachel to do his dirty work, and when we got too close, he betrayed him. He then eliminated Solomon to relinquish all ties with the operation."

"What operation?" Megan asks.

"You remember the drug trafficker we brought in for questioning?"

She nods.

"Well, he'd mentioned Operation Flashback."

"Operation Flashback?" Megan is shocked. "I never heard of it."

"That's not surprising, Megan. Few people have. It was aborted over twenty years ago."

"Well, if Megan never heard of it," Harrison says, "I know I haven't. But, twenty years? What did a project that old have to do with pressnell? He wasn't even around back then."

The chief leans forward. "That's where you're wrong, Harrison. You see, twenty-two years ago, the government initiated an operation that was designed to eliminate drug trafficking. They began by flooding the market with drugs. So much in fact, that they were practically giving them away."

"I don't understand, Chief. How would that help?"

"The traffickers were spread thin, financially speaking. They were banking on future business, and couldn't afford the cost of competing with the government. They drove the prices so low it wasn't worth the trouble of staying in the business.

"The preliminary results looked promising, but as Megan can attest, drug lords aren't that easily liquidated. They reinvented and refined their drugs. A complete line of new drugs having entirely different effects was put on the open market. They called them 'enhancement drugs.'" Boyd states. "Suddenly, you can be anything you want — everything from increased strength to superior intelligence. You can gain weight or lose it, feel and even look younger. As with most things there is a drawback. The improvements are short-lived. This makes the drugs even more addictive." Boyd stands and walks out from behind his desk.

"Needless to say, the government couldn't compete, so the operation was cancelled and the traffickers were back in business ... with an even larger clientele."

Harrison ask. "So that's how the drugs we're fighting now got started?"

Boyd nods. "And following the failed operation, there was a major shakedown in government. We didn't know it till recently, but that's when our present head councilor seized the opportunity to gain complete power ... all his people were put in place. That's the reason I've had to fight so hard to accomplish so little."

"Where did Pressnell fit into all this?" Megan asks.

"I checked the records and found that Pressnell was the brains behind Operation Flashback. He acted as a sort of purchasing agent: arranged the buying and selling for the government. When the operation ended, I believe Pressnell never stopped. I suspected that he'd been involved with traffickers ever since, but I needed solid evidence. So I had a warrant drawn up and presented it to him."

The chief looks away. "Of course, I never told Pressnell that he was under arrest. I simply stated that I had a warrant. He just assumed he was under arrest. Actually, all I could do was bring him in for questioning. If he hadn't resisted, I might have been able to gain enough information from him to take down the head councilor."

"How could you, or anyone, get a warrant signed for Pressnell? He was second-in-command," Harrison asked.

"There's only one person, the head councilor."

"So Pressnell thought the head councilor had betrayed him."

"Just like he betrayed your admiral. Kind of suspicious, isn't it?" The chief raises his eyebrows.

"Well Chief, maybe this will end the drug problem," Megan says, hopefully.

He looks at her. "It won't, Megan. As long as there are people willing to pay for it, we can never stop it. Only the people themselves can end it. But for now, we do have an opportunity to get it under control."

Harrison hands his folder over to the chief. "I think you'll find my report is complete."

Boyd walks back to his desk and tosses the folder on it, looking into Harrison's one bloodshot eye. "I'll study this later. What I need to know right now are your plans. Classes for the DEA training start next week. Commander Benson wants you back ... says things will be different with the admiral gone. I don't want to push you into anything, but the Wingate has plenty of good pilots. On the other hand, we badly need good agents."

Megan holds her breathe.

Harrison looks from Megan to Boyd. "Well, Chief, I think I'd like to stay where I'm needed."

"Yes!" Megan squeals with delight, and springs from her chair to hug Harrison.

When Harrison is able to pull away, he looks at the smiling Boyd, who says, "I don't think I'll be able to match that, but let's just say I'm very happy with that decision, also."

¤ ¤ ¤

The mood is grim inside the head councilor's office as he turns to the man sitting across from him. "Very soon, Mr. Kane, you will be designated as the current director for our space program. As you well know, Mr. Pressnell is no longer with us. A shame, since he was on a mission of grave importance. This obligation now falls on you. Pressnell gave his life for it ... I'm asking if you are willing to do the same."

Kane nods. "I understand, sir, but what of the Wingate?"

"I know you were being trained to replace the admiral, but that position is no longer necessary. We'll eliminate it. The DEA has just released the Wingate and her shuttles. I want you to begin transferring your men and supplies. It's scheduled to depart for Sector GI-10 in ten days. When everything is ready —"

The viewer bleeps, the head councilor reaches out to answer it.

"Sir, my apologies for interrupting, but you have an urgent call."

The head councilor nods at his secretary's image, and then says, "Yes. Give me a moment, then put it through to my office."

"Yes, sir."

As her image fades, his gaze returns to Kane. "That will be all for now, Mr. Kane. By the way, congratulations again on your promotion."

"Thank you, sir. And don't worry. Everything will be ready for departure in ten days."

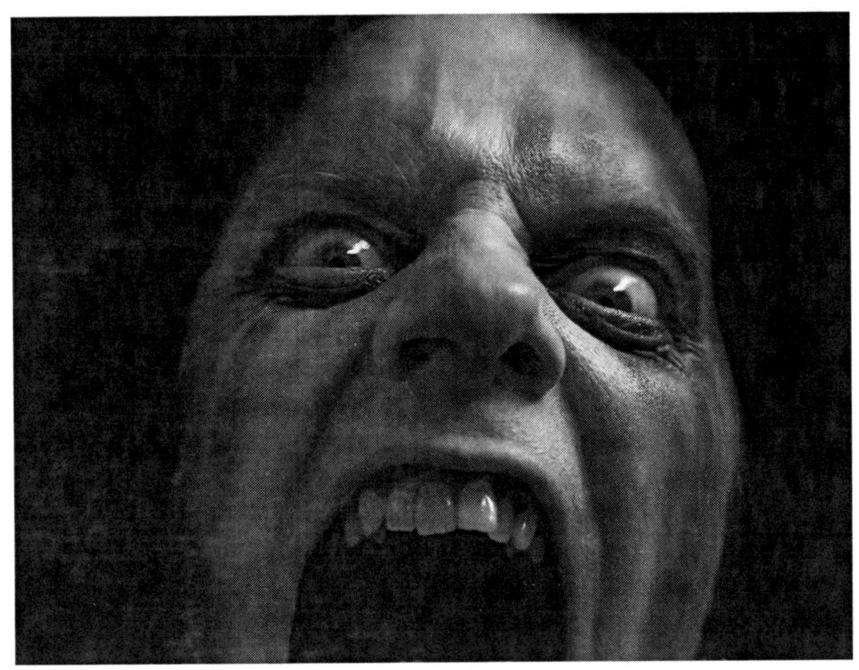

Chapter Eighteen

The head councilor revives his communicator. The screen is overflowing with at least five dwarf-like faces, each accompanied by a pair of hauntingly dark eyes. It appears as if someone has forcibly squeezed them into his monitor; their faces press against the glass, all trying desperately to get what might be their only look at the one man who controls their destiny. The councilor recognizes the half-breeds, as well as the voice in the background demanding that all of them return to work.

A calloused hand reaches out and pries the half-breeds free of the viewer. Followed by a thin, grungy-looking man that emerges from the dark background.

"I see you survived the DEA, Mr. Campanelli," the head councilor says, smiling.

"Yes, no thanks to you," Campanelli replies, as he glares through the badly smudged viewer.

"But you did survive."

"Only because I wasn't there. My fields, my crop, the workers ... my entire complex is gone, dammit, everything is gone." His words fade to a whisper as the vein deep in his forehead bulges. He sounds as though he's just minutes from a stroke.

"No, you can't be serious!" The head councilor is shocked. "The DEA isn't suppose to destroy anything unless a trafficker is present. I'll have to talk to Boyd about this." He doesn't hide his smirk.

Campanelli's face reddens even more. "Don't patronize me, Councilor. We have a contract! You agreed to keep me one step ahead of them, and for that, your people have enjoyed an uninterrupted flow of drugs — the same people that work on your little project. The one with the exorbitant appetite for funds. Oh, I see. You found the money to pay everyone, and now you don't need me." Campanelli begins to laugh at that thought, knowing it could never happen.

"I no longer have control over the DEA, Campanelli. Since their discovery of the modules, they suspect everyone. So you see, there is nothing more I can do. Goodbye."

His red face looking even nearer a stroke then before, Campanelli leans toward the monitor. "We have a contract, damn you!"

"No, we *had* a contract!" The head councilor's voice is taunting. "You're forever telling me how powerful you are. If you want the DEA neutralized, why not do it yourself?"

"I just may do that, and while I'm at it, we'll see how long you maintain control without this." Mr. Campanelli holds up a serum bottle that the head councilor recognizes as an enhancement drug. "Consider the government facilities no longer off-limits to druggies. They can be very troublesome, as you will soon discover, Councilor. But in time, you will learn to cope. Besides, the government workers will need to purchase their substance like everyone else: from the pushers, I mean, associates. I'll see to it that someone is scheduled to accommodate their needs."

Campanelli falls back in his chair laughing loud, then springs back to the viewer. "If the DEA wins, I'm dead. If I win, I control everything. Just think of it."

He slams his left hand down hard on the control panel in front of him, striking the heat-activated sensor that shuts off the viewer. Still laughing, he stands and walks over to the half-breed sitting motionless on the console, trying to look inconspicuous in light of his father's bizarre behavior.

Campanelli sneaks his hand on top of his half-breed son's head, leans over and levels his eyes to his. "Good news, is it not? The druggies will keep the military busy while we eliminate the DEA and their clean-up crews."

He releases his grip on the terrified half-breed and turns for the door. "I want you to contact all of our people. We must concentrate our strength. Tell them Mr. Campanelli wants a meeting. Tell them Mr. Campanelli says it's time the many take power from the few." As he exits the small dark room, without looking back, he yells, "Mr. Campanelli will control everything and everyone!"

¤ ¤ ¤

One week later, Harrison enters the DEA control room. Megan spies him and grins. "Harrison, I'm glad you finally came in. It's good to see you. Who've you been seeing latly? I know it's not been me."

He drops into the empty chair beside her. "In case you've forgotten, I've been somewhat busy the past week, with the academy and all."

She beams. "Yeah, I know. Just ribbing you a little. So what are you doing here? Not that I'm complaining, but I thought you weren't scheduled for duty until after your training was completed."

He rubs his forehead. "Actually, I don't know what I'm doing here. The Chief just left a message for me to report in as soon as possible."

Now it's Megan's turn to look befuddled. "I don't know, either. There's been little drug activity. The chief's main concern has been the build-up of arms."

"Huh? What arms?"

Megan sighs. "It seems the remaining traffickers have their mercenaries out arming the druggies. The chief calls it 'The Antagonistic Army.'"

Harrison looks up. "That's not a DEA assignment. Militia, I mean. Besides, I'm sure the military already knows all about this."

Megan shrugs. "All I know for sure is that the chief's talking with the head councilor right now, and I guarantee you one thing: Before he's through, they'll all know."

¤ ¤ ¤

Inside Chief Boyd's office, the viewer is crackling. "Talk fast Boyd, I'm a busy man."

"You're going to be a dead man if you don't deploy the military before it's too late."

"Before what's too late? Boyd, what are you talking about?"

Boyd gives the Councilor a hard look. "The traffickers are building an army, and you know it."

"What makes you think they're after the Council?"

"I know what you're thinking, Councilor. Do you actually believe they'll stop with the DEA?"

The answering sigh comes slow. "The military is occupied. At the present time, they're protecting government facilities."

"Well, there's one government facility you forgot," Boyd snaps. "Its headquarters is located in Houston."

"It seems we ran short of men. We have, as you well know, an overflow of druggies. A problem you yourself, Boyd, should have resolved some twenty years ago."

"And if you had selected your Council more wisely, we would definitely not have this problem, Head Councilor."

"Nevertheless, your people are on their own, at least for a few weeks. Then I might possibly free up some auxiliary help."

"Listen to me, Councilor." Boyd slams his fist down on the desk. "It's the military's designation to put down any and all civil uprising, not the DEA's."

"That's just it, Boyd. I don't see a civil uprising. It looks to me as if there's a serious drug problem, and considering you have complete authority concerning drugs, that makes it your problem." As the Head Councilor lectures, he smirks.

"So that's what it's all about?" Boyd growls. "Everyone knows the Council has been trying to eliminate the DEA for years. And this is how you plan to do it — by allowing the traffickers to arm the druggies?"

"Don't take it so personally, Boyd. You should've anticipated that eventually I'd win."

"Listen to me, you bastard, you haven't won."

Boyd turns off the viewer and heads for the control room.

"Megan, send a communication out to all agents and crews. I want everyone to report in with their personal articles. They'll be residing here at the complex until further notice."

"Is that what you called me in for, Chief?" Harrison asks.

Boyd glares at him. "No. I want to see you in my office." He ushers Harrison back to his office while Megan passes on the order.

¤ ¤ ¤

"Harrison, I know you just started training and I despise the thought of pulling you out. But nevertheless, I have a clean-up crew aboard the Wingate, and I'll need every man I can get. I want you to retrieve them."

"Of course, sir ... but didn't you release the Wingate last week?"

Boyd nods. "I left a crew onboard intentionally ... to observe the change of command and collect any evidence they could find. I have a ship scheduled to retrieve them in a couple of days, but I need them now."

"Is it the arms build-up you're worried about?"

Boyd sets down at his desk. "I just spoke to the Head Councilor. We're going to be up to our armpits in druggies, and soon. Druggies with weapons. And we can expect no help from the military."

"Isn't there anyone on the Council you can reason with?"

Boyd shakes his head. "No one goes against the head councilor. Furthermore, with Pressnell's replacement and a few other new faces, the Council is principally family, if you know what I mean. So, I'm afraid we're on our own. I want you to leave as soon as possible. Everything's cleared at Houston Control. You can use any one of the Wingate's shuttles you want. Most of them are supposed to be here."

Harrison frowns. "Down here?"

"Yes," Boyd replies, reading Harrison's expression. "Is there something strange about that?"

"It's just that ... The admiral would never have allowed that. What if they have an onboard emergency? No one could get off the ship."

Boyd's brow furrows. "I don't know. The Wingate is under new command now. There's been a lot of activity onboard, but nothing that concerns the DEA." He straightens in his chair. "Harrison, our job is finished up there. Just get the crew back as quickly as possible. One more thing. I ... I'm sorry I talked you into this. Maybe you should have stayed a fighter pilot with the Wingate. At least there, you would be away from all of this."

"Chief, I made my choice, and I'm glad to be here."

Boyd looks up at him, raising his chin with pride. "No more than I am to have you here. I just hope you don't live to regret your decision."

¤ ¤ ¤

Harrison stops off at Megan's desk to say his goodbyes, which takes a little longer then he had planned. He now must head straight for his vehicle on the upper landing deck. It takes him just minutes to reach Houston flight control. From the air, the facility looks to be well protected by the military.

On a flyover of the shuttle holding area, he realizes that the chief is right: all the Wingate's shuttles and some others are indeed on the ground.

Since the shuttles are all the same, Harrison simply selects the nearest one. After a routine inspection, he's ready to leave — with one exception. He contacts flight control and advises them that he will have no copilot. After acknowledging the request, flight control relays all essential information to the shuttle's computer. This is a precautionary measure: If something happens to Harrison, the shuttle will stay on course and notify the Wingate of a problem. It also makes possible a computer link-up with the Wingate, permitting the director to land the shuttle if needed.

Soon, Harrison is en route to the Wingate.

Even with the help of the onboard computer, which is programmed to keep the pilot occupied, the hours drag. No matter how he tries, the same two thoughts haunt him: what the chief had said, and what the admiral told him just before he died. Both men said he would have been safer on the Wingate. And their statements brought a second image to mind: What is so important that Pressnell and the admiral would die for it?

It's becoming apparent to Harrison that everyone the DEA comes into contact with dies. "There's something going on, and everyone knows it … except me," he believes.

¤ ¤ ¤

At DEA Headquarters, Chief Boyd addresses the office personnel at a special meeting within the ground-floor auditorium. "I've asked all of you to bring in your personal belongings, since it is no longer safe for you beyond the confines of headquarters, at least until this thing is over. We've already had several agents killed, in the field and at their homes. I have the crews out collecting the latest … and possibly the final bits of information from our agents stationed in various precincts throughout the city. And the preliminary results don't look good.

"Here is everything we know at this time. The drug cartel has been stockpiling arms for the past six months or so. The weapons were seized from government shipments and purchased by the drug lords. We don't know why the sudden change of heart, but at this point, they have their mercenaries out distributing military grade weapons among the druggies, mainly within the city."

He holds up his hand to forestall the questions that immediately begin. "I know what you're thinking, and yes, the military is securing all government facilities: except one."

The spoken words "Why not us?" dies on one staffer's lips as the chief continues without addressing the question.

"I don't want to go too deeply into the reasons why, but I fear that no one associated with the DEA is safe right now. I've seriously thought about giving them what they want ... that is, disbanding the DEA ... but even that would not ensure your safety. So I'm giving you an option: Stay here and continue working, or leave now while you still can. If you choose to leave, we will of course eliminate any record of you ever working here. But we can not be responsible for you. If you're recognized, it could be ... no, it would be fatal."

An androgynous voice blares over the intercom. "Chief Boyd, you are needed in the control room."

He turns back to the now-silent group. "That's all I have to say. Those of you who wish to remain may return to what you were doing. The others will need to give their names to Susan. She'll take care of the files."

¤ ¤ ¤

In the control room, Boyd asks, "What is it, Angie?"

"We've lost contact with a clean-up ship. Crew Nine."

"What do you mean 'lost contact'?" Boyd demands.

"No radar, no cell or microwave, no satellite track, no direct link. It's vanished. In their last communication, they reported, and I quote, "foreign radar has a tracking grid locked on", and then we lost it."

"Ground radar can't hold a clean-up ship on screen!" Boyd roars. "They can't be hit. Contact Houston and find out what they know about this."

Chapter Nineteen

The shuttle's communicator briefly blinks, and then a voice says, "Identify yourself."

It's the face of a young man Harrison doesn't recognize. The man's uniform is also unfamiliar. But he sees no reason to refuse the query. "Agent Harrison, DEA."

"Activate your computer link-up."

Whoa now, Harrison thinks, unsure who's going to land his ship. "This mission has been pre-authorized, and I am perfectly capable of docking my own shuttle," he says.

"Ah, yes, I have you on register," the young officer states, changing tacks. "You're cleared for Portal Four starboard side, no reported activity."

The communication officer's inexperience becomes obvious when Harrison has to ask what the Wingate's orbiting speed is. So maybe the link-up request is only a precaution. Now, cleared by the director, Harrison maneuvers the shuttle into its assigned location and patiently waits for the docking ramp that will allow him access to the starboard wing.

Immediately upon sealing the enclosed walkway to the shuttle docking doughnut, Harrison is on his way. His first stop, as usual, will be Commander Benson. When he arrives at the commander's office, it definitely isn't Benson he meets there. "Where's Commander Benson?" Harrison asks the older overweight man standing outside Benson's office.

"Oh, you must be here to collect your men," he says without identifying himself. "Well, you'll find them in Barracks Three, straight down the hall, turn right, third door on your right." The man turns and steps inside the office.

Harrison has never experienced antagonism aboard the Wingate. For the first time, he is being treated as an outsider. He wonders if it is because he is no longer with the space program, or because he's now part of the DEA.

"Wait!" He quickly squeezes out the word.

With the door now only partially open, the man bellows, "Can't the DEA follow the simplest instructions, or do you need someone to lead you?"

"I've spent several years of my life onboard this ship, and I am quite capable of finding the barracks."

"Good, then you won't need me," as he tries to slam the door again.

Suddenly, everything that Harrison has acquired, everything he considers to be civilized begins to boil up inside of him. He fears for just a moment, a fleeting moment that he might lose touch with his culture and erupt into a hollow assassin. He yells back, "Need you. Oh, yes I do!" and lunges for the office door. His flying body makes a solid impact; the door is knocked free of the man's hand and hits against the wall. Harrison grabs his right arm and forces it behind his back. He groans through clenched teeth as he tries to undo the arm lock, but Harrison places his left arm securely around the neck of his new found enemy, cutting off his air.

"The DEA has their own means of dealing with people like you," Harrison grunts, further forcing the right arm up. The man senses a lessening of pressure on his windpipe and seizes the opportunity to gulp some much-needed air.

Harrison is so startled he almost loses his grip on the traitor. It's as if someone different has materialized. But it isn't someone else choking the man, it's Harrison. After nearly four months, he suddenly realizes why the DEA is so brutal. For the first time, he's seen the other side of the coin, and now fears that, through necessity, he will become as callous as they are.

Harrison lets go of the man's neck and thrusts him forward. At the same time, he frees his arm. The man stumbles into the far wall and turns to face Harrison. Leaning against the wall and cradling his right arm, he stares up at Harrison.

Harrison looks down at the gray-haired man and wonders what has come over him. Either way, he has gotten his attention, and they both know Harrison is blameless for what has just happened, or for what might yet happen. He now realizes the power and the reason behind having it. People don't just fear the DEA … they hate the DEA.

"All right. What do you want?"

"Where is Commander Benson?"

"I don't know. He's been transferred."

"He's been assigned to another ship?"

"I don't know."

Harrison walks toward him, hands out. "Of course you know. He's no longer with the space program, is he?" Harrison doesn't really expect a reply. Incoming command can always access the whereabouts of the last commander. The man is lying to him.

He moves closer. "Who's the new admiral?"

"There is no admiral. The position has been eliminated."

"Then who has operating authority?"

There's a long pause. He straightens up and looks down at Harrison's weapon. "I know what you expect from me, and I can't tell you what I don't know."

Harrison realizes he'll get nothing more from him.

A familiar thought races over him. Another one willing to give his life for the cause, whatever that might be. Well, all right then.

Harrison slowly pulls his weapon and points it at the man, who closes his eyes. Within the first seconds of knowing he's going to die, sweat begins to form just above his eyebrows and his breathing turns to a ragged pant as he waits for the blast that everyone says the victim never hears. Moments pass, before he opens his eyes, only to find himself alone in the office.

Harrison is halfway down the hall, inspecting every room as he continues on, with the hope of locating a familiar face, someone he can talk to … or at least someone who will tell him what's going on.

After checking barracks one and two and finding nothing but newcomers wearing military uniforms, he arrives at barracks three. The men here seem to be pre-assembled and ready for departure. One wears lieutenant's bars on his DEA uniform. Harrison presumes this to be the crew he's supposed to retrieve.

"Where's the captain?"

The lieutenant moves forward. Harrison recognizes him as Captain Raynor's lieutenant. "There was an urgent call from Chief Boyd. He went somewhere more private."

"There is no place private on the Wingate," Harrison says, scoffing. "They monitor all communications."

"That may be, but by the time they unscramble the message, it'll be old news," replies one of the men.

"Any communication from the chief can only be decoded by the captain," adds the lieutenant."

Harrison nods. "Tell him we're scheduled to depart in thirty minutes. I'll be back before then."

Harrison starts down the hall, heading directly for the admiral's private chambers, but suddenly returns to the barracks. With a determined look, he says. "I'll need three of your men, Lieutenant."

"Well, Harrison, you're starting to sound like DEA now." He waves three fingers. "Full combat gear, I want to see everything."

One of the men nods and taps his helmet, indicating that their communicators are set so he can listen in as well.

Harrison silently guides them down the turning and twisting halls toward the ship's interior. Although the three men are hopelessly lost, Harrison knows exactly where he's headed. He's planned it that way.

The closer they spiral to the admiral's quarters, the more people they encounter. Harrison notes they have confronted no one from the space program, likewise no civilians. It's been strictly soldiers guarding doors, patrolling the halls, and even some high-ranking officers. But no one gives them a second glance. Apparently, the military has become accustomed to DEA agents.

As expected, Harrison finds the admiral's quarters secured by two guards, both with weapons at their side. Harrison, knowing he could never obtain permission to enter the admiral's private quarters, decides to do it his way. Or maybe it's more the DEA style, he believes. He waits for a moment when the hallway is clear of traffic, then places one clean-up man in front and the other two behind. All four quietly walk down the hall. Stopping directly adjacent to the closed door, the man in front as well as the two behind raise and point their weapons at the guards.

"We're with the DEA, open the door." Harrison stands back to give the men a clear shot, if needed.

The guards, looking despairingly at each other, are embarrassed at how easily they have been subdued. The younger one speaks first. "We were told that the DEA no longer has control of this ship. That you'd already departed."

Harrison smiles. "As you can clearly see, you're wrong on both counts. Open the door and step inside."

The two clean-up men relieve the guards of their weapons and motion for them to enter the admiral's quarters; the third remains outside to watch the hall.

Once inside, Harrison finds that most of the admiral's belongings have been removed, and the accommodations prepared for a new occupant. The first room, off the main hall, is a nicely furnished office. He knows it's just the place to look if one has to catch up on recent activity. With a little luck, he'll find out just where Commander Benson and everyone else was transferred to.

However, the files and desk drawers only contain general data on the ship's classification. He's about to leave when he runs across an average-looking black electronic book, which holds a list of names. The list seems endless. There must be at least ten thousand names here, Harrison thinks as he scrolls down the list.

The list is alphabetical, and it's obvious that entire families, including spouses and children, are named. There is one name he recognizes: the dead Mr. Solomon. With that, he begins reading more intently.

He's not yet finished when one of the clean-up men confronts him. "There's someone in the main hall demanding to be let in. Also, Captain Raynor has returned to the barracks and ordered us back."

Harrison nods. "We're finished here. Let them in."

Before the steel door is fully open, Harrison slips the book inside his suit and zips it up. At this time, two high-ranking military officers' storm into the room and head straight for the desk.

"Who gave you permission to enter this office?" asks the first officer, as the other one begins searching frantically through the desk.

"Oh, we were just leaving." Harrison keeps his tone casual.

He assumes they're looking for the book, but can only watch and wait for their next move. He has no plans of giving it up, since it is obviously of great value to someone.

After looking through the desk drawers and having nothing to show for all his trouble, the officer looks straight at Harrison. "You're not leaving this room."

Behind them, Harrison can see that the two clean-up men have activated their helmets; their clear shields have already begun a slow transition to black. Apparently, they've been given permission to terminate. In a heartbeat from now, the military will have two fewer officers; the clean-up men won't hesitate to squeeze the trigger.

The door opens again, and a well-dressed man enters, accompanied by the third clean-up man. "I thought the DEA was scheduled for departure," the newcomer says.

Harrison nods. "We'll be leaving as soon as I assemble the men."

"Good. I'll notify the director that you'll be departing very soon now."

The first officer tries to explain, "But, Mr. Kane, we think they have the—"

Mr. Kane holds up his right hand. "It doesn't matter."

Harrison feels the book digging into his waist and wonders if it is still important, or if Kane is lying when he says it doesn't matter.

He leaves the office expecting trouble around every corner, but finds none. He and his three escorts make their way back to the barracks safely.

When they enter the corridor where Barracks Three is located, most of the men are standing at attention in the hall, with several more guarding the barracks door. The men are suited up; bearing weapons and shields, they look ready for something.

Approaching, the first thing that Harrison notices is the door. A steel bar has wedged it open. He glances around and sees a large black hole where the room monitor was once located. Both the captain and the lieutenant are leaning over a table studying a diagram of the Wingate.

Raynor looks up with a grave face. "Harrison, come in."

"Is everything ready?" Harrison asks as he walks closer.

"It seems there's been a change in our status. We're no longer here just to observe."

"What sort of change?"

"Well, as you know, I've been in contact with Chief Boyd. We now have a new objective: that is, to decommission the Wingate."

"What? The military will never let us take control of the Wingate."

"You misunderstand. We're not taking command. Our orders are to permanently disable the Wingate."

Harrison knows the DEA's up to something, and his lack of concern for the military leaves him ambivalent about what kind of pain the captain inflicts on the soldiers. But to destroy the Wingate? "That's impossible. Why?" Harrison's voice cracks.

"No, it is possible with your help. The Wingate's designed to withstand an attack from the outside, but not from within. The Chief knew you would help us."

"Yes, I guess. But you realize, if we succeed in destroying the Wingate, we might not get back. And you still didn't answer my question: Why are we doing this?"

Raynor looks him straight in the eye. "If we don't succeed, we'll have no reason to return. Chief Boyd just informed me that the military is using the Wingate to lock onto our clean-up ships and DEA offices. They're intercepting our traffic, and relaying that information to the mercenaries — who have the weapons and means to destroy our clean-up crews. According to Chief Boyd, they've eliminated five of our crews already, which they know of. We've cut off communication to keep the remaining crews from being targeted. The only way we can stop them is to disable this ship. So we must succeed."

Harrison now realizes why he'd been permitted to leave the admiral's quarters without a fight. "They plan on destroying our shuttle as soon as we depart," Harrison says, clutching his weapon.

Raynor nods. "You know this ship better than anyone onboard, so I want you to lead the lieutenant and his men to the main power terminal in ... " He glances at the blueprint. " ... Sector One. According to this, Sector One is the only location where we can undermine the ship's power."

Raynor looks at Harrison, who looks up and nods. "Yes, that's right, Captain. That would leave only auxiliary power, mainly life support and lights. They're drawn from Power Plant Two. But to get to the main terminal, we'll need to get close to Power Plant Two. Too close. The radiation will be unbearable."

"That's a chance we'll have to take. Lieutenant, get your men ready to move out. We'll be five minutes behind you. Remember, we have to move quickly, before Kane figures out what we're doing."

¤ ¤ ¤

Two DEA clean-up men with shields move quiet as possible down the unnaturally empty hall, with Harrison, the lieutenant, and eight other heavily armed men close behind. As Harrison directs them to Sector One, he begins to feel that familiar sensation in the pit of his stomach — the one he's had ever since he signed on with the DEA. With the space program, everything was planned in advance for him, and the outcome was evident. Unless he encountered a pirate who had more than the usual number of weapons, there were no surprises. It flowed parallel with his life: slightly productive, but boring. Achieving this mission would mean an uncertain conclusion. Even accomplishing it might not guarantee success: When they disable the Wingate, Boyd's battle down on the surface will continue, maybe even escalate. But maybe that's the price one pays for independence, not knowing the outcome, Harrison thinks.

His heart is divided on another issue as well. Cutting the Wingate's primary power terminal will be like severing a main artery and watching the victim slowly die — and he, the one responsible for the final cut, had sworn loyalty to the victim previously. But, based on what Raynor has just told him, this is the Chief's direct order. And if nothing else, Harrison always tries to follow orders.

¤ ¤ ¤

The military learns quick what the DEA is planning and organizes a blockade in the hall leading to the main power terminal.

"Harrison!" the lieutenant yells as the remains of one agent devoured by laser fire crashes to the floor. "The captain needs you. He's in Corridor Two."

"It looks like I'm needed here," Harrison shouts back as he grabs the dead man's weapon.

"No, we'll hold them back. You return to the captain."

The lieutenant's words are nearly drowned out by the military's surge of firepower. Harrison slides the weapon to him just as a laser blast flashes in front.

"Get going and keep your head down," the lieutenant yells back. "That's an order!"

¤ ¤ ¤

After exiting the hallway on hands and knees, Harrison turns the corner and heads for the captain's location at a dead run. When he arrives at Corridor Two, he finds the men strategically placed like a second line of defense. Harrison locates Raynor halfway down the corridor. "Captain, your men are cut off from the main terminal."

Not bothering to look up from the map he's studying, Raynor replies, "Which of these walls is opposite Power Plant Two?"

"Didn't you hear me? Your men are being killed off."

"Yes, I know Harrison, now which wall?" Raynor shakes the map at Harrison.

Harrison has never dealt with the military before. He just now realizes their plan. "You knew what would happen, didn't you? You used your own men as decoys."

"What did you think; we could just walk in and pull the plug? Yes, I know they're dying. Everyone knows. This will be our last mission together."

Raynor speaks loud to reassure Harrison that the men knew the situation. "And I couldn't have asked for a finer crew or better men to die with. Don't you see? They're doing their job, and now it's time for us to do ours." He thrusts the map at Harrison again.

Harrison searches the faces of the remaining men who are distributed up and down the corridor, wondering if they feel the same as him and just aren't showing it. He'd always considered himself an individual who liked challenges, even a risk-taker at times. But to make such a decision is inconceivable. He'd always been a loner, never wanting to be solely responsible for someone else's life — or death. To knowingly give his life, or ask anyone to give their life for him ... this is extraordinary to him. Harrison disliked, even hated the captain at their first introduction, but at this moment, he has more respect for the man and his crew than anyone he has ever known.

Harrison shoves the map away. "You won't be needing that. I'll escort the men."

Raynor's eyes measure him. "You don't have to. You could just tell me."

"Yes, I do. If you got lost, it would be my fault." Harrison starts back down to Corridor Two with the captain and ten men trailing.

They move quickly through Corridor Two, but slow as they near the fighting in Corridor One. The corridors run parallel with connecting halls. Harrison stops to listen to the battle. It sounds as if military reinforcements have arrived and the fight is escalating.

He turns and starts down a narrow hallway with a steel door at the end. He punches in several numbers and the door opens into a long entranceway. The danger is evident: Signs are posted everywhere, warnings of heat radiation and contaminated air.

Raynor immediately wedges the door open, then assigns three men to stay behind and maintain the open hallway. As the remaining men near the chamber located at the end of the hall, Raynor asks, "How much further?"

"This is it." Harrison turns to open the door on his left. The large, dimly lit room inside looks as if it hasn't seen action for quite some time: There are several computers, monitors, and other instruments that are shut off and covered up.

"What, this the back of Power Plant Two?" Raynor says, puzzled.

Harrison shakes his head. "This is the auxiliary monitoring room. If a problem develops, the engineers retreat to this room. It's protected by the containment wall behind there." He points to the far end of the room. "That's where we've got to go. Solid titanium."

Raynor nods, and then steps out into the hall and motions for his remaining men to enter. The last man, guiding the box-weapon in front of him. Or at least that's what Harrison calls it; no one has ever told him the actual name of the weapon.

"Place it at the far wall," Raynor barks, and then turns to Harrison. "Is there an alarm?"

Harrison nods. "Yes, you'll need to barricade the door open."

Raynor thinks for a moment, and then tells the man, "Set it to cut a hole two meters in diameter. That should be sufficient."

Once activated, the laser calculates the wall's mass and begins its task. The needle-sized white beams waste no time cutting away at the wall. A static discharge arcs from the titanium wall as if in retaliation. The electric charge soon covers every portion of the box, searching out a ground that doesn't exist. The beams continue disappearing into the titanium wall until a ruddy, dark break appears.

The sudden rise in temperature activates the silent main alarm system, which attempts to seal off the room. Harrison can tell the men are nervous, and understandably so, as they watch the obstructed door trying repeatedly to close itself. Nevertheless, they hold their positions. They all know the military will soon arrive.

A few minutes later, the laser weapon shuts down, meaning the cycle is complete. The men begin blasting away at the circle until it falls inward; they have completed unveiling the containment wall for Power Plant Two.

As the tremendous rampart of heat from the containment wall floods through the open hole and into the room, Harrison believes for the first time that the destruction of the Wingate is possible.

The men thrust the weapon as near to the opening as possible, considering the heat, and reset the laser to cut a one-meter hole. Several men, including Raynor, race from the room. Harrison, being the only one without a communicator channel for the clean-up crew, has no idea why. He follows them into the hallway. "What is it?"

Raynor turns to him, his face blank. "The military will be here soon. They broke through our first line."

Harrison knows that's the captain's way of saying the lieutenant and his men are dead.

Raynor speaks. "What do you know about this containment wall?"

Harrison thinks for a moment. "It's designed to retain heat for several hours after a break appears. The heat extractors will keep it cool enough for the engineers to shut down and jettison the power plant."

"Can they still do that?"

"Not unless they stop that." He points at the box-weapon standing alone in the scorching-hot room. "When the oxygen hits that power plant, there's going to be one hell of an explosion. It'll start a chain reaction with the other three plants, which will thoroughly destroy this ship." He glances at Raynor, then over at the nearby men.

Raynor slaps his shoulder. "Well, Harrison, I can't thank you enough for what you've done. You better get going while you still can."

An alarm begins blaring overhead. Harrison has to yell to be heard over it. "I thought I'd stay and see this thing through. You may need me before it's over."

Raynor shakes his head and yells back, "See it through? It's already through. Besides, you won't last long enough to help."

The captain points to Harrison's suit. Unlike the clean-up crews' suits that are designed to resist the heat of a laser blast, Harrison's pressurized flight suit will soon be rendered useless from the tremendous heat.

Raynor yells once more. This time it's more like an order. "I told the three men in Corridor Two that you're on your way."

The alarm stops abruptly. After what seems like an eternity of silence, a recorded message plays over the intercom: "All personnel evacuate the area. Radiation has reached the 03 level."

Harrison knows this is his cue, the perfect time to get out, the last opportunity he'll have to leave. The military will be pulling back, and one man armed with only a laser pistol wearing a pilot's suit might slip through during the excitement. He reluctantly turns and begins walking.

Reaching the entrance, Harrison turns and takes one long look back. The clean-up men are crouched down along the wall. He can see Raynor standing beside the open door, watching the box weapon.

He presumes the immense heat is beginning to affect him everything seems to be moving in slow motion. The room is emitting a red glow that reflects off the captain's shiny black suit.

He knows there's no way to get the clean-up crew out, Harrison thinks numbly. The shuttle's their only way out, and they won't be able to reach it. They know that, and still they're right there fighting.

With a great respect and even greater sense of loss, Harrison turns again and walks away. This time, he doesn't look back.

¤ ¤ ¤

He makes his way to the pilot's barracks without incident, after which it's a short and familiar ride up the emergency chute to the Number One Port, his docking position for several years. As he straps himself in and prepares for takeoff, it hits him, and he whispers, "Guess I'll never be on this ship again — no one will."

As soon as the fighter powers up, it shoots down the emergency exit and into open space, leaving behind the captain, crew, and the place Harrison once thought of as home. When the explosions begin, he tries hard not to think about what's happening.

¤ ¤ ¤

After the first series of explosions, Harrison sets a new course in the hope of avoiding the blast zone and outrunning the final shock. He advances on several evacuation ships that have exited from the orbiting space station the Wingate is docked to. The space station had no warning, and Harrison knows they have no chance of outmaneuvering the final blast.

His fears are abruptly confirmed when the Wingate lets loose with the final devastating blow. It consumes the late jumpers in its intense retribution. The larger, more cumbersome ships are next to go; it takes several minutes before the tremendous pressure destroying everything in its wake reaches out and seizes the smaller, quicker ships.

As Harrison fears, his instruments erratically indicate the size and magnitude of the approaching explosion. Any hope of outrunning it fades when the fighter's outer temperature shoots up to nearly five hundred degrees Celsius and continues to steadily climb. He can see a white haze like a cloud in the viewer. The blast has engulfed his fighter. The instruments repeatedly warn of power plant and cockpit temperatures high enough to inflict damage.

Harrison knows the "damage" would be fatal. The inside temperature has reached 200 Celsius, well above the designer's expectations. Once again, his pilot's suit is put to the test.

For the next several minutes, Harrison can hear the fuselage groan as he fights to maintain stability; he feels certain it will fly apart at any moment. Suddenly, an alien code he's never encountered scrolls down the screen. It's mostly numerical mumbo-jumbo, but it brings to life the seriousness of his position. He has never pushed anything this hard before. For the first time, he actually believes he might have overstepped his limitations.

The fighter exceeds its maximum operating range. Knowing this should be the end, Harrison reaches to shut it down. Suddenly a green "down" arrow indicates a drop in the outside temperature, and the cockpit temperature stops rising. But it will be several minutes before the life-support system can begin cooling down the inside. Even so, for the first time, Harrison feels hopeful that if he can't outrun the explosion, maybe he can outlast it. He knows as the distance from the Wingate increases, the density of the particles decrease, resulting in a lessening of pressure, which defines steadily cooling temperatures.

¤ ¤ ¤

By the time the cockpit begins to cool, Harrison has set his course for Houston and immediately initiates systems check of the ship's functions. The inoperable list is quite long, but the most important is the ion tracker. He hopes it won't be needed.

He knows shock, heat exhaustion, and grief will settle in soon. He begins mentally slipping away. Just now realizing how very little of this government plot he knows, and even less of the damage it's done. He wonders how much is yet to come, and what the outcome will be. Knowing he needs a plan, but it's hard to focus on things that might have been, and things that were, but are no longer. He drifts in and out of consciousness for several hours, until he's crudely awakened by the blare of the re-entry warning horn. The small fighter is coming in much too fast. He needs to react quickly. Because he doesn't trust Houston Flight Control, his computer isn't linked with theirs. The re-entry will be his job alone.

Chapter Twenty

Houston's airspace shatters with a turbulent blaze created by the depleted fighter and its pilot, the sole survivors of what was once the most dominant vessel ever built. Ignoring Houston Control, Harrison heads straight for the DEA. Saturated with sweat inside his heat-stiffened suit, his first obligation is to contact headquarters.

"I can't talk right now," Megan declares. "The entire compound's on full alert. After you left, the mercenaries began an all-out attack on the civilian population. We barely have two crews remaining, and they're both on the ground. The chief has them guarding the outer entrance."

"Maybe we still have a chance with the Wingate destroyed. It was acting as a —"

Boyd steps in front of the viewer.

"Harrison, we don't know how large the attacking force will be, but we do know they possess heavy-caliber weapons appropriated from the space program."

"I'll be there in a few minutes, I have one of the Wingate's fighters, so I'll need you to clear me with Houston Control."

"No, no, I don't recommend it. Several of the less-adequate facilities have already been seized. I'm afraid it's not an isolated assault, as the Council believed it would be. I fear not even the military can stop it now. The traffickers' army is multiplying at a dramatic rate. Every time they evacuate a complex, their numbers increase. They've acquired druggies from various communities, and nearly every complex between here and Houston. We've already lost contact with several of the branch offices, and most of the agents. We might be forced to abandon this facility as well. So you see, one more person won't make a difference. ... I was informed you're alone?"

The chief's hopeful question hits Harrison like a slap. But he has to reply. "Yes. I'm sorry to say, I ... had no means of rescuing the crew."

Boyd nods, his eyes full worry. "Houston Control has already informed me of the Wingate aftermath. I can't tell you where to go, but Houston Control seems to be safe, at least for now."

"No, I'm coming in, but ... there's something I have to do first."

Boyd assumes Harrison means the Houston re-entry checkpoint, a mandatory first stop. He looks on. "Well, just in case, I want to commend you on your part in helping the clean-up crew achieve its mission."

"Thank you, sir."

Harrison doesn't intend to squander what little time he has at Houston flight control. Against Chief Boyd's advice, he heads straight for the complex where the guard once lived.

During the return flight, Harrison had time to examine the electronic book salvaged from the admiral's quarters. It wasn't difficult to see that the people and their families were singled out for a reason. The list covers government and corporate leaders, scientists and space program personnel, and of course, the entire council.

That must have been why the occupants were forced to abandon the complex, he thinks. It's the logical place to house thousands of dignitaries.

Also, it's the farthest, most isolated complex from Houston, but close to flight control and all the Wingate shuttles— shuttles that seem to be just quietly waiting. Now, Harrison has a good idea what they're waiting for.

He suspects that the assault on DEA headquarters is nothing more than a decoy to keep the only uncontrollable branch of government occupied. It's apparent that some type of grand-scale plot has been conceived, and the people in this book are involved. Something genocidal, considering entire families are involved — powerful families, and if he's right, they're at the deserted housing complex right now.

Harrison is hopeful he can get to the bottom of the plot and possibly even save the DEA, but mentally he prepares for the worst.

There is no activity on the landing deck of the abandoned complex. He lands and steps out of his vehicle onto the deck. There are no vehicles or guards anywhere on the facility's roof. He expected this.

After removing his flight suit, he decides to use a stairway on his left in the hope of being less conspicuous — as unobtrusive, that is, as one can be in a DEA uniform. It doesn't take very long to work up a sweat zigzagging down what seems to be an endless stairwell. Finally, he arrives at the door marked Main Level, which opens into a long, empty hallway leading to the center of the complex. As he approaches the end of the hall, automatically the set of double doors parts.

He expected the complex would be fully occupied, but the size of this crowd is shocking. The complex is literally overflowing with people trying to look as important as they can. Large groups traveling in all directions, filling the moving walkways, and going in and out of the shops and eateries.

The open-air ceiling, which extends to the landing deck several hundred meters above, only amplifies their noise. Combined with conversation, their clamor echoes around until it sounds like a roar. No one seems to pay any attention to Harrison as he slips in behind the main body of a large group shuffling past. He hopes to pick up some bits of information. After a few minutes of eavesdropping on their mundane conversations, he turns off and starts down another walkway, but stops to take a good look around.

Massive crowds flow past glass-enclosed walkways above him. Harrison spots a familiar face he can't place. When the man catches him staring, he bolts from the crowd and Harrison begins his chase.

The man gains a good lead, but as he pushes and shoves his way through the crowd, he leaves a trail for Harrison to follow.

He glances back when his flight ends at a brick wall, then turns left and heads for an open doorway approximately fifty meters down one side. Harrison also starts for the door, hoping to head him off. After stumbling around several people eating at tables, Harrison comes to a small open area that gives him a clear view of the man and the doorway. His heart jumps in his chest; there's no way he can overtake the man before he reaches the exit.

Harrison pulls his laser pistol from its holster. The scope automatically flips up and the light indicating adequate power beams. He squeezes off a single shot. The blast impacts several meters ahead of the man, blowing the cement outward and opening a new hole in the wall. The concussion knocks the man to the floor and shatters the second-story windows just above him.

The complex falls abruptly silent. Harrison can hear his heart pounding; the echoing blast has been consumed by all the ears and eyes that are now on him. No one ventures to move; the people now have nowhere else to run. The man Harrison was chasing is lying on the floor, covered with shards of glass.

Security personnel are moving past the windows just above Harrison. They act as if they don't see him and haven't heard the laser blast. He walks to the man and pulls him up by one arm, then slams him against the wall. The curious crowd disperses when they see the murderous look on the face of the man wearing a DEA uniform.

Harrison now knows the man. *Like recalling a bad dream, it came to him during the chase. A figure stands over him, holding his head up by his chin because he's strapped to a heavy metal chair. The man, with a cynical grin, moves into the light, and Harrison gets a good look at Mr. Solomon.*

"You move unpleasantly fast for a dead man," Harrison says, wheezing.

"You owe me, Harrison. I saved you from the furnace," Solomon pants. He tries to smooth his hair and straighten his suit coat.

"I didn't miss by accident," Harrison roars. "Now we're even."

The look on Harrison's face frightens Solomon. "What — what are you going to do?"

"That depends on you, and the answers I get."

"Answers? I can't tell you anything."

"Oh really. Come on, let's go." Harrison pulls Solomon by the arm.

"No, no, I — I can't leave now."

Harrison doesn't say a word, just stares at the several small bleeding cuts on Solomon's face from the shattered windows.

"All right," Solomon says after a long hesitation. "I'll tell you what I know, but you have to keep quiet. I must stay here. You can't make me leave!"

¤ ¤ ¤

Chief Boyd storms into the control room accompanied by several men — the last of the clean-up crews.

"Megan, I want you and the remaining operators to prepare for evacuation, now. They've broken through our defense, there's just too many to hold back. A clean-up vehicle is waiting on the roof."

Megan stands. "Where are we going?"

"That's not important, just get everybody ready."

"What about you?"

"I have some emergency matters I need to take care of first." He sees her alarmed look and adds, "But I'll be finished in sufficient time to leave." Boyd marches to his office. Megan notifies the remaining personnel of the critical situation. Most of them are ready to leave within minutes. The first group consists solely of operators, who are escorted by the clean-up crew to the vehicle waiting on the roof. Megan and a handful of analysts stay behind. They expect to leave with Boyd when the crew returns.

Hearing the sound of fighting in the outer hall, Megan runs toward Boyd's office. Boyd steps out into the main control room; he sees the last of the analysts huddled against the wall, with two lone guards standing near them.

"Megan, what are you doing here? I told you to see that everyone evacuated this office. 'Everyone' meant you, too!"

"I sent the operators that were ready up first. The rest of us have been waiting, but the crew never returned. And I hear shooting outside, in the hall!"

Boyd glances around the control room, then turns back to Megan. "In order to survive, your group must reach the vehicle now." He motions for the guards to start up. "You go with them, Megan."

She sets her chin with resolve. "What about you, Chief? I'm not leaving without you."

"Don't worry. I'll be right behind you."

The first guard steps out into the hall and is mowed down by laser fire. The one remaining closes and locks the door. Within seconds, the solid steel door is burnished red. A small hole begins to emerge in the center of the melting door, and rapidly swells. The waiting personnel move to the opposite wall while the guard fires at the open hole in the faint hope of deterring the intruders. Then all the shooting stops suddenly and the room is dead quiet. It appears the attack has been repelled.

A small, black, disk-shaped projectile sails through the open hole. Striking the floor, it glides halfway across the room, coming to rest in the center of the office. Chief Boyd shoves Megan into his office and pushes the button to seal the door, then dives for the black disk. But it is too late. The disk explodes with the fury of a blast furnace. The tremendous heat lasts several seconds, initially turning the room white hot; then slowly it cools to reveal blackened walls.

¤ ¤ ¤

Harrison has to warn Megan and the chief, but he receives no reply on the communicator after several attempts. Twenty anxious minutes later, he's approaching the near empty DEA rooftop landing port. He uses the vehicle's heat scanner to verify the area is deserted.

After setting down among the abandoned vehicles, he makes his way to the only operating elevator, which delivers him down one level to the floor housing the control room. The elevator doors open to unrecognizable body parts littering the hallways and the overwhelming stench of burnt flesh.

"No ... NO!" Harrison's whisper becomes a shout as he runs to the control room. The door has been knocked off its hinges and is lying in the middle of the floor with a hole in it. He steps over it and looks around, but it takes his eyes a moment to adjust to the dark. When they do, he wishes they hadn't. The control room is no longer recognizable. The desks are molten pools on the floor. Even the glass covering the maps has liquefied and streaked the walls, he can feel the heat still emanating from them. He wants to believe Megan and the Chief have escaped unharmed, but knows no one could survive such devastation. If their bodies had not been burned to ash, they were probably in pieces, out in the hall. Stunned, Harrison turns and moves toward the doorway. Maybe someone is alive on another level.

"Rod?"

He whirls to meet her quivering voice, while removing his helmet. "Megan, is that you?"

She doesn't reply. Just saying his name has used up all her strength. She'd forced open the office door, and seeing what lay before her has sent her into shock. Harrison approaches. "Megan, are you all right?"

She still doesn't answer.

He doesn't dare ask what's happened, but knows he needs to move her in case whoever did this returns. "Come on, let's go, Megan. Let's get out of here."

Tears from her blue eyes have washed black soot down her cheeks and trickled down her chin, "Go? Go where? Where is there to go, Rod?"

"I don't know, but we can't stay here. Everybody's leaving. I found Mr. Solomon. He's still alive. He told me everyone's boarding the shuttles." Harrison knows more than he's telling, but thinks Megan is in no state to hear it right now.

He reaches out to her, but she jerks away. "I don't want to leave," she shouts, sobbing. "D — don't you see? This is my home. I have to stay here, the Chief needs me!"

"I know," he says. His voice is gentle; he's thinking how unlikely it is that Boyd would have left Megan behind. "But we need to leave, Megan. Just for a little while, all right? The Chief would tell you the same thing."

That strikes a chord. Only then does she allow Harrison to escort her to the landing deck.

Megan begins to respond after a few minutes of fresh air. But Harrison is still unsure of her decision-making abilities, or his own. Could he give up his newfound freedom and return to a life in space, breathing recycled air, never seeing the planet again? That's what he's expecting her to do.

He finds an abandoned personal transport and presets the instruments to deliver her to Houston flight control. Once there, she can board a shuttle and leave with the others. Or, she can stay. He has no doubt many will chose to remain on the planet.

When she begs him to go with her, he tries to smile but it's a sad smile at best.

"No, you go on. Catch a shuttle," he says. "I'll follow soon." Harrison gives her what he hopes is a reassuring hug. "There's something I have to do first. I'll find you. I promise."

"That's … the same thing the chief said right before the bomb, and I—"

Moments later, her tears subside. Still shell-shocked, she accepts his decision and climbs aboard the transport that will deliver her to Houston flight control, and hopefully safety.

He hasn't lied to her. He does have one final detail to attend to. After obtaining a new flight suit from downstairs, he carefully departs the rooftop landing port hoping Megan will be happy with whatever choice she makes — even though he may never know of it.

¤ ¤ ¤

Once in the air, Harrison pushes the fighter close to its breaking point. He's confident that it will take just over an hour to emerge on Capitol City. He can't imagine spending the rest of his life in space, especially with people like Mr. Solomon. He has decided, assuming he isn't killed, to stay and make the best of it. He hopes Megan will, too, but realizes he can't make her decisions for her. Stay here and live with the situation, or leave with the others: That's a decision they both need to make on their own.

¤ ¤ ¤

As he descends onto the head councilor's normally well-guarded building, only a single sentry approaches. The guard closely examines the steaming fighter, as Harrison climbs down to the landing deck. He looks down at his handheld monitor, then once again at the DEA uniform. "What business do you have here?" he shouts. "I have no Wingate fighters on my display, and no DEA is supposed to be here."

Harrison reaches into a zippered pocket and draws out the electronic book. "This must be delivered to the head councilor immediately," he says.

"The head councilor is busy. Can't you see we're in the middle of an evacuation?" He waves one arm as if to drive Harrison away, occasionally glancing behind him as he walks away.

Harrison senses the guard is nervous about something, possibly afraid to be left behind. He catches up to the man.

"The head councilor can't leave until he has this book." Harrison opens the book and allows the guard to see the first page of names.

The guard's eyes widen. "I — I'll accept responsibility for it."

The guard grabs at the book, but Harrison is too fast. "I was instructed to deliver it in person."

"All right, but make it fast. The head councilor has no time to waste."

The guard points Harrison to the proper door. At the same time, he's on his communicator, informing someone inside the building to open the outer door.

Once inside, Harrison has no trouble finding the head councilor's chambers. The hallways outside bustle with people deciding what to take and what to leave. Bits of their overheard conversations frequently use the head councilor's name.

Thick wooden doors with the hand-carved words "HEAD COUNCILOR" stand undefended. Harrison walks through the empty reception office to find the head councilor sitting behind his desk with his face obscured by the satchel he's filling with items from his desk drawers.

Harrison draws his weapon and hurls the book toward him. It lands in the center of his desk with a loud crack. The councilor jumps from his chair to a standing position, knocking the satchel over in his panic.

Then, unbelievably, the man smiles at him.

"Harrison, I might have known. When the report came in that a lone fighter had escaped the Wingate, I knew, I just knew it had to be you. I see you found my book and your name inside as well."

Harrison takes a careful look around the large, lavish office. "You were expecting me?"

"Yes, sooner or later. Don't worry. We're not going to terminate you. We don't kill our own here." The councilor's words are hasty.

Harrison can't decide whether to shoot first or listen to him. He knows the man couldn't have sustained power this long without knowing how to manipulate people or conversations.

"Yes, Harrison, I know what you're thinking ... we're all deranged. But you're one of us. We developed you. And if we're wrong, that makes you wrong as well."

Harrison examines the room, the loudly states.

"I am not one of you".

The head councilor turns and faces the wall behind him, which is composed entirely of glass. After a minute of looking down fifty stories to the shuttles loading below, he swings back around with pride. "No, Harrison, you're wrong. Your training began the day your father gave you to us. Your father was a good man, an intelligent man. He knew something would have to be done, and soon. He wanted you to be part of it. I knew him well. He was one of us, just like you, and this is his wish. We taught you everything you know. You are here because of our ingenuity. You are one of us."

"What about Admiral Kachel?" Harrison shouts. "Wasn't he one of your own?"

The councilor's face hardens. "It's unfortunate about Kachel. But the DEA wouldn't stop until they incarcerated someone, thanks to you. Besides, Kachel overstepped his bounds when he attempted to eliminate you. That wasn't in the plan. He had to be sacrificed. He was jeopardizing the entire project."

"So you had Pressnell set him up?"

"But you killed him," the councilor replies. "Are we any more vicious than you? Pressnell died by the hand of your unwillingness. And your rebelliousness has caused us several unintended variations to the project. You should have stayed put. We only needed a few more months."

"Two people have died on account of me," Harrison says. "Indirectly. That's true enough. But you ... you've ordered thousands, maybe millions to their deaths. Don't compare me to you."

"Yes, but they're not our people. Those people are out of control, strained by their burdens and limited by their drugs. They're different than you and I."

Something Winston once said echoes through Harrison's mind. He'd said it wasn't training, but government brainwashing, is that what this is.

Harrison glares at the councilor. "So your goal is absolute control over everyone. And if you can't possess them, you simply let your drug syndicate do the exterminating. Do I have that right?"

The head councilor nods. "Yes, we conspired with the drug cartel. We had no choice. They have control of the drugs, and the drugs have control of the majority. And we needed them." He sighs. "You're wasting precious time, Harrison. People are waiting."

"Personally, I don't care if you and I stand right here until hell freezes over," Harrison states. "So, now what? You fly around with your handpicked race until the war is over? Then, assuming the military wins, you return and establish your own government?"

"I see you don't know as much as I had anticipated Rod. No, we're migrating to a planet in the G1-10 sector. A perfect planet, perfect as we can locate on such short notice. We won't be coming back. You see, the military will never win."

"Why couldn't you just take the military with you?" Harrison asks.

The councilor chuckles. "The military is far from drug-free, Harrison. And that is our goal: to start fresh on a new planet, one without drugs or polluted minds of any kind."

"You know the DEA is drug-free." Harrison doesn't realize he's yelling.

The councilor takes the tone of a friendly teacher talking to a wayward student.

"Yes, but they are uncontrollable, and we don't need them on a drug-free planet, now do we?"

Harrison fights the urge to pull the trigger. "Let's see if I understand this," he says. "You're running off to an unspoiled planet that you located in Sector G1-10, and taking with you only those you need and control. You've allowed the DEA to be eliminated because you can't control it, but you're willing to take me with you. And oh, how are we supposed to reach G1-10 without the Wingate, might I ask?"

The councilor gazes off into the distance.

"The Wingate, yes. I despised destroying her, but she was much too powerful. Whoever governed the Wingate would have the power to dominate everything. We'll just have to make do with the shuttles. It'll be a rather lengthy trip, stopping at every outpost." He smiles. "But then, thanks to you and the others, they've been well-supplied."

Harrison's face reddens as his anger grows.

"You tricked and used me to do your killing. You removed the Wingate's personnel knowing I wouldn't destroy it with them onboard, and allowed the military to take the loss."

"Don't think of it as 'tricked and used,' but as trained and utilized." The councilor chuckles again. "I knew Boyd couldn't resist the opportunity to strike once he discovered the military was using the Wingate to eliminate his precious clean-up crews. And you performed excellently. I expected no less. With the engineers reassigned, you knew they couldn't stop you from destroying the Wingate. I even made sure the DEA was finished while you were absent, to ensure your safety."

He places his hands flat on the desk, his urgency gone for the moment. "You see, you still have the option to come with us. I've made many alterations to keep you alive. Your name is still on the list. We need people like you. Remember, we trained you, and hundreds like you, especially for this day. In fact, I had planned for you to be head of my security … our security. Responsible for the government's protection, the planet's protection. It's a crucial undertaking. Are you up to it?"

Harrison hesitates. The speech is getting to him, but he realizes he dare not believe a word of it. "No. No, thanks. I'll take my chances here," he says.

"I am afraid that won't be much of a chance."

Harrison glares at him. "What do you mean?"

"You don't expect us to leave knowing this drug-infested population has the technology and manpower to follow? How long do you think it would take them to find us? A year? A decade? A century? How long before they come falling from the sky, bringing with them their vile poisons? They would come, you know. They're like parasites. They thrive off us. They need us. We're their only source of life."

The councilor turns back to the wall of windows and the evacuation below. "The power-plant waste facilities weren't picked at random. The sites are strategically located. … Buried deep within each is a detonator." There's a long pause as if the words had escaped involuntarily. "The explosions will obliterate anyone nearby. Those people who endure the desert hardships will be the first ones to go. Ironic, isn't it? However, the winds will carry the contamination around the globe. In a few short months, life on this planet will cease to exist."

"You've been planning this all along." Harrison grunts through clenched teeth. "And you let the drug problem get out of hand as a means of killing off millions, knowing the rest would have to follow you to this new world that you so conveniently discovered. You allowed the drug crisis to become what it is for the sole purpose of playing God." Harrison points his weapon at the head councilor.

"No, no, you're not blaming me for the entire world's weakness. It was out of control long before my time. Centuries before." The councilor turns back to Harrison. He doesn't flinch when he sees the weapon, but speaks in a calm voice. "You have no alternative. You need me. The people boarding those shuttles need me. I'm giving them their only chance to be free from it. You can't kill me, so put that weapon away, Harrison. That's an order."

Harrison's hand is steady. "You've forsaken the people on this planet. They're the ones who don't need you."

The head councilor has carefully thought out every segment of his master plan, except one. During Harrison's brief period of independence from the totalitarian government rule he'd always lived under, he has acquired something of greater importance, something that changed his life forever. He's learned what life is meant to be, and what freedom is. Right or wrong, he's able to make his own decisions. Free to live his own life, to be whatever and with whomever he chooses. It's something he can't bring himself to let go of — a thing he would die for.

"I can't let you live," he tells the councilor. "You'll just enslave and contaminate another planet. They might be free of drugs, but they'll be suffocated by government rules, submerged in your egotistical ideals of how their life should be. That's not living. Without their freedom, they'll have no life."

"Now who's playing God?" the councilor shouts.

"I guess we are a lot alike. But now, it's your time to go."

The councilor grabs for an open desk drawer. Harrison fires. The blast severs the councilor's left shoulder; it whirls him around, and then continues on to strike the window directly behind him. The glass explodes outward into thousands of pieces, which vanish into the unobstructed view and are followed closely by the head councilor, who's dragged out by the pressure change released from the open hole.

Harrison hears the emergency alarm, but can't move. He stands watching as the councilor's papers rush through the hole; one by one they disappear until the satchel is empty. Harrison hears a noise behind him and realizes that the heavy wooden doors are about to close. In a few seconds, the room will be sealed. He needs to leave now.

¤ ¤ ¤

Harrison's bearing is Houston flight control, in the hope of finding Megan before its too late. Now, he knows their decisions have been made for them — neither can stay.

He approaches Houston's air space an hour and a half later; nearly four hours since he'd left Megan. All he can do is hope she boarded the personal transport he had obtained for her, then caught a shuttle at Houston flight control.

When he arrives, he sees flight control is covered under a shroud of black smoke. Things look even worse the closer he gets. Apparently, the death of the head councilor has delayed his people's departure; the military has no hope of holding them back. The druggies, led by the mercenaries, have broken through the south wall and are overtaking the military. A few shuttles too close to the fighting, now burn out of control. Several others still in the holding area have been destroyed also. A vicious battle is raging for the remaining shuttles that haven't yet attempted launch stratum.

Harrison has no way of knowing just how many shuttles escaped, or Megan's current location. It would be certain suicide for him to attempt a landing now. Pushing the fighter to full power, he sets a course for G1-2, the first outpost, in the hope of tracking Megan and the initial shuttles. It's not what he wants to do, but he has no choice.

Several hours later, Harrison leaves behind any opportunity for a normal life and enters deep space. However, he does have several things to look forward to. The best is his dream of settling on the new planet with Megan by his side. If she survived what he'd seen earlier. He knows it will take days to reach the first outpost. If he's to catch the shuttles before they refuel and move on, he needs to keep moving. Finding the right shuttle will be difficult, but he won't stop until he finds her.

He sets the instruments to signal him when they encounter an object or locate the shuttle's heat trail, then prepares for an extended rest, that will prolong life support. The longer his inactivity, the better chance he has to bridge the gap.

It's been over a full day since Harrison last slept, so the transfer to a dormant rest is welcome. He thinks of Megan and how badly he needs to find her as he lays back and closes his eyes. He can't help thinking of the planet, technically his home, but one he's barely known. How truly beautiful it was; he will miss the colors and smells. How could anyone destroy a thing of such beauty? Why would intelligent people allow a substance so addictive to continue uncontrolled? Or try to cover it up? Everyone knows a thing that serious will only perpetuate its own problems. Or perhaps that was the plan all along, and we were taught lies to control us. Then everything went as planned.

Harrison believes the head councilor was truthful about one thing: A single person in a thousand lifetimes can't destroy an entire planet ... but millions of individuals in a few short generations can.

Printed in the United States
131634LV00001B/44/P